James Hadley Chase and The Murder Room

>>> This title is part of The Murder Room, our series dedicated to making available out-of-print or hard-to-find titles by classic crime writers.

Crime fiction has always held up a mirror to society. The Victorians were fascinated by sensational murder and the emerging science of detection; now we are obsessed with the forensic detail of violent death. And no other genre has so captivated and enthralled readers.

Vast troves of classic crime writing have for a long time been unavailable to all but the most dedicated frequenters of second-hand bookshops. The advent of digital publishing means that we are now able to bring you the backlists of a huge range of titles by classic and contemporary crime writers, some of which have been out of print for decades.

From the genteel amateur private eyes of the Golden Age and the femmes fatales of pulp fiction, to the morally ambiguous hard-boiled detectives of mid twentieth-century America and their descendants who walk our twenty-first century streets, The Murder Room has it all. **>>>**

The Murder Room
Where Criminal Minds Meet

themurderroom.com

James Hadley Chase (1906–1985)

Born René Brabazon Raymond in London, the son of a British colonel in the Indian Army, James Hadley Chase was educated at King's School in Rochester, Kent, and left home at the age of 18. He initially worked in book sales until, inspired by the rise of gangster culture during the Depression and by reading James M. Cain's *The Postman Always Rings Twice*, he wrote his first novel, *No Orchids for Miss Blandish*. Despite the American setting of many of his novels, Chase (like Peter Cheyney, another hugely successful British noir writer) never lived there, writing with the aid of maps and a slang dictionary. He had phenomenal success with the novel, which continued unabated throughout his entire career, spanning 45 years and nearly 90 novels. His work was published in dozens of languages and more than thirty titles were adapted for film. He served in the RAF during World War II, where he also edited the RAF Journal. In 1956 he moved to France with his wife and son; they later moved to Switzerland, where Chase lived until his death in 1985.

No Orchids for Miss Blandish
Eve
More Deadly Than the Male
Mission to Venice
Mission to Siena
Not Safe to Be Free
Shock Treatment
Come Easy – Go Easy

What's Better Than Money?
Just Another Sucker
I Would Rather Stay Poor
A Coffin from Hong Kong
Tell it to the Birds
One Bright Summer Morning
The Soft Centre
You Have Yourself a Deal
Have This One on Me
Well Now, My Pretty
Believed Violent
An Ear to the Ground
The Whiff of Money
The Vulture Is a Patient Bird
Like a Hole in the Head
An Ace Up My Sleeve
Want to Stay Alive?
Just a Matter of Time
You're Dead Without Money
Have a Change of Scene
Knock, Knock! Who's There?
Goldfish Have No Hiding Place
So What Happens to Me?
The Joker in the Pack
Believe This, You'll Believe Anything
Do Me a Favour, Drop Dead
I Hold the Four Aces
My Laugh Comes Last
Consider Yourself Dead

You Must Be Kidding
A Can of Worms
Try This One for Size
You Can Say That Again
Hand Me a Fig Leaf
Have a Nice Night
We'll Share a Double Funeral
Not My Thing
Hit Them Where It Hurts

Not Safe to be Free

James Hadley Chase

An Orion book

Copyright © Hervey Raymond 1958

The right of James Hadley Chase to be identified as the author of this work has been asserted in accordance with the Copyright, Designs and Patents Act 1988.

This edition published by
The Orion Publishing Group Ltd
Orion House
5 Upper St Martin's Lane
London WC2H 9EA

An Hachette UK company
A CIP catalogue record for this book is available from the British Library

ISBN 978 1 4719 0336 6

www.orionbooks.co.uk

CHAPTER ONE

JAY DELANEY lay back in the canvas slung chair, a book in his lap, and listened to the voice that was speaking to him in his mind.

He had grown used to listening to this voice. It had been urging him to do various acts of violence now for the past eighteen months, but up to now, he had resisted the voice's cajoleries.

But this afternoon, as he relaxed in the hot sunshine, the suggestion the voice was making to him tempted him.

The idea of murdering a girl had been in his mind for some time. It would be, he had told himself over and over again, the ultimate test of his wits, his intelligence and his courage.

From behind his heavily tinted blue sun-glasses, he had been watching a girl seated on the sand some thirty yards or so from him.

The girl was wearing a sky-blue bikini, and she was posing on the sand before a group of sweating photographers who stood or knelt in a semicircle around her while a big crowd along the Croisette stared with insatiable curiosity at the spectacle.

The girl was blonde and very young with a body conforming to the standard requirements of the movie world, and her skin was the colour of honey from the comb. She was pretty with small features and a bright, animated expression that would come out well in a photograph.

Sexually the girl didn't interest Jay. No girls had ever interested him that way. The qualities that made her attractive to him were her freshness, her vitality and her animation.

The voice in his mind said persuasively, "This is the girl you have been waiting for. This is the girl you should kill. It won't be difficult. She is a film star. It won't be difficult to get her alone. You have only to tell her that your father wants to meet her for her to go anywhere with you."

Jay reached in his shirt pocket and took out the gold cigarette-case that his step-mother had given him for his twenty-first birthday, four months ago. From it, he took out a cigarette and lit it.

1

The girl had turned over now, her chin cupped in her hands, her legs lifted, her ankles crossed, while photographers took pictures of her long slim back and the curve of her hips, scarcely concealed by the skimpy bikini she was wearing.

It was true, Jay thought, it wouldn't be difficult to get her alone. Being the son of Floyd Delaney, who was to Pacific Motion Pictures what Sam Goldwyn was to M.G.M., made it easy to approach her without arousing her suspicions.

He was suddenly glad that his father had insisted that he should accompany him to Cannes. He hadn't wanted to go and he had raised all kinds of objections, but finally his father, who always got his own way in the end, had persuaded him to come along.

The Cannes Film Festival was fun, his father had said: lots of pretty girls, wonderful food, swimming and good movies. Besides, he needed a vacation.

So he had reluctantly tagged along as he had always tagged along wherever his father went.

It was a lonely business, this trailing along in the wake of his father's glory. Twelve years ago, Jay's mother had thrown herself out of a hotel window. Since her death, his father had married twice, divorcing his second wife after two years of constant bickering. His present wife, Sophia, was five years older than Jay: a fragile, dark beauty with enormous blue eyes, a slender lovely body and the face of a Raphael Madonna. She was an Italian, and had been a celebrated film star before Floyd Delaney had married her. Now, because of his possessiveness and his millions, she had retired from the screen.

Jay was always a little uneasy in her presence. Her beauty disturbed him, and he avoided her as much as he could. When they did get a few minutes alone together, he had an uneasy feeling that she suspected there was something a little odd about him. He had often caught her looking at him, a quizzing, puzzled expression in her eyes as if she were trying to probe into what was going on in his mind.

She was always kind and pleasant to him, and she always made an effort to include him in the conversation when a crowd surrounded his father, and this bothered him. He much preferred to remain on the fringe of his father's activities rather than to be forced to talk to people who obviously weren't interested in him.

The Delaneys had been at the Plaza hotel now for three days. From there they were going on to Venice and then on to

Florence with a camera unit to shoot background material for a new movie that was going into production in the late autumn.

During these three days in Cannes, his father and Sophia had spent most of their time watching the best films Europe had to offer. His father's own film offering, an all-colour, star-studded, glittering musical, was to be shown on the last day of the Festival, and Floyd Delaney had no doubt that it would take the first prize.

Jay had said he preferred to remain on the beach, rather than watch a series of foreign movies. Reluctantly, his father had agreed. He would have liked his son to have taken more interest in the film business, but, as it was the boy's vacation, he told him to go ahead and please himself.

Jay looked over at the girl in the sky-blue bikini. She was standing now, her long, slim legs apart, her hand shielding her eyes while she laughed at the group of photographers who grinned back at her because they thought she was a nice, cute kid, and because she didn't throw her weight around like some of these little bitches who didn't know enough even to wash their feet before putting on their swim-suits, and who behaved as if they had talent instead of just a body in search of a job.

A press photographer, shambling across the sand, recognized Jay and paused.

"Hello there, Mr. Delaney," he said. "Giving the movies a miss this afternoon?"

A little startled, Jay looked up and nodded.

What a specimen! he thought, looking at the shabby figure before him, and what a complexion!

The man looked pickled with drink, but Jay smiled at him. He made a point always to be polite to anyone who spoke to him.

"Who wants to watch a movie in this weather?"

"I guess that's right, but your father's in there." The man moved a little closer, and Jay could smell the whisky on his breath. "Your father's keen: the keenest man in the business. I don't reckon he's missed one picture since he's been here."

"I don't think he has." Jay nodded over to the girl in the bikini. "Who's that? Do you know her name?"

The man turned and peered at the girl.

"Lucille Balu: pretty nifty, huh? She's working with a small independent French unit right now, but in a year, she'll be up at the top. She's got a lot of talent."

"Yes," Jay said, and having got the information he wanted, he pointedly picked up his book.

3

The photographer studied him. A good-looking kid, he thought. He would make quite a movie actor, and how the girls would rave about him!

"Look, Mr. Delaney, could you fix an exclusive for me with your father?" he asked hopefully. "I'd like to get his views on the future of the French cinema and take some pictures. Could you put in a word for me? My name's Joe Kerr."

Jay shook his head, smiling.

"I'm sorry, Mr. Kerr, but you'd better talk to Mr. Stone. He handles that side of my father's business."

The red-raw face tightened in a grimace.

"I know, but I can't get anywhere with him. Couldn't you put in a good word for me?"

"It wouldn't help. My father doesn't listen to any suggestions I make." Jay's smile widened and he looked very young and boyish. "You know what fathers are."

"Yeah." Kerr's raddled face fell and he shrugged his shoulders. "Well, thanks anyway," then, seeing Jay made another pointed movement with his book, he went shambling away across the sand.

Jay looked at the girl again.

The photographers were thanking her, and then they moved off towards a red-haired girl who was lying seductively on the sand, impatiently waiting for them.

Lucille Balu came across the sand and entered the Plaza enclosure. She sat down at one of the tables within ten feet of where Jay was sitting.

A small, compact, powerfully-built man with wiry black hair came over to her, carrying a wrap and a beach bag which he put on the table.

"Nice work," he said. "Well, that'll do for to-day. I'm going to catch a bit of this movie. Do you want to come?"

The girl shook her head.

"I'll stay here for a while."

"All right, but don't hide yourself: let the people see you. I'll meet you in the Plaza bar at six."

Jay listened to this conversation, and he watched the little man stroll away. Turning his head, and behind the dark screen of his sun-glasses, he watched the girl as she opened the beach bag to take out a powder compact.

She is very attractive, he thought.

"Why not now?" the voice in his mind asked. "This thing has been with you for a long time. Why don't you do it? She will make a perfect subject. You could take her up to the hotel suite. You have two hours before they will be back. You will have plenty of time to arrange things."

Jay glanced around the enclosure. There were only a dozen or so people sitting at the tables. At this hour in the afternoon most people were in the cinema or sight-seeing. No one was paying any attention to him or to the girl.

He decided he would do it, and without giving himself a chance to change his mind, he shut his book and stood up. His heart was beating a little faster, but otherwise he felt surprisingly calm and relaxed.

The girl was touching up her lips, looking at herself in the mirror of the compact as Jay came up to her.

"It's Mademoiselle Balu, isn't it?" he said in his impeccable French.

The girl glanced up, stiffened a little and then immediately smiled.

"Yes. You are Monsieur Delaney."

"Junior: it makes a lot of difference," Jay said with his charming, boyish smile. "This is fortunate. My father was talking about you this morning. He wants to meet you."

The expression of surprise and excitement that spread over the girl's face amused him.

"Mr. Delaney wants to meet me? Why, how wonderful!" She cocked her head on one side and smiled at him. "You're serious? You're not joking?"

"Why, no. He said if I happened to run into you to bring you to meet him," Jay said. "If you have nothing to do, why not come now?"

"Now?" The girl was becoming flustered and she stared at Jay, her eyes very wide, and he thought how vulnerable she looked, and that pleased him. "But where?"

"At the Plaza hotel, of course. He thinks you have a lot of talent." Jay smiled. "I don't often agree with my father, but this time, I think he is absolutely right."

The flattery didn't have the result he expected. The girl continued to stare at him.

She had a sudden wish that she could see beyond the two blue screens that hid his eyes. Somehow, even though his smile was charming, she felt a little uneasy about him.

But, she told herself, if his father wanted to see her, this expensive trip down to Cannes would be justified. Her agent,

Jean Thiry, the little man who had just left her, had insisted that she should go to Cannes.

"You never know," he had said. "It's a gamble of course, but then one of the big shots from Hollywood might spot you. Cannes is a shop window for a girl like you."

Then she remembered seeing Floyd Delaney and his beautiful wife leave the Plaza about an hour ago and go over to the cinema.

"But Mr. Delaney is in the cinema now."

Jay took this in his stride.

"My father doesn't sit through many of these films. He sneaks out the side exit. He's back at the hotel now." He looked at his gold Omega. "I know he is going out just after four. It's half past three now, but if you have something else to do, perhaps some other time."

"But I haven't a thing to do," the girl said, getting hastily to her feet. "I'd love to meet him."

"You will want to change, won't you?" Jay said. It amused him to see the panic that had jumped into her eyes. He saw she was wondering what she should wear, how she could possibly change in half an hour and still look her best. "Are you staying at the Plaza?"

She shook her head.

"The hotel next door. The Metropole."

"You don't have to be formal," he said. "My father already knows how beautiful you are."

She laughed nervously.

"Well, I'd better hurry if I have only half an hour," she said and slipped on her beach wrap.

Jay watched her.

When she had been posing for the photographers she had been very self-possessed, but now, at the thought of meeting his father, she had lost her poise. She was pathetically eager and like any other young girl in a fluster.

"There's just one thing," he said, and his intimate, boyish smile widened. "Perhaps you'd better not tell anyone that you are seeing my father. There'll be time for that later. People here do gossip, don't they? My father's moods are very unpredictable. I think he has plans for you, but it would be as well not to count too much on him."

She realized how damaging it would be to her career and her reputation if it got around that the great Floyd Delaney had given her a personal interview and then nothing had come of it.

6

But suppose he made her an offer? She wished Jean hadn't gone to the cinema. She would have liked to have had a word with him first.

"No, of course. I won't say anything to anyone," she said "Suite 27? I must fly."

"At four o'clock then."

He watched her hurry up the steps on to the Croisette, then he lit another cigarette and sat down.

He had now to consider how he was to kill her. It would be done in the suite. Obviously there mustn't be anything messy: no blood. He thought of the silk curtain cords that held back the drapes at the big windows of his father's lounge. It shouldn't be difficult to drop one of these cords over her head and tighten it around her throat before she could scream.

He flicked ash off his cigarette, again conscious that he was calm, and that pleased him.

The excitement and the tension he needed would begin after he had killed her. The mere act of killing her was nothing – a means to an end. The excitement would begin when he had a dead body on his hands in a suite in the famous Plaza hotel. That would be the test of his ingenuity; a challenge to his power of inventiveness, when one slip would put him into the hands of the police.

He sat there, letting the sun beat down on his upturned, handsome young face, his mind deliberately blank, aware that his heart was now beating faster and his hands were a little damp.

At ten minutes to four o'clock, he got up and walked slowly up the steps to the Croisette.

The crowd staring at the starlets in their scanty swim-suits ignored him. Even if they had been told that he was the son of one of the most famous motion picture makers, they wouldn't have given him more than a glance.

A few of the film executives nodded to him as he crossed the road to the hotel and he nodded back with his customary politeness. He was sure these men, who had often been ruthlessly treated by his father, were thinking he was a nice kid who hadn't been spoilt by his father's millions and the thought amused him.

He collected the key to his father's suite, acknowledging the nod and the smile from the clerk who handed him the key. He walked up the stairs to the second floor that was reserved for the important executives attending the festival. The long corridor was deserted as he had expected it to be deserted.

7

At this hour none of the executives would be in their suites. They would either be in the cinema or else on the terrace discussing their affairs.

He unlocked the door of suite 27 and walked in.

The suite consisted of a large lounge, a dining-room and three bedrooms. It had been completely redecorated for Floyd Delaney's arrival.

Jay crossed the lounge and removed one of the scarlet silk cords that held the cream curtains in place. He ran the cord through his fingers. It felt smooth and strong to his touch. He coiled the cord and then placed it on the settee, putting a cushion over it to hide it from sight.

He looked down at his watch. The time was one minute to four.

He sat down.

In another minute she would be here. In five or more minutes she would be dead and then what was to be the most exciting experience in his life would begin.

He remained motionless, his eyes on the hands of his watch while he listened to the thump-thump-thump of his heart.

As the minute hand of his watch centred exactly on the hour, there came a gentle rap on the door.

II

The Festival offering for that afternoon was a documentary made in India, and Sophia Delaney found it unbearable.

The background music set her teeth on edge, the scenes were of poverty and squalor, and it went on and on and on. She thought longingly of the beach and the sea and the sunshine. Finally, when the picture switched to an Indian hospital to show men and women suffering from tropical diseases with close-ups of revolting sores and gigantic limbs swollen out of all recognition, her spirit rebelled.

She glanced at her husband, who sat huddled down in his seat, his eyes riveted on the French subtitles while he strove conscientiously to follow the action of the film. She realized there was no hope of getting him to leave. He would nevet set the bad example of walking out on another man's film. She knew he had always at the back of his mind the possibility that one day, someone as important as himself might be tempted to walk out on one of his films and she knew how superstitious he was about tempting providence.

8

A man with a deep sore on his chest appeared on the screen, and this picture revolted her. She touched Floyd's hand.

"Darling, do you mind? I think I've about had enough of this," she said softly.

In the semi-darkness she saw his look of surprise, then because he loved her and treated her like a child, he nodded, patting her hand.

"Yeah. You skip, honey doll. I'll have to stay with this thing, but you go. Have a swim or something."

His eyes were drawn back to the screen as the camera tracked up to a close-up shot of the sore.

She brushed his cheek with her lips.

"Thank you, darling," she murmured, and then slipped past him into the aisle.

The nine hundred odd men and women in the cinema observed the kiss and enviously watched her leave.

Sophia sighed with relief as she left the dark auditorium. She glanced at her wrist-watch. The time was ten minutes to four o'clock.

She would return to the hotel, get her swim-suit, and then drive down to the bathing station by the Casino, away from the activities in front of the Plaza and have a bathe in peace.

Floyd would be tied up with that ghastly film, and then with the discussion that would inevitably follow until six o'clock, so she had plenty of time.

She walked from the cinema to the Plaza, along the crowded pavement, smiling at the people she knew, and once stopping to exchange a few words with a famous Italian star who Floyd was anxious to sign up but who was showing temperament and demanding an outrageous sum for his undoubted talents.

The Italian star caressed her body with his eyes and conveyed to her by his direct, insolent stare that he would be amused to have her in his bed.

Sophia, long accustomed to this kind of approach, said the right thing, smiled the right smile and kept out of reach of the star's wandering hands, and then moved on, hoping the greasy little beast would be more amenable when Floyd's casting manager approached him again.

The lobby of the Plaza hotel was as usual crowded with celebrities as Sophia made her entrance.

Over in a corner was Georges Simenon, pipe clenched tightly between his teeth while he listened to Curt Jurgens discussing his latest movie.

9

Eddie Constantine, his peak cap at a rakish angle, waved to Sophia and pantomimed that he would like to join her only he was tied up with a producer who seemed determined to talk him into something.

Michele Morgan and Henri Vidal were arguing amiably while photographers stalked them with their cameras.

Jean Cocteau in his short dark cloak swept through the lobby and out into the sunshine without paying attention to anyone.

Henri Verneuil, the famous French director, was listening with a broad smile to the gentle cajolings of Marese Guibert, who was trying to persuade him to make an appearance on the Monte Carlo television.

Sophia moved through the crowd to the reception desk. The hands of the wall clock stood at four o'clock as she asked for the key to suite 27.

"Mr. Delaney junior has it, madame," the clerk told her. "He went up a few minutes ago."

This surprised Sophia, but she thanked the clerk, and then made her way across the crowded lobby, smiling and nodding and giving her left hand the way the Italians have to show special intimacy, but not stopping.

The elevator whisked her to the second floor, and she noticed as she stepped out of the cage that the hands of the wall clock now stood at seven minutes past four.

She crossed the corridor, turned the handle of the door to suite 27, then frowned as she found the door locked.

She rapped sharply.

"Jay! It's Sophia," she said and waited.

There was a long pause of silence, and with a little movement of exasperation, she rapped again.

She had been Floyd's wife long enough now to have acquired the veneer of a millionaire's wife, and to be kept waiting in a hotel corridor was insufferable to her.

"Jay – please, for heaven's sake!"

Again the silence and this time, becoming angry, she rattled the door handle and rapped again.

"Excuse me, madame."

The floor waiter had come from the still room.

"Have you a key?" she asked, controlling her irritation and smiling at him. "I think my step-son must be sleeping."

"Yes, madame."

She moved aside and the waiter unlocked the door with his pass key and pushed the door open.

Sophia thanked him and walked into the big lounge, closing the door sharply behind her.

The first thing she noticed was a perfume in the air that was unfamiliar to her.

She came to an abrupt standstill, sniffing at the fragile, almost imperceptible perfume, her lovely blue eyes narrowing.

Their suite was strictly private. Floyd made a point of never having anyone up there, so the unfamiliar perfume meant that there had been an intruder in the room.

Was it possible that Jay had brought a girl up here? Sophia wondered. Had she walked in on some sordid sexual adventure?

Floyd had told Jay that they would not be back to the suite until after six. Had the boy dared to take advantage of this to bring to their suite one of those ghastly, half-naked little morons who paraded in the lobby of the hotel like lost souls in search of financial salvation?

Sophia felt hot, indignant anger surge through her.

"Jay!"

She heard a movement in Jay's bedroom and then the door opened.

Jay came into the lounge and very carefully closed the bedroom door. He was wearing his heavily tinted sun-glasses. This habit of his, wearing sun-glasses indoors, always irritated Sophia.

The glasses made a barrier between them. She never knew of what he was thinking or how he was reacting to what she said to him. When speaking to him she always had the impression that she was talking over a high wall to a voice that answered her from the other side.

But this time, although his face was, as usual, expressionless, she was immediately aware that he had brought into the room an atmosphere of extreme tension, and she also noticed that his upper lip glistened with tiny beads of perspiration.

"Why, hello, Sophia," he said and his voice was just a shade too casual. "You're back early, aren't you?"

Had he got a girl in his bedroom? Sophia wondered with a feeling of disgust. Was there some wretched little slut trapped in there, listening against the door panel to what she was saying?

"Didn't you hear me knocking?" she asked, and because his tension made her uneasy she spoke sharply.

He moved further into the room and she noticed that he kept between her and his bedroom door.

"I did think I heard something," he said, "but I didn't imagine it was you."

He took out his gold cigarette-case she had given him and as he lifted his left arm, she saw on the inside of his forearm three ugly red scratches, one of them bleeding slightly.

"You've hurt yourself," she said. "Be careful: it's bleeding."

He glanced at the scratches, then put the cigarette-case on the table and took out his handkerchief and wiped the blood away.

"There was a cat in the corridor," he said. "It scratched me."

The stupid, transparent lie made her very angry.

She bit back a sarcastic retort and moved away from him, crossing to the window, turning her back on him.

Should she accuse him of bringing a girl up here? Her position as his father's third wife made such an accusation difficult. He might well tell her to mind her own business. Also she might have made a mistake, although she was sure she hadn't. Perhaps she had better tell Floyd and let him deal with the boy.

"Wasn't the movie any good?" Jay asked.

"No."

There was a pause, then he asked, "Where's father?"

The anxious note in his voice tempted her to say his father was on his way over. If there was a girl trapped in the bedroom, the idea of his father walking in might frighten him enough not to dare do such a thing again, but she resisted the temptation.

"He's still in the cinema."

Impatiently, she pushed aside the right-hand curtain that was hanging loose, looking for the curtain cord to fasten back the curtain.

She saw the cord was missing.

"Are you looking for something, Sophia?" Jay asked, and his voice sounded very gentle.

She turned quickly.

His handsome young face was still expressionless. He was smiling, but it was a meaningless smile of a shop-window dummy.

She could see the twin reflections of herself like miniature snapshots in the lenses of his sun-glasses. She noticed how very still she stood and how tense she seemed.

"There's a curtain cord missing," she said.

"How observant you are!" he said and pulled from his hip pocket the scarlet cord. "You mean this? I forgot to put it back. I've been amusing myself with it."

She didn't know why, but this remark had an oddly sinister sound.

"What do you mean?" she asked sharply.

"Oh, nothing. I was bored. I was just fooling with it."

He began to move slowly and deliberately across the room towards her. The scarlet cord hung limply in his hands and it formed a noose.

There was something about his silent approach that suddenly alarmed her. It seemed stealthy and somehow threatening.

She moved away from the window, her heart beating fast and she stepped around the table that stood in the middle of the room so that it was between him and her.

Jay paused, looking at her across the table, the cord still held in a loop between his slim brown fingers.

Sophia realized that she was beginning to be frightened. She felt instinctively that something had happened in this room. The smell of the unfamiliar perfume, the scratches on Jay's arm, the loop made by the curtain cord formed a pattern that she couldn't bring herself to analyse.

She wanted now badly to run out of the room, but she controlled the impulse. This was absurd, she told herself. Nothing had happened. Why should she be suddenly afraid of Floyd's son?

She forced herself to remain where she was, aware that her heart was now thumping and she was slightly breathless.

"Jay – have you brought a girl up here?" she demanded and she was surprised to hear how harsh her voice sounded.

Jay released one end of the cord and let it swing like a scarlet pendulum. He continued to stare at her.

"Did you hear me?" she said, raising her voice.

"How did you guess?" he said. He waved his hand towards his bedroom door. "You are quite right. As a matter of fact – she's in there now."

CHAPTER TWO

I

THERE had been a time when Joe Kerr had been considered by editors and agents as a top-flight journalist: probably the best in the game.

There had been a time when Joe could call his agent, tell him he was going over to London or Paris or Rome or wherever it was to cover some special event, and, within the hour, his agent had sold the article, sight unseen, and had also got a generous expense allocation to cover the cost of the trip.

At that time Joe could not only write brilliantly but he was also a class photographer and that made a very lucrative combination.

He reached the peak of his success in 1953. He not only had a book chosen by the Atlantic Book of the Month Club, but he also had a profile running for three weeks in the *New Yorker*, and *Life* had given a five-page spread to his remarkable photographs of the birth of a baby.

But the highlight of that year for him was his marriage with a nice but thoroughly ordinary girl, whose name was Martha Jones.

Martha and he set up home at Malvern, which was a little over an hour's run from Philadelphia, Joe's working headquarters.

Married life agreed with Joe. Martha and he were as happy together as two people really in love can be happy.

Then something happened that was to alter completely the rhythm of Joe's life.

One night coming back from a rather wild party, Joe, not exactly drunk, but certainly fuddled, accidentally killed his wife.

They had driven back to their home in Joe's Cadillac, with Joe driving. He knew he was a little high, and he had driven the thirty odd miles with extreme care. He was carrying with him his most precious possession, and he wasn't going to put her in the slightest danger just because he had had one whisky too many and was a little dizzy in the head.

They arrived home without incident, and Martha got out of the car to open the garage doors while Joe slid the automatic gear into reverse and had his foot on the brake pedal.

As Martha was about to open the garage doors, Joe's foot slipped off the pedal and the car began to move backwards.

Fuddled, and realizing Martha was directly behind the car, Joe stamped down hard on the brake pedal, missed it and his foot descended on the accelerator.

The massive car swept back at a speed that made it impossible for Martha to jump clear.

She was smashed against the garage doors and, with the splintered and broken doors, hurled into the garage and crushed against the back brick wall.

Joe never recovered from this experience. From the moment he got out of the car and ran to the lifeless body of his wife, he began to go downhill.

He began to drink. He lost his touch, and editors soon discovered he could no longer be relied on. After a while, the assignments didn't come to him and the articles he wrote lost their bite and didn't sell.

Anyone knowing him in 1953 wouldn't have recognized him as he shambled up the drive of the Plaza hotel after his brief conversation with Jay Delaney when he had hopefully asked if Jay could arrange an interview for him with Jay's father.

Joe Kerr was a tall, thin man who looked a lot older than his forty odd years. He stooped as he walked, and he was always a little short of breath. His hair, the colour of sand, was thin and lank, but it was his raddled plum-coloured face that shocked people meeting him for the first time.

Since the death of his wife, he had been drinking two bottles of whisky a day, and his face was now a mass of tiny broken veins. With his ruined face, his watery frog's eyes and his shabby clothes, he looked beaten and broken, and people moved out of his way when he approached them.

Somehow, he still managed to scrape up a living. He was now employed by a Hollywood scandal sheet called *Peep* that paid him enough to buy his drink and the bare necessities.

Peep had a large circulation. It specialized in near-pornographic photographs and an outrageous gossip column. In his heyday, Joe wouldn't have dreamed of contributing to such a paper, no matter what he had been offered. Now he was thankful to do so.

As he walked into the Plaza lobby, his Rolliflex camera hanging around his neck and bumping against his chest, Joe was thinking of the letter he had had that morning from Manley, the Editor of *Peep*.

Manley hadn't pulled his punches. If Joe imagined he had paid his fare to Cannes to get the insipid junk that Joe was turning in, Joe had another think coming.

"How many more times do I have to tell you that we have got to have something that'll stand our readers on their ears?" Manley wrote. "Cannes is a cesspit: everyone knows that. The dirt's there. If you'll only lay off the booze and dig for it, you'll find it. If you can't find it, then say so, and I'll wire Jack Bernstein to take over."

This letter had shaken Joe's nerves. He knew no other paper

would employ him, and if Manley dropped him, he might just as well walk into the sea and keep on walking.

Ever since Floyd Delaney had arrived in Cannes, Joe had been desperately trying to get a personal interview with him.

Floyd Delaney was the most colourful character at the Festival, and Joe hoped that, if he could get him talking, he could trap him into saying something indiscreet. He had worried Harry Stone, Delaney's publicity manager, to get him an interview, but Stone had been brutally frank.

"If you imagine F.D. wants to talk to a rumdum like you, Joe," he said, "you must be out of your mind. That pickle puss of yours would give him a nightmare."

Joe's drink-sodden mind glowed with resentment when he remembered Stone's words. If he could only dig up some dirt on Delaney, he was thinking, something really hot with photographs, maybe the snoot wouldn't be quite so sensitive about how a man looked if his own face was turning red.

It was a quarter to four when Joe took up his position in an alcove window that gave him an uninterrupted view of the door to suite 27. He was out of sight of anyone going into the suite and also out of sight of the occasional waiter who passed up and down the corridor.

He sat on the window seat, his Rolliflex at the ready, satisfied that there was enough light in the corridor to get good pictures without using his flash equipment.

He had had four double whiskies since two o'clock and his mind was a little fuddled. He wasn't quite sure what he was waiting for, for he knew Delaney and his high-hat wife were in the cinema and they wouldn't be out much before six o'clock. He had seen Delaney's good-looking son sunning himself on the beach, and he looked set to remain there some time. So, on the face of it, Joe was wasting his time sitting outside this door. Nothing seemed likely to happen in suite 27 until around six o'clock, and, even then, the chances of anything of value to Joe happening was remote.

But that didn't bother Joe. It simply supplied him with an excuse to sit still for a while and to get away from the mad crush downstairs.

The Cannes Festival had exhausted him. The competition had been unbelievably fierce. Joe felt old and washed-up when jostling with the other photographers for position when some famous star condescended to pose for a very brief moment to allow the photographers to go into action.

16

These photographers were young men, smart in their Riviera clothes, with hands that were rock steady, and their ruthless keenness dazed Joe. His drink-fuddled mind made him clumsy with his camera, and he had trouble in keeping it steady. They jostled him to the back of the crowd, yelling at him: "Get the hell out of the way, grandpa! Let a man work!"

At five minutes to four by the corridor clock immediately above the door to suite 27, Joe snapped out of a doze and peered down the corridor.

He saw Jay Delaney come down the corridor and pause outside the door to suite 27.

Without thinking much about what he was doing, Joe lifted the Rolliflex, glanced quickly into the view-finder, adjusted the focus, and then gently pressed the shutter release. He had already set the aperture, and he was satisfied that he had taken a printable picture should Manley want to print a picture of Floyd Delaney's son which, Joe knew, was extremely unlikely.

He shifted on the window seat as he watched Jay unlock the door and disappear into the suite.

Joe shrugged and groped for the half-pint bottle of whisky he always carried around with him in his hip pocket. He took a long pull, sighed and put the bottle away. He was just beginning to wonder if he should waste any more time outside this door when he saw a girl coming down the corridor.

He recognized her immediately. She was the up-and-coming French starlette, Lucille Balu, in a blue and white off-the-shoulder dress and a string of fat blue beads around her lovely brown throat.

Automatically, Joe wound on a new strip of film, wondering what she was doing on this floor reserved for film executives only. He felt a tiny prickle of excitement as she paused outside the door of suite 27.

He lifted his camera as she raised her hand to knock on the door and the shutter clicked as she rapped.

As he lowered the camera, he thought the right caption to that picture should be: *Opportunity Knocks. Lucille Balu, the French starlette, knocks on the door of Floyd Delaney's luxury suite at the Plaza hotel. Is this the beginning of a Hollywood career for this talented young beginner?*

Not the kind of material Manley was looking for, of course, but there was a chance he might sell the picture to some other rag.

He watched the door open and Jay appear in the doorway.

17

He heard Jay say, "How wonderfully punctual! Come on in. My father's waiting to meet you."

He watched the girl enter and the door close.

It took several seconds for Jay's words to sink into Joe's fuddled mind.

My father's waiting to meet you.

That couldn't be right. Floyd Delaney was at the cinema. Joe had seen him with his wife walking up the steps leading to the cinema and he knew they wouldn't be back until at least six o'clock.

Joe ran his fingers through his thinning hair.

What did this mean?

He remembered Jay Delaney had asked him who the girl was, and he suddenly stiffened to attention.

Was there more to this good-looking, pleasantly mannered youngster than he had imagined?

Joe had already noticed that Jay seemed to live a pretty solitary life. He had noticed, too, that he spent his days alone sitting on the beach, reading, and kept away from the fun and games that made the drudgery of the Festival worth while.

Had this boy tricked the girl into coming to the suite on the pretext that his father wanted to see her? Any ambitious starlette would jump at the chance of meeting Floyd Delaney. Was the boy going to attempt to seduce her?

Joe broke out in a hot sweat of excitement. Suppose he did and she screamed for help: that would give him the right to burst in there with his camera. He might even catch them struggling together: the girl with her clothes up around her neck! How Manley would eat a picture like that! It would wipe out all Joe's past mistakes! He would be in solid with Manley for life!

He leaned forward and listened, but he couldn't hear anything. Then just as he was about to leave his hiding-place and go and listen at the door, he saw Sophia Delaney coming briskly down the corridor.

For a moment he couldn't believe his eyes. His run of bad luck had been so consistent that he couldn't believe he was getting a break, and what a break!

Step-son lures starlette up to Papa's luxury suite, then, at the psychological moment, step-mother arrives! It was the kind of stuff *Peep* lived on!

Joe lifted his camera as Sophia knocked on the door.

II

As Jay swung the scarlet cord, he saw Sophia follow each swing.

He felt very sure of himself. He had seen that he had frightened Sophia, and he knew it wasn't easy to frighten his father's wife. He had also seen that he had disconcerted her by his bare-faced admission that he had brought a girl to the suite.

I had better not overdo it, he thought. I'd now better begin to reassure her. I mustn't let her imagine that there is anything seriously wrong. I had her worked up just now so badly she looked as if she were going to bolt out of the room. She must be very sensitive to atmosphere. I wonder how she guessed about the girl. Maybe it was the perfume. Women notice things like that. The girl had been over-scented.

"Do you mean to tell me you have a girl in your bedroom?" Sophia said, and he could see she was now trying to whip up her anger again, which had been cooled by her fear.

"I'm sorry, Sophia." He spoke gently. "It was one of those stupid impulses."

He moved away from her, tossing the curtain cord onto the settee; then he sat on the arm of a lounging chair.

He had now to persuade her to come over to his side. He had to appeal to her sympathy and understanding. He must get her to promise not to tell his father.

It was fantastic, he thought, that she should have returned like this. For three days she had remained with his father throughout all those dreary performances, but on this day, when it had been so vitally important that he shouldn't be disturbed, she had to return.

But, now he had recovered from the shock of hearing her angry rapping on the door, he found the situation exhilaratingly exciting.

It had certainly been a shock when she had rapped on the door. He had been kneeling beside Lucille's lifeless body, loosening the cord around her throat. The knocking sound had paralysed him. His heart seemed to stop beating. The blood in his veins seemed to congeal. His mind had gone blank with panic. It had been a bad moment, but it also had been a test.

He had known from the beginning that if he did this thing, sooner or later, he would be challenged, and he would have to rely on his nerve and his wits to save himself, but who would have imagined the challenge would have come so quickly? The girl was scarcely dead when the knocking had come on the door.

He had got his panic quickly under control. He had known that he had only a few seconds in which to act. He had picked up the girl's body. She had been surprisingly heavy and awkward. He had staggered with her into his bedroom and dumped her on his bed. Then he had returned to the lounge and snatched up the curtain cord and stuffed it into his hip pocket.

There had been an added complication: during the very brief but violent struggle, the string of the girl's necklace had broken and the beads had shot about the floor.

They were big blue beads, the size of small walnuts, and although they were easy to retrieve, he had had to do it at lightning speed.

He had just picked up the last bead in sight when he heard a key being pushed into the lock of the door.

He had darted into his bedroom and closed the door soundlessly as the door leading into the suite had opened.

He had had no time to compose himself when he heard Sophia call him.

He had been thankful for his dark glasses. He was confident that he could control the expression on his face, but he knew that his eyes would have given him away could she have seen them.

"A stupid impulse," he repeated. "I'm really sorry, Sophia. She looked so attractive and I was bored." He reached for his cigarette case lying on the table and opened it. "Will you?" He offered the case.

She shook her head.

"I can't understand you doing such a thing," she said and her voice was cold.

He lit a cigarette, and he was pleased and not a little proud to see how steady his hands were.

"I don't think you realize how lonely I am sometimes," he said, feeling sure this would be the right approach. "After all, Sophia, you have father, but I have no one. Father doesn't care about me. He's too busy to care about anyone but you. This girl was on her own in the lobby. She looked lonely too. So I talked to her. It was she who suggested we should go somewhere together. Don't think I'm trying to excuse myself. She appealed to me, and, if I had had the nerve, I would have made the suggestion. I didn't know where to take her, so I brought her up here." He looked at Sophia from behind his dark glasses. She was relaxing, and she had moved over to the table and now rested her hips against it. He could see he had her interest. "It's a funny thing, but although I thought she was attractive down in the lobby, as soon as I got her here, I realized she wasn't attractive at all. I suppose it was seeing her in this familiar room. Anyway I realize now what a fool I've been to have brought her up here."

"I can understand that, Jay," Sophia said, and he was quick to notice that her voice had softened.

"My one thought was to get rid of her," he went on. "I didn't know how to do it. I was scared she would make a scene. Then you knocked. I can't tell you how glad I was that you came back. I honestly don't know how I would have got her out of here without making a scene."

"Can she hear what you are saying?" she asked and looked at his bedroom door.

"Oh, no." He leaned forward to flick ash into the ash-tray. "I bundled her into the bathroom and locked the door." Then he couldn't resist making the gruesome joke. "She can't hear anything – she might just as well be dead."

Sophia wasn't listening. She walked over to the window and stared down at the sea glittering in the sunshine.

"I must say this does surprise me, Jay," she said. "It wasn't nice of you to bring a girl up here."

"I know and I'm ashamed of myself. I'm sorry, Sophia."

She turned then and her lips made a movement of a stiff smile.

"Let's forget it. I'm sure it won't happen again." She began to cross the room to her bedroom. "I'm going for a swim. I just looked in for my swim-suit."

Jay felt a surge of triumph run through him. He had come through the first test. It has been unbelievably easy. He was willing to admit it had been a very dangerous moment. If he had lost his nerve, it would have been disastrous.

"Thank you, Sophia, for being so nice about it," he said, and gave her a lost, very young smile. "Will you have to tell father?"

"No, I won't tell him."

A blue object lying under a chair caught her attention, and she bent and picked it up.

"Where did this come from?" she asked and put on the table one of the beads from the broken necklace.

Once again panic nibbled at the edges of Jay's mind as he looked at the bead.

"It's a pretty thing, isn't it?" he said, trying to speak casually. "Are you sure it isn't yours?"

"Of course it's not mine!"

The snap in her voice warned him not to overdo his casualness.

He pointed to his bedroom door, lowering his voice as he said: "It must be hers. She probably dropped it."

Sophia gave him a questioning, uneasy look, then she walked quickly into her bedroom, leaving the door open.

Jay picked up the bead and dropped it into his trousers pocket, where the other beads were.

He would have to search the room very carefully after Sophia had gone to make sure there were no other beads lying around. It was unfortunate she had seen it. If she thought about it she might realize it was a bead from a string of beads and that, together with the scratches on his arm she had seen, might make her think there had been a struggle.

Sophia came out of the bedroom carrying her swim-suit and her *peignoir*.

Jay opened the door for her.

"I'll be back in an hour," she said and looked pointedly at his bedroom door; then she went quickly down the corridor, as if she were anxious to get away from him.

Jay stood in the doorway looking after her, then he turned and shut and locked the door.

He glanced at his wrist-watch. The time was exactly half-past four.

Moving quickly, he began to search the room for any more of the blue beads. He found yet another under the settee, and then, after a further search, he was satisfied there were no more to be found.

He replaced the curtain cord, and then stood back and surveyed the room.

There were no signs of the struggle that had taken place. The room looked exactly as he had found it when he had entered forty minutes ago.

He lit a cigarette, and, moving over to the window, he examined the three ugly red scratches on his arm.

The girl had tried desperately to save her life. The cord had choked back her screams, but she had managed to reach behind her and had clawed his arm just before she lost consciousness. He had been surprised and alarmed that such a frail-looking girl could have had such desperate strength. There had been a moment when he had begun to doubt if he could subdue her.

He went into his bedroom, crossed the room without looking

22

towards the bed and entered the bathroom. He bathed his arm and put on some disinfectant ointment. Then he washed his hands and, while he was drying them, he considered his next move.

It wouldn't be safe to get rid of the body until the early hours of the morning. The Plaza hotel went to bed around half-past three a.m. He had twelve hours to make up his mind what to do with the body. But during those twelve hours, unless he did something about it, the girl would be missed.

He remembered overhearing the conversation between the girl and the man with the wiry black hair who, he guessed, would be her agent. They had made a date to meet in the bar downstairs at six. If she didn't turn up, this man might make inquiries about her, and this, Jay decided, he would have to prevent.

He went back into the lounge, again not looking towards the bed as he crossed the room. He went over to the row of reference books his father always had by him and, after a quick search, he found, in a copy of *Who's Who in the Film World*, a scrappy entry covering Lucille Balu's brief career as a movie star. He learned that she was twenty-one, had appeared in five movies, that she had an apartment in Paris, and her agent's name was Jean Thiry.

Jay closed the book and replaced it on the shelf, then he picked up the telephone receiver and asked the girl on the switch board to connect him with Information and Messages.

He had no fear that his call could be traced. The two men dealing with messages were coping with a steady stream of callers throughout the day. They would not be likely to remember one isolated call.

"Will you please deliver the following message to Monsieur Jean Thiry, who will be in the bar at six o'clock?" Jay said. "The message is: I am spending the evening in Monte Carlo. Will see you in the morning. Lucille Balu."

The man repeated the message, said it would be delivered to Monsieur Thiry and then hung up.

At about six o'clock, Jay knew the maid came to prepare his bed for the night.

He went into his bedroom, shutting and locking the door.

He looked at the dead girl lying on the bed. She lay on her side in a slightly curled up position, her back turned to him. She looked as if she were sleeping.

He glanced around the room for a place in which to hide her.

23

There was a big cupboard against one wall, and he went over to it and opened it, noting there was a lock on the door. He decided to put her in there.

For a brief moment his nerve faltered at the thought of touching her, but only for a moment. He opened both doors of the cupboard, then went over to the bed and took hold of her.

Again her dead-weight sui rised him, and he was breathing heavily by the time he had got her into the cupboard.

He was glad when he had shut and locked the cupboard doors. He took the key from the lock and put it in his pocket. Then he went to the chest of drawers, took from it a pair of swimming trunks and, unlocking the bedroom door, he went into the lounge. He paused to fill his cigarette case from the box on the table; then he left the suite, locking the door after him.

He crossed the passage to the elevator and pressed the buzzer.

Joe Kerr watched him.

Joe was puzzled and disappointed. What had seemed to be the situation of a life-time had mysteriously fizzled out to nothing. Instead of a first-class row and scandal, and a chance for him to have walked into the suite with his camera, nothing had happened at all.

Sophia Delaney had left, taking with her a swim-suit, and now young Delaney had also left with a swim-suit.

But where was the girl? Why hadn't she left?

Joe had seen the boy lock the door: that meant the girl couldn't leave even if she wanted to. What was the idea?

Joe wiped his red-raw sweating face with a grubby handkerchief and tried to puzzle out what it all meant.

The girl had gone in there and she hadn't come out, so she must still be in there. Then why had young Delaney locked her in?

This was now developing into an intriguing situation.

Joe peered up and down the long, deserted corridor, then he left his hiding-place and crossed over to the door of suite 27.

He listened intently, his ear against the door panel, but he could hear nothing. He hesitated for a moment, then, lifting his hand, he rapped sharply on the door. He knocked several times, but he heard no movement nor sound from within the suite, and he stepped back puzzled.

He was certain she was still in there. Had young Delaney warned her not to answer a knock?

Then he suddenly became aware that he was being watched,

and he moved casually away from the door and glanced down the corridor.

At the far end, leading to the stairs, he saw the short, bulky figure of the hotel detective.

With the resourcefulness of years of experience as a newspaper man, Joe started down the corridor towards the detective, who eyed him suspiciously as he came.

"Mr. Delaney doesn't seem to be in," Joe said as soon as he was within a few paces of the hotel detective.

"No, he isn't," the detective snapped. "Didn't you inquire at the desk?"

"Why, sure," Joe said blandly. "I was told he was in his suite."

"That was the young Mr. Delaney, but he's out now. You don't want him, do you?"

Joe sneered.

"What should I want him for? Never mind. I'll come back." He moved around the hotel detective and started down the stairs, whistling softly, aware the detective was staring after him.

That was bad luck, Joe thought, as he edged his way through the crowd in the lobby. I wonder how long he's going to remain up there? Anyway, the girl can't get out until young Delaney returns.

He crossed over to the hall-porter's desk.

"When any of the Delaneys go up to their suite, let me know, will you?" he said to the hall porter. "I'll be in the bar." Reluctantly he parted with a thousand franc note. "Don't forget: it's important."

The hall porter said he'd let him know, took the note and then moved away.

Joe crossed over to a telephone booth and asked the girl on the switch board to connect him with the Delaneys' suite.

There was a long pause, then the girl said, "I'm sorry, monsieur, no one answers."

Joe replaced the receiver and edged his way through the crowd into the bar. As he pushed open the swing door, he saw the hands of the clock above the bar stood at five minutes to five.

At that hour the bar was almost empty. Joe shocked the barman by asking for a plate of ham, a roll and butter and a double whisky.

He was sure the girl was still in the suite. No point in going hungry, he told himself as he began to butter his roll. The wait could be a long one, but he was determined to see the girl leave, even if he had to wait outside the door of the suite all night.

CHAPTER THREE

I

JEAN THIRY walked out of the cinema a few paces behind Floyd Delaney.

Delaney was talking to his business manager, Harry Stone, a big, heavily built man who wore rimless glasses and a fawn light-weight suit. Sweat beads made his bald head glisten.

Thiry wondered if this might be the opportunity he had been waiting for to approach Delaney. If only he could get Delaney interested in Lucille, his financial troubles would be over. There were now only three more days of the Festival, and then his chances of getting Delaney to sign Lucille up would be gone.

Lucille was Thiry's one great hope. His agency had been going down-hill now for the past two years, and Lucille was the only promising star on his shrinking list of clients. The others were has-beens: good, efficient actors and actresses who at one time had been names, but now were too old for anything but bit parts, and the commission he got from them wasn't enough to take care of the office overheads.

Thiry glanced at his wrist-watch. It was just on six. He had told Lucille to meet him in the Plaza bar at six. If he hurried on ahead of Delaney, he could fix it that he and Lucille were in the lobby when Delaney entered the hotel.

As he was about to move towards the cinema exit, Delaney walked directly past him.

Grabbing at the opportunity, Thiry said, "Good afternoon, Mr. Delaney."

Floyd Delaney gave him a quick, sharp stare and then paused.

Delaney was tall and broad with blond, wavy hair, turning white at the temples. His deeply tanned face was arresting rather than handsome. He had grey eyes, a cleft chin and a sensitive mouth. He looked a lot younger than his fifty-five years.

He frowned, trying to recall where he had seen Thiry before.

"Let's see . . . you are . . . ?"

Harry Stone moved up.

"This is Jean Thiry, Mr. Delaney. Lucille Balu's agent."

Delaney's face showed sudden interest.

"Yeah, that's right. I remember." He offered his hand to Thiry. "You have a nice little property in that kid, Thiry. I've been thinking I might do something about her. How's she fixed?"

Thiry took Delaney's hand as if it were made of egg shells.

"She's just finished a picture, Mr. Delaney. She's free right now."

"Suppose we all have a drink together?" Delaney said. "I'm not free until nine. Bring her along then. Nine in the bar, eh?"

"Yes, Mr. Delaney," Thiry said, scarcely believing his good fortune. "We'll be there, and thanks."

Delaney nodded and, taking Stone's arm, hurried with him across the foyer and down to where his big Bentley was standing in the sunshine.

His heart thumping with excitement, Thiry ran down the cinema steps and started along the Croisette towards the Plaza hotel.

What a break! he was thinking. Delaney wouldn't be wasting his time buying us drinks if he wasn't really interested. This could be a thirty million franc contract! A ten per cent cut on that figure would be a life saver!

He had difficulty in stopping himself from breaking into a run. What a bit of luck for Lucille too! he thought. Well, she deserved it. She had worked hard, hadn't given herself airs, hadn't been hard to handle, had done just what he had told her to do, and now this looked as if both of them were going to reap their reward.

He pushed his way through the crowd in the Plaza lobby and entered the bar.

The clock above the bar told him it was now five past six. The bar was pretty crowded. He looked around but he couldn't see Lucille.

Not like her to be late, he thought, elbowing his way to the bar. Feeling it was a moment to celebrate, he ordered a whisky and soda, and, while he was drinking it, he leaned against the bar and watched the entrance.

Joe Kerr, sipping his third whisky, watched him.

A page put his head around the bar door and called, "Monsieur Jean Thiry, please."

Thiry signalled to the boy, who came over and gave him a slip of paper.

Frowning and watched by Joe Kerr, Thiry read the message.

Telephone message for Mr. Jean Thiry. Received 16.45. I am spending the evening in Monte Carlo. Will see you in the morning. Lucille Balu.

Thiry stared at the message, then, as the page began to fidget, he tipped him and then moved over to one of the big windows that overlooked the Croisette.

Why in the world had Lucille gone to Monte Carlo? he wondered. Who had she gone with? She wouldn't have gone all that way alone.

He again looked at the clock over the bar. The time was now twenty minutes past six. He had two hours and forty minutes to find her and get her back to the Plaza hotel. Well, it wasn't impossible. Monte Carlo was a small place. She was certain to be in the Casino.

He crumpled the message slip and tossed it from him, then he hurried from the bar, through the lobby and out of the hotel to where he had parked his shabby, overworked Simca Verdette.

Before Thiry had reached the bar door, Joe Kerr had slid off his stool and had picked up the crumpled message slip. He carried it back to the bar and carefully smoothed out the paper. He read the message, and his red-raw face puckered into an expression of blank bewilderment.

Had the girl left the suite after all? Had he missed her somehow?

He put the message slip into his wallet, finished his whisky and, leaving the bar, he went to the hall-porter's desk.

"Have you seen Mademoiselle Balu leave?" he asked.

"She hasn't left the hotel, monsieur," the hall porter returned, and, knowing the man's efficiency, Kerr didn't doubt him for a moment.

"None of the Delaneys been in yet?"

"No, monsieur."

There was a side exit near the entrance to the Television Studios that was housed in the Plaza and Joe decided it would be worth while to check there. He hurried down the long corridor to where a couple of pressmen were sitting outside the studio, patiently nursing their cameras.

"Seen Lucille Balu go out?" Joe asked.

28

They shook their heads.

"She didn't come this way."

She must still be in Delaney's suite, Joe told himself as he returned to the lobby. Then why the message? Had she sent it? Maybe she was planning to spend the night in the boy's bedroom. Was that it? It seemed odd to Joe that the girl should get herself locked in the suite as early as this.

He saw Floyd Delaney and Harry Stone come into the lobby.

Stone went over to the desk and got Delaney's key while Delaney paused for a moment to have a word with Edward G. Robinson, who was passing through the lobby.

Joe heard Delaney say to Stone as Robinson moved on: "I'll go on up. See you in the bar at nine, Harry. If we can come to terms I'd like to get this Balu girl under contract."

Moving quickly, Joe crossed the lobby and ran up the stairs to the second floor. He paused at the head of the stairs to make sure the hotel detective wasn't still prowling around, then he hurried to the alcove window and had just got out of sight as the elevator door opened and Delaney came out and crossed to the door of suite 27.

Delaney unlocked the door and entered, shutting the door behind him. He went over to the telephone and called his secretary, Miss Kobbe, who had a room on the third floor.

"Come on down, will you?" he said, then dropped the receiver back on its cradle and, going into his bedroom, he stripped off his clothes and put on a dressing gown.

He heard Miss Kobbe come in.

"Get Sanson," he called. "I'll be out in a moment," and he went into the bathroom and took a cold shower.

When Sophia came into the suite, she found Floyd talking on the telephone. He waved to her and she went over and kissed his forehead, then went into her bedroom.

Miss Kobbe, a tall willowy girl, began to mix a batch of martinis in a silver shaker.

With a speed born of long practice, she poured two drinks, put one of them on the table where Delaney could reach it, and then, carrying the other, she rapped on Sophia's bedroom door and entered.

Sophia was sitting at her dressing table. She had taken off her frock and now, clad only in panties and brassière, she was painting her lips with a fine-haired brush.

"Thank you," she said as Miss Kobbe put the martini on the dressing-table. "Do you know if Jay is in his room?"

"I don't think he is, Mrs. Delaney," Miss Kobbe said. "I haven't heard him. Do you want me to see?"

Sophia hesitated, then shook her head.

"No, it's all right. Will Mr. Delaney be tied up for long?"

"He's waiting a call from Hollywood. Mr. Cooper is coming up at six forty-five."

"What's happening to-night?"

"Mr. Delaney is meeting Miss Lucille Balu in the bar at nine. He then wants to catch the last part of the film showing to-night. You and he are having supper at half-past twelve with the van Asters at the Château de Madrid."

Sophia sighed.

"When Mr. Delaney is off the phone, please tell him I want to speak to him."

"I will, Mrs. Delaney."

Miss Kobbe went out.

Sophia drank half the martini, then, lighting a cigarette, she slipped on a wrap and lay down on the chaise-longue by the open window.

She had been uneasy and worried since she had left Jay. His explanation about the girl in his room hadn't satisfied her. It had been too glib: too calculated. She was sure he had been lying, and she had an instinctive feeling that something was seriously wrong. The scratches on his arm, the way he had held the curtain cord, the blue bead she had found on the floor, and the atmosphere and tension that had been in the room had formed a sinister impression in her mind.

The more she thought about it, the more uneasy she had become. She felt that Floyd should be told, and yet she was anxious that he shouldn't go off the deep-end, as he so easily did. She knew he didn't take much interest in his son and that he was inclined to be unfairly critical of him. She didn't want to make the already big rift between the two any bigger, but she was now so uneasy in her mind that she felt compelled to shift the responsibility on to her husband.

She heard the telephone bell tinkle as Floyd hung up, and then, after a pause, her bedroom door opened and he came in.

"Well, honey, did you have a nice swim?"

"Yes, it was nice. Sit down, darling. I want to talk to you."

He moved over to the chaise-longue, his half finished martini in his hand and he sat down by her side. He put his glass on the side table and then rested his hand, under her wrap on her knee, smiling at her.

"What is it? You looked worried. I don't like to see my baby doll worried. Is there anything wrong?"

For a moment she hesitated. Floyd was unpredictable. Was it her business to talk to him about his son? Would he be offended? Then she thought of the way Jay had moved across the room, the curtain cord in his hands and the sudden frightening feeling she had had that perhaps he meant her harm. This recollection decided her.

"Not exactly wrong, Floyd. It's about Jay. . . ."

Delaney's smile faded and two deep lines of disapproval appeared above the bridge of his nose.

"Jay? Why should you be worrying about him?"

"Floyd, this is in strict confidence. Please. . . ."

His hand slid over her knee and along her thigh and he smiled again.

"Of course. What is it?"

"He had a girl up here."

Delaney stared at her, then took his hand away and rubbed his jaw, his eyes hardening.

"A girl? Up here?"

"Yes. When I left you, I came back here to pick up my swimsuit. I found the door locked. When I finally got in, there was a smell of perfume in the room. I knew at once someone had been in here. I asked him if he had brought a girl up here and he admitted it."

"Well, for the love of mike!" Delaney said and got to his feet. He began to prowl around the room, his face set in a heavy frown. "Who was she?"

"I don't know. She was in his bedroom. He said he was lonely. He met the girl in the lobby and thought she was attractive and brought her up here. Then he decided she wasn't so attractive and was wondering how he could get rid of her when I arrived."

"Well, I'll be damned!" Delaney said, his voice suddenly harsh. "I'll kick his tail for him! Where is he?"

"Floyd, please . . . I promised him I wouldn't tell you. You mustn't say anything to him, but I thought you should know about it."

Delaney moved over to his drink, picked up the glass and finished the martini.

"There's not much point in knowing if I can't do anything about it," he said impatiently. "I don't object to him fooling around with a girl. At his age, that's natural, but I'm damned if I'll stand for him bringing some tart up here."

"He won't do it again, Floyd. We had an understanding about that," Sophia said quietly.

Delaney ran his fingers through his hair.

"Well, then. . . ."

He glanced at his watch. His mind was already beginning to move away from the subject of his son, which never interested him for more than three or four minutes at a stretch. He had a lot to do this night. The Hollywood call bothered him. He had made an offer for the new Atlantic Book of the Month choice and he had just learned that M.G.M. were also interested in the book. If his agent, Brennon, didn't hurry up, the book might cost him more than it was worth.

"Floyd . . . Jay is a little odd, isn't he?" Sophia said. "Ever since I've known him I've thought he was – well, a little odd."

Delaney looked sharply at her.

"Odd? I wouldn't say that. Perhaps he's a bit too quiet for his age and maybe he doesn't mix enough, but I wouldn't say he was odd. What exactly do you mean?"

What exactly did she mean? Sophia wondered. She really had nothing to go on except this instinctive feeling the boy wasn't entirely normal.

"It's a feeling I have." She hesitated, then went on. "Sometimes I think he's a little sinister. Why does he always wear those dark glasses? It's as if he is hiding away his real thoughts from everyone. There's an atmosphere about him. . . ."

Delaney was suddenly bored with all this. His mind was too absorbed in his own affairs to be bothered with abstract impressions.

"For heaven's sake! Jay, sinister? You're imagining things. There's nothing sinister about the boy . . . nothing at all."

Again Sophia hesitated, then, compelled to go further because of her genuine alarm, she said quietly, "His mother was a little queer, wasn't she, Floyd?"

Delaney's face hardened.

A little queer was an understatement.

Harriette would have been certified as insane had she not thrown herself out of a tenth-floor window of a hotel in Los Angeles. Although it was now twelve years since that fatal day, the thought of it still made Delaney flinch.

His mind shied away from the memory of the years he had

spent with Harriette. Admittedly the first year had been enchanting. She had been breath-takingly beautiful, vivacious, wealthy and exciting. But from the very first, she had been eccentric, but amusingly so. To anyone with any insight the hint of mental instability was there but Delaney had no insight. Her fits of crying, her outbursts of violent temper and her sudden hysterical elation made her to him interesting and unpredictable. Her passion for dangerously fast driving, her long periods of sulky brooding and her restlessness were things that Delaney shrugged off as part of her personality.

Jay was born a year after the marriage, and Harriette gave the boy over to a nurse, taking no interest in him. As the years went by, she developed such an active dislike for him that Delaney sent him to boarding school and during the vacations arranged that Jay didn't come home.

Harriette's mental condition slowly deteriorated. Although Delaney's friends had long realized that she was mentally sick, Delaney himself, absorbed in his work, was still unaware that there was anything seriously wrong with her. His married life was no longer happy. Whenever they were alone together, which was seldom, they invariably quarrelled, but this he shrugged off as inevitable.

Then one night something happened that brought the facts brutally home to him.

The memory of that night, although now twelve years ago, still had the power to increase his heart-beat whenever he allowed himself to think of it.

He had returned from the Studios late to his luxurious home in Beverley Hills and had settled down to read the script of a film he was planning to produce.

Harriette sat away from him, silent and brooding. He had spoken to her, but she hadn't replied, and, mentally shrugging, he put her out of his mind and concentrated on the script.

He had read for about an hour, then suddenly he had become aware of an extraordinary tension in the room. He had looked across the room to where Harriette had been sitting, but she had left the chair and had moved behind him out of sight. There was a mirror on the wall facing him and he had glanced at it. What he saw reflected there gave him the shock of his life.

Harriette was creeping up behind him, a carving knife in her hand and an expression on her face that still haunted his dreams.

He realized in those brief seconds as he stared at her in the

33

mirror that she was insane and the shock momentarily paralysed him.

It was only when she was within a few feet of him and had lifted the knife that he threw aside the script and jumped to his feet.

She had come at him with the ferocity of a wild cat and he had been appalled by her strength. Before he had managed to get the knife away from her, she had slashed his arm and inflicted a long, deep scratch down the side of his face.

She had broken away from him, and before he could stop her, she had run out of the house.

That was the last time he had seen her alive.

She had taken his car, driven to a hotel in Los Angeles, taken the elevator to the tenth floor, entered an empty bedroom and had thrown herself out of the window.

Yes, 'a little queer' was an understatement, and Delaney was irritated that Sophia should revive such a painful memory.

"Yeah, I guess she was," he said frowning, "but that doesn't mean . . ."

He broke off as he heard the telephone bell ring.

"That's my call. Look, honey, forget it. There's nothing to worry about. Jay's all right. Damn it! I've lived with him for twenty-one years. I know he's all right."

Miss Kobbe put her head around the door.

"Mr. Brennon on the line, Mr. Delaney."

"I'm coming."

Delaney patted Sophia's cheek, then went into the other room, closing the door behind.

Sophia stared up at the ceiling, frowning.

She again thought of Jay, picturing him as he had moved towards her, the scarlet cord betwen his fingers, his eyes hidden behind the dark glasses, and she moved uneasily.

Where was he? What was he doing? Who had been the girl he had brought up to the suite?

Miss Kobbe looked in.

"Another martini, Mrs. Delaney?"

Sophia nodded.

"Yes, perhaps I will. Has Jay got back yet?"

"Not yet, Mrs. Delaney."

A sudden impulse made Sophia get to her feet and walk into the lounge.

Delaney was talking on the telephone. His assistant producer, Jack Cooper, sat on the arm of a lounging chair, smoking.

He smiled at Sophia as she crossed over to Jay's bedroom door.

She nodded to him as she turned the handle and entered the room.

Shutting the door, she leaned against it and looked around.

The hotel maid had been in. She had turned down the bed, put Jay's blue pyjamas on the bed and had half lowered the blinds.

The smell of perfume was noticeable still in the room.

A photograph in a silver frame of Harriette, looking very lovely and very innocent, stood on the dressing table.

Sophia studied the photograph. She could see how like Harriette Jay was. They had the same mouth and the same facial bone structure and the same beguiling innocence.

From the photograph she looked at the big cupboard against the wall and noticed the key wasn't in the lock. She crossed to the cupboard and tried to open it, but found the doors locked.

Then suddenly, for no reason at all, she felt an urge to get out of the room. The same sharp feeling of fear she had experienced when Jay had moved towards her, the scarlet cord in his hands, took hold of her.

She stepped away from the cupboard, her heart beating fast. She paused by the door, staring at the cupboard, trying to control this inexplicable feeling of panic. Then she jerked open the door and walked into the lounge.

She came to an abrupt standstill when she saw that Jay was in the room. He was standing by one of the big windows, looking towards her. She could see herself, very tense and still reflected in the dark surfaces of his sun-glasses.

Delaney was saying over the telephone: "Fine, Ted, get the contract signed and fast. Get it done to-night." He seemed oblivious of the tight, strained atmosphere.

Sophia moved quickly to her room. She felt Jay's hidden eyes on her as she pushed open the door.

She looked back at him and he smiled at her. It seemed to her it was a sinister, threatening smile and it sent a chill crawling up her spine.

II

Jay leaned against the polished bar, a tomato juice in his hand. He watched the small group of men standing a few feet from him. There was his father, Harry Stone and Jack Cooper, all in tuxedos. They surrounded Jean Thiry, who was wearing a beach shirt, fawn slacks and sandals. He looked hot and tired and bothered. The gay beach shirt stuck to his back in black patches and his face was shiny with sweat.

He was saying: "I'm sorry, Mr. Delaney, I don't know where she's got to. I've hunted everywhere. She left a note saying she was spending the evening in Monte Carlo, but there's no sign of her there. I've only just got back."

Jay sipped his tomato juice. He listened and watched with concentrated interest.

Floyd Delaney snapped his fingers impatiently.

"Well, for heaven's sake! Don't you take care of that girl better than that? Okay, if she's not here, she's not here." He turned to Stone. "Handle this, Harry. I want to catch the film."

"Yes, Mr. Delaney," Stone said.

"I'll see she's here for you to-morrow any time, Mr. Delaney," Thiry said miserably. "It's just one of those things. Someone must have invited her. . . ."

But Delaney wasn't listening. He moved away from Thiry and walked over to where Jay was standing.

"You come along with me," he said. "I want you to see this movie."

Startled, Jay groped for an excuse. He was surprised to see how hostile his father's eyes were. Had Sophia told him? She had promised not to, but she might have changed her mind. Why had she been in his room? That was a question that had puzzled and disquieted him all the evening. He was thankful he had thought to lock the cupboard and take the key away with him.

"And, look, take those glasses off," his father went on. "You don't have to live in them, do you?"

Jay took the glasses off and tucked them into his top pocket.

"I'd rather not see the movie, father," he said. "I'm not dressed. I was thinking of going over to the Eden Roc for a swim."

Delaney's face tightened.

"I want you to see this movie. I want your opinion. What's the matter with you? You'll be coming into the Studio next year. How the hell do you expect to get anywhere if you don't show some interest in your career?"

"All right," Jay said meekly. "If you really want my opinion, of course I'll see the film. I'll go up and change."

"Yeah, do that." Delaney's face relaxed and he grinned, slapping his son on the shoulder. The kid was okay: a little lazy perhaps, but, if you handled him right, he was co-operative. Sophia had said he was odd. That just showed you. Women were always going off at half-cock. Odd? Nonsense! "I'll tell the guy at the door to keep you a seat next to me. Snap it up, boy. It's due to start in twenty minutes. See you," and leaving Jay and ignoring Thiry, he walked fast from the bar, waving to right and left to people he knew.

As soon as his father was out of sight, Jay put on his glasses again. He finished his tomato juice and edged a little closer to where Thiry and Stone were standing.

He heard Stone say, "You can take it or leave it. She hasn't any name in the States."

Jay was tempted to tell Stone he was wasting his time. He thought of the girl lying in his cupboard, and he felt a little prickle of excitement crawl up his spine. He had still six hours before he could attempt to move her. He might just as well sit in the cinema as wander about waiting for the time to pass.

Leaving the two men still talking, Jay left the bar, crossed the lobby to the elevator.

He said casually to the elevator attendant: "What time does the elevator go on automatic?"

"Three o'clock, sir," the attendant told him.

Jay nodded.

It was as he had thought. He would need the elevator when he moved the girl. The thought that, within six hours, he would have to get her out of the cupboard, across the lounge, across the corridor and into the elevator, made his heart-beat quicken. There was a risk that Sophia or his father would hear him take her across the lounge. There was a risk someone would see him cross the corridor. He was ready to take the risk: it was all part of this intense excitement he had to have.

He was a little startled to find the door to suite 27 unlocked, and he opened it cautiously and looked into the lounge. The lights were on, and he heard movements in Sophia's room.

He moved silently to his room, opened the door and stepped into the room, shutting the door before he turned on the light.

Sophia would be going to the movie. She would be leaving in a minute or so. He took the cupboard key from his pocket, unlocked the door and opened it.

The dead girl lay exactly as he had left her. He stared at her for a moment, then he reached down and touched her bare arm. The flesh felt cool and hard and he grimaced. She would be awkward to handle unless by the time he was ready to move her

37

the rigor had passed off. He vaguely remembered reading some-where that rigor did pass off after some hours, but just how long he couldn't recall.

He took his tuxedo from the cupboard and tossed it on the bed, then, unable to wait, impelled by the urgent need to know for certain, he took hold of the dead girl's arm and experimented in trying to pull her upright.

He was shocked by her weight and awkwardness. He felt a doubt that perhaps he wouldn't be able to get her from his room to the elevator.

He put his hands under her armpits and, straining, he managed to lift her upright. Then, as he propped her up against the wall of the cupboard, he heard a knock on his door.

His heart gave a painful little kick, then began to thump so violently he had trouble in breathing. He heard the handle of his bedroom door turning. Letting go of the girl's body, he slammed the cupboard doors shut as his bedroom door swung open.

He turned, feeling cold sweat on his face.

Sophia stood in the doorway. She was wearing a flame-coloured evening dress, cut low and tight in the bodice and flaring out at the skirt. There was a large diamond brooch in her hair and diamonds around her slender throat.

They stood staring at each other.

Sophia hadn't expected to find him in his room. Her uneasi-ness had increased while she had been dressing, and, imagining she was alone in the suite, she had decided to take one more look at Jay's room in the hope of finding something that would either reassure her or confirm her suspicions that something was badly wrong.

Seeing Jay, motionless, white-faced and so obviously fright-ened, she knew she had caught him in some guilty act.

She watched him take hold of himself.

"Hello," he said and there was a slight quaver in his voice. "I was just going to change. Father wants me to see the movie tonight."

"Does he?"

There was a pause, then he said: "I'll have to hurry. You're going, aren't you?"

"Yes, I'm going."

He moved away from the cupboard and, going over to his chest of drawers, he began to empty his pockets, putting his gold cigarette case, his lighter, handkerchief and money on top of the chest.

Sophia drew in a long, slow breath.

"Jay . . . is there something wrong?"

He stiffened, then slowly turned his head. The dark lenses of his glasses gave him a sinister appearance.

"Wrong? Why, no. What do you mean?"

"It's a feeling I have," she said, not moving. "This girl . . ."

"You don't have to worry about her," Jay said. "She has gone now."

"But is she likely to make trouble?"

"Why should she?"

"She might try to blackmail you."

Jay smiled: at least his lips curved into a smile but the rest of his face was stiff and tense.

"She won't do that. What makes you think she would do such a thing?"

"A girl like that . . ."

The words hung in space. Sophia saw that Jay's eyes were riveted on the cupboard and she looked too.

Very slowly, the cupboard doors were opening.

Sophia suddenly felt very frightened.

She saw Jay make a movement forward and then stop. His face had gone the colour of tallow.

The doors of the cupboard swung fully open.

Lucille Balu's rigid body swayed uncertainly, then as Sophia's hands went to her mouth, stifling her scream of horror, the dead girl slid to the floor at Sophia's feet.

CHAPTER FOUR

I

No one, not even her husband, suspected that under the veneer of Sophia's beauty there was a core of armour-plated hardness forged there by the misery and horrible squalor of her childhood. Very few people knew that Sophia was the product of the slums of Naples.

As soon as she had been able to walk, she had roved the Naples waterfront with a band of other filthy, ragged children, preying on tourists, surrounding them, dirty hands outstretched, while chanting the only English word she knew: "Money – money – money."

At night she returned to the tiny hovel constructed out of two wooden crates and a strip of corrugated iron that served as her home.

She lived there with her father, a short stocky Italian, with the flat black eyes of a gangster, who had never done a day's work in his life.

If Sophia failed to bring home less than five hundred lira a day, her father would seize hold of her, raise her ragged dress and savagely flay her naked flesh with his belt.

This existence continued until she was thirteen years old. Then one night, on returning home with less than the required five hundred lira, her mind and body cringing at the thought of the thrashing she would receive, she found her father curled up on the bundle of rags that served him for a bed, a dagger buried to the hilt in his heart.

She stared down at him for a long time, savouring the joy of finding him dead, then moving up to him, she had spat in his dead, snarling face and had left, happy to realize she was on her own, that she had now only herself to think of, and the bite of the strap into her flesh was now a thing of the past.

Even in rags and under a coat of grime, Sophia had been a beautiful child. It was not long before she attracted the attention of a man who called himself Giuseppe Francini, a pimp, who worked the cafés in the festering alleys off the Via Roma. He saw her possibilities, took charge of her, dressed her, found her a reasonably clean room and launched her on the career of a prostitute: all this before she had reached the age of fifteen.

Realizing the money that could be made from this profession, Sophia had entered into her new career with an enthusiasm that astonished and delighted Francini. He quickly realized that he was wasting her talents by allowing her to work the low class cafés. He arranged with a friend of his to share the expense of sending her to Rome and renting an apartment there for her.

By the time she reached the age of seventeen, Sophia was a highly successful prostitute. She had shaken off Francini, had taken a luxury apartment in the fashionable quarter of Rome, she was making a substantial income, owned an Alfa-Romeo car and had a wardrobe full of expensive, fashionable clothes that included a mink stole.

A few months after her seventeenth birthday she met Hamish Wardell, a movie director on vacation from Hollywood. Wardell, impressed by her beauty and her enthusiastic love making, took her back to Hollywood with him and arranged for her to have a small part in the movie he was making.

Sophia made an immediate hit in the movie. Her beauty, her strident sex appeal, wiped all the other actresses and actors out of the picture. She made such an impact on the public that she was immediately signed up on a six-figure salary to do three movies and an increase on a further three.

From then on, money flowed unceasingly into her various bank accounts, the public's adoration was hers and the horror of her childhood and the memories of the brutalities of her past clients when she had been walking the streets of Rome became a blurred memory

She had met Floyd Delaney when she was twenty-four. He had fallen in love with her and they had married within six months of their first meeting.

She was now the wife of one of the richest and most powerful men in Hollywood. She had everything she could wish for. Her position in life was secure, and security to Sophia was her most important possession, next to life itself.

She sat on the settee in the lounge, her knees pressed tightly together, her hands in fists as she stared at Jay who sat opposite her, his face set and pale, a muscle close to his right eye twitching.

She had no doubt that he had murdered this girl, and she realized this mad act had jeopardized her own position.

If ever this thing hit the headlines of the world's newspapers, the security and her position she had suffered so much to gain would go.

She was now recovering from the shock of seeing the girl's body falling at her feet. The fibre in her was tough, and after the initial shock of horror, she was now able to cope with the situation. Her mind was already searching for a way out. She had no intention of weakly surrendering to the situation, but before she could decide what she could do, she had to know all the facts.

"She was Lucille Balu?" she asked, staring at Jay.

"Yes."

He too was recovering from the horrible moment when he had seen the doors of the cupboard slowly opening. His mouth was dry as he wondered what Sophia was planning to do. He was surprised that her nerves were obviously stronger than his.

"And you killed her?" Sophia said, her hands turning into fists.

"It was an accident," Jay said, and forced his lips into a tight, meaningless smile.

"How – an accident?"

The tip of his tongue moved over his lips as he hesitated, then he said, "What I told you was the truth. When I saw her in this room I knew I had made a mistake. I suppose I was tactless. I told her to get out. She became angry. She threatened to scream. I was frightened someone would hear her. I put my hand over her mouth. There was a struggle. She was stronger than I imagined. I – I must have used more force than I realized. Suddenly she went limp. I thought she had fainted. When I tried to revive her, I found she was dead."

Watching him and listening to the flat tone of his voice, Sophia knew he was lying. She recalled the picture of him threatening her as he moved across the room, the scarlet curtain cord in his hands, and she knew the girl had been deliberately strangled.

She studied him.

The dark screens of his glasses covering his eyes gave him a protective camouflage.

"Take those glasses off," she said.

He stiffened and frowned. His hand went to his glasses, hesitated, and then he took them off.

His pale, washed-out blue eyes with their lost, furtive expression gave her confidence. They told her he was more frightened and shocked then she was.

"You're lying," she said. "You deliberately brought her up here and killed her. You killed her with the curtain cord."

Jay's eyes went completely blank. They looked like the eyes of a blind man. Then his lips curled upwards and he made a little choking sound as if he were suppressing a giggle.

"You are quite right," he said. "You're much cleverer than I had imagined. Yes, of course. It wasn't an accident."

Sophia drew in a deep breath and got to her feet. She crossed the room and took a cigarette from the box that stood on the table. As she lit it she noticed her hands were quite steady and that surprised her.

She now had no doubt that the boy was insane. She had always suspected that he had inherited his mother's mental instability. She was alone with him in this room. Was she in any kind of danger? Would he suddenly turn on her? She would have to be careful not to antagonize him.

She moved back to her chair and sat down.

"Why did you do it?" she asked, her voice gentle.

He looked sharply at her, reacting to the sympathetic note in her voice.

"Why did I do it?" he repeated, and he slid further down in his chair. "Because I was bored, Sophia. You wouldn't know what real boredom means. You wouldn't know what it means to be always playing third fiddle: not even second fiddle. I've been unwanted ever since I was born. My mother hated me. Father has always regarded me as a nuisance. All my life I have been farmed out to please him or my mother or his second wife or whenever I happened to be in the way."

Sophia nodded.

"Yes, I know. I had a rotten childhood myself. That's why I've always tried to make you feel you are wanted and that you're not in the way. Don't think I don't understand. I do. Your life hasn't been much fun."

Jay's eyes lit up. He suddenly looked very young and eager.

"I've always admired you, Sophia. You are the only one who has come within any distance of understanding me, but your kindness has come a little late. Twenty years of playing third fiddle isn't very exciting." He leaned forward, staring at her. "Being pushed aside, unwanted and only trotted out to be shown off when it was convenient isn't very exciting either. For years now I have searched for something in life that really means something. I have come to the conclusion that taking risks is more important than anything else in life. At first I thought that risking my freedom would be enough. When I was at school I became a burglar." His pale lips moved into his boyish smile. "I didn't steal anything. I broke into houses and crept into people's bedrooms. That was quite exciting, to sit by their bedsides watching them sleep, not knowing if they would suddenly wake up and catch me. But after a time I got bored with that. I realized I didn't put enough value on my freedom to care if I were caught or not. After a lot of thought, I decided the one thing was irreplaceable and of most value to me was my life."

Sophia touched off the ash in her cigarette. Her mind was active. She let Jay talk, but she was only half concentrating on what he was saying. He was trying to excuse himself. Before long, they would come to the dead girl. It didn't matter to her why he had done it. What did matter to her was what would happen once the news broke. Jay was Floyd's son. The thought of the publicity, the scandal, the horror of the newspaper men, the effect on Floyd's film, the resurrection of Harriett's suicide, the trial, the pity of their friends and the frightful newspaper headlines that would go on and on and on made her blood run cold.

"I tried Russian roulette," Jay was saying. "Do you know what that is? You put a cartridge in the cylinder of a revolver, spin the cylinder so you don't know if the cartridge is or is not under the firing pin, then you put the gun to your head and pull the trigger. But it is a gambler's risk and although it provided intense excitement at the first attempt, I realized it wasn't the kind of risk I was looking for. If I was to risk my life, I wanted to be sure that it wouldn't be blind chance but my own planning, my own wits, my own intelligence I had to rely on. That brought me to murder. I have thought of murdering someone now for quite some time. This afternoon I decided to do it." He was leaning forward now, his face tense. "I saw this girl. It was easy enough to persuade her to come up here; as easy to kill her. She was so pathetically unsuspecting. Of course I could have arranged it differently. I could have made it much safer and easier for myself, but I didn't want that. I wanted a genuine risk. It seemed to me that to be landed with a dead body in this hotel would test my inventiveness to the limit. I made no plans. Even now, I don't know what I am going to do with the body." He ran his fingers through his hair as he continued to stare at Sophia. "I didn't anticipate that you would be so clever, Sophia. I didn't include you in my plan. Just what are you going to do about this thing?"

Just what was she going to do about it? Sophia asked herself. Tell Floyd? Call the police? Deliberately cut her own social throat?

Once the news hit the headlines, there would be no more dinners at the White House, no more exciting evening parties in London when it was possible that members of the royal family might look in on an unofficial visit, no longer would the rich hostesses in New York fight among themselves for the privilege of having the Delaneys on their dinner list. And Floyd? He had sunk millions in this film of his. Could the film be shown while his son was standing trial for murder?

She knew it would be fatal to confide in Floyd. His reaction would be unthinking and instinctively correct. He would call the police and hand his son over to them without hesitation. She loved and admired Floyd. He always did the right thing, but this thing couldn't be handled like that. This was something special. A wrong move could ruin their future, and she was very conscious that, at this moment, she held the destinies of Floyd, herself and this insane boy in her capable, shrewd hands.

She hedged a little because she wanted more time to think about this thing.

"What do you expect me to do?" she asked.

"Tell father," Jay said.

"If I told him, you know what he would do."

"Yes, I know. He would call the police."

She looked at her wrist-watch. The time was twenty-five minutes to ten. The movie would be running now and Floyd would be wondering where she was.

"I want to think about it, Jay. I can't keep your father waiting any longer. It's a thing one can't make a decision about in a moment. You're not the only one involved. There's your father and myself."

Jay took his dark glasses from his pocket and put them on. She became immediately alert. She felt that this action of his was a declaration of war.

"There isn't much time," he said.

"I'll come to your room after dinner," Sophia said. "I'll have decided by then."

Half smiling, Jay slid out of his chair, moved quickly to the door, turned the key, took the key from the lock and dropped it into his pocket. He leaned against the door and looked across the room at her.

"I'm sorry, Sophia," he said, his voice gentle, "but I can't leave the decision to you. Unless you are prepared to be co-operative, I shall have to make my own arrangements."

"Is that a threat, Jay?" Sophia asked, a little surprised that she wasn't more frightened.

"I'm afraid it is," he said apologetically. "This is very important to me. I can't have you spoiling it."

Sophia crossed her long, shapely legs.

"But wouldn't you be in difficulties if you had two bodies on your hands?" she said.

"Of course, that is why I hope you will be co-operative."

"What do you expect me to do, then?"

He moved back to his chair.

"It's to your advantage and father's advantage too if I get away with this. I think I can get away with it. If you tell father, he will rush off to the police. If you say nothing, there is a reasonable chance that no one will even find out what I have done, so I'm asking you not to say anything."

Sophia didn't hesitate. What Jay had said was true. If she told Floyd, the horrible thing would be newspaper headlines within hours.

"All right, Jay. I won't say anything. I give you my word."

He nodded.

"I shall have to trust you, but I think you are clever enough to see that it won't help any of us if I am caught."

"You can trust me." Sophia lit another cigarette. "But what are you going to do with the – the body?"

"I thought I'd put it in a trunk and leave it somewhere," Jay said. "I haven't really got down to making a plan."

"The trunk would be traced to you," Sophia said. "Besides, you couldn't handle it yourself. No, that's not a safe idea."

"Perhaps you can suggest a better one?" Jay said, watching her.

"When you brought her up here, someone must have seen you."

"Oh, no. We came up separately. It was around four o'clock. There was no one up here."

"But you can't be sure she wasn't seen. She may have told someone she was coming here."

"No, she didn't. I warned her not to tell anyone. No one knows she came here. I'm sure of that."

"What makes you think you won't be found out? The police are clever. When her body is discovered, there will be an investigation. You may have left clues. Murderers always do."

Jay put his head on one side. He was enjoying this. Sophia was showing unexpected intelligence and interest. He was surprised that she was taking this so calmly. It was as if she were dissecting the plot of a movie. He had often listened to her discussing movie plots with his father, and he had been impressed by her shrewdness and her quick fault-finding.

"I don't think I have left any clues," he said, "but that's part of the risk. It's my wits against theirs. The one thing that helps the police more than anything is the motive. There is no motive to this murder. If I can get rid of the body, I should be safe."

"I hope so." Sophia glanced at her watch. "I think I should join your father now."

Jay nodded.

"I'll come too. Will you wait a moment while I change?"

"All right."

He put the key of the door on the table.

"I won't be a few minutes. I'm trusting you, Sophia."

46

She watched him go into his bedroom and close the door, then she picked up the key.

At this moment the reaction hit her and she suddenly felt faint and sick. She fought down her faintness, and, making an effort, she got up, crossed over to the liquor cabinet and poured out a stiff shot of brandy. She drank it, and then moved to the open window.

A big crowd circulated in front of the hotel on the watch for the Stars who were coming out now onto the terrace for an aperitif and to display themselves.

It was a hot night and the big moon made a glittering patch of yellow on the sea.

She stood there, leaning against the wall, staring at the active scene below.

If I can get rid of the body, I should be safe.

Jay's words echoed and re-echoed in her mind.

How was he going to do it?

Safe? Could anyone ever hope to be safe after doing such a thing?

She heard him come out of his bedroom, close and lock the door and she turned.

He looked very handsome in his tuxedo.

He paused by the door and smiled at her.

"Shall we go?"

"Yes."

She unlocked the door and they left the suite.

From his hiding-place, Joe Kerr watched them.

II

Jay sat in the cinema seat, his eyes staring blankly at the lighted screen. He was sharply aware of Sophia, sitting next to him. He could smell her subtle perfume, and from time to time when she moved, her skirts brushed against his leg.

On her other side, his father was sitting, slightly leaning forward, his face set as he struggled to follow the action of the film by the inadequate sub-titles that kept flashing onto the screen.

They were watching a Swedish film. The photography was splendid, but neither Sophia nor Jay, who had arrived too late to pick up the thread of the plot, had the slightest idea what the film was about.

A sudden sub-title, trite in itself, gave Jay the solution to the problem he was trying to solve: the problem of how he was going to get rid of the girl's body in reasonable safety.

When the sub-title appeared, Floyd Delaney, his schoolboy French failing him, leaned across Sophia and whispered irritably to Jay: "What the hell does that say?"

Jay translated without conscious effort: "There's safety in numbers."

His father grunted and settled back in his seat.

There's safety in numbers.

Jay remembered reading somewhere – probably in the *Michelin Guide* – that the Plaza hotel had five hundred bedrooms. That must mean at a guess that there were a thousand people staying in the hotel. It seemed to him that a thousand to one risk of discovery was an acceptable hazard.

He decided he wouldn't attempt to move the girl's body out of the hotel. He would carry it into the elevator, take the elevator to the top floor and leave it there.

The body wouldn't be discovered for several hours. How could the police find out if the killer was someone staying in the hotel or one of the hundreds of non-residents who had the run of the hotel during the Festival? How could they guess on which floor the girl had met her death, let alone in which of the five hundred bedrooms?

The solution was so obvious he was surprised he hadn't thought of it before.

The tension that had been gnawing at him now went away, and for the first time since he had killed the girl he relaxed.

He was able, too, to think more clearly of the situation as it was so far. Everything depended on whether he could trust Sophia to keep silent.

Would she lose her nerve? Would she tell his father?

He thought not. Her behaviour when the girl's body had tumbled out of the cupboard had been astonishing. She must have nerves of steel to have reacted as she had done.

Of course she had been shocked, but she hadn't lost her head or screamed or even fainted as most women would have done. She had gone white and her hands had covered her face but she had quickly recovered. She had gone out of the room, and he had seen her sit down and light a cigarette.

A woman who could do that after what had happened was not likely to lose her nerve. He looked slyly at her. Her face was expressionless as she watched the film. There was a resolute set to her mouth he hadn't noticed before; otherwise she looked as she always looked when watching a movie.

She must know it would be disastrous for his father and herself if he were discovered. He was pretty certain that he could rely on her silence.

The film finished a few minutes to midnight.

As they made their way along the Croisette back to the Plaza hotel, Floyd questioned his son about the film. His questions were technical and Jay floundered in trying to answer them.

"Oh, for heaven's sake!" Delaney snapped, losing patience. "You're talking through the back of your neck. You don't seem to have learned the first thing about your trade. Look, have a talk with Cooper, will you? Get him to wise you up." He turned his attention to Sophia. "I have a call to Paris before we meet the van Asters. At this hour we shouldn't be held up." He snapped his fingers at Harry Stone who was walking behind them. "See the car's waiting, Harry. I want to talk to Courtney. We're getting scarcely any coverage in the French press for our picture."

"I'll run along," Jay said. "I feel like a walk."

"Go ahead," Delaney said curtly. He was still angry with his son for his poor showing when he had questioned him. "See you in the morning."

"Good night, Jay," Sophia said and she looked directly at him.

"Good night," Jay said.

He tried to read a message in her eyes without success. He stood back and let them go on ahead.

Then, crossing the promenade, he paused for a moment to look back at the dense crowd, standing behind the crush barriers erected outside the hotel. He watched his father and Sophia walk up the drive and heard the buzz of voices start up as the crowd, intent on spotting the Stars, identified Sophia.

He turned away and began to walk slowly along the promenade towards the Casino.

He made a lonely figure walking on his own away from the centre of activity, moving against the stream of people who were heading towards the Plaza.

Because he was wearing a tuxedo, the Star-spotters stared inquisitively at him, making sure they weren't passing a celebrity whom they could pester for an autograph.

Jay was too preoccupied by his thoughts to notice how he was being stared at. He was beginning to wonder if perhaps this idea

49

of his mightn't have misfired. Now the first excitement had passed, it wasn't as tense or as thrilling as he imagined it would be.

It was the waiting that spoilt the tension.

If he could have moved the girl's body now; if the body could have been discovered a few minutes later, and if the police could have arrived immediately and begun their investigation, the rhythm of the excitement would have been maintained. But when he realized that her body might not be discovered for another five hours the long wait for further action depressed him.

The crowd moving towards the Plaza hotel was thinning out now. He passed the Casino, and, as he moved towards Quai St. Pierre that ran alongside the harbour where the yachts and motor-boats were moored, he heard a street clock strike one.

The quay was deserted and he walked slowly, looking at the yachts and the motor-boats, lit up by the moon.

Reaching the end of the harbour, he sat on a bollard and lit a cigarette.

He sat there for maybe twenty minutes, smoking and staring emptily across the oily moonlit water in the harbour; then he heard the sound of someone approaching, and, frowning, he turned his head to his left.

A girl had just got off a bicycle, and she was pushing the machine as she walked to the edge of the quay.

She stood in the full moonlight as she propped the cycle against a coil of rope. She was wearing a pair of dark blue jeans, a white sleeveless singlet and a pair of heelless slippers. She looked about his age: possibly a little younger, which would make her nineteen or twenty. She was blonde. Her hair that reached her shoulders hung free. She was pretty without being beautiful, and her figure was charming without being sexually blatant.

Wondering what she could be doing on the deserted quay at this hour, Jay watched her.

The girl glanced at him as she paused at the edge of the quay, then squatting down, she took hold of a mooring rope and began to draw an open boat, equipped with an outboard motor, close to the quay.

Seeing she intended to get into the boat, Jay got to his feet and walked over to where she was squatting.

"May I help you, mademoiselle?" he asked, pausing beside the girl.

She looked up. The moonlight fell directly on her face. He was struck by the clearness and brightness of her eyes. She gave him a half smile, shaking her head.

"I can manage, monsieur, thank you."

There was a trace of the Midi accent in her voice.

He reached down and took hold of the rope.

"I'll hold it steady," he said.

"Thank you."

She slid down into the boat.

He watched her as she took the waterproof hood off the outboard engine.

"Are you going out at this hour?" he asked.

"Yes. In a quarter of an hour the tide will be just right."

"For what?"

"For fishing, of course."

"You are going fishing alone?"

"Of course."

He was struck by her matter-of-fact, independent air. He watched her wind the cord around the starting wheel. By the way she pulled the cord, swinging the wheel, he saw she had more strength than he had thought.

After three attempts, the engine failed to start and she gave an exclamation of annoyance.

"The points are probably dirty," he said. "I'll clean them for you."

She shook her head.

"It's all right, thank you, monsieur. I can do it. You would get dirty." She began to hunt in a locker for tools. "Have you just come from the cinema?"

"Yes. Look, I don't mind getting dirty. I'd like to help you."

"No, please. I can manage. Was the film good?"

"Not very. The photography was excellent, but the rest of it bored me."

She found a screwdriver and began to loosen the screws holding the engine cover in place.

"Are you something to do with the movies?" she asked.

"Well, I suppose so. I'm learning."

"You speak French very well for an American."

He was pleased and flattered.

"I spent two years in Paris. Are you sure I can't help you?"

"It's all right, thank you. It must be interesting to work in the movies. I'd like to work in a Studio. Do you know many of the Stars?"

"A few."

She paused in her work, looking up at him.

"Did you ever meet James Dean? I have a signed photo of him at home. I think he was wonderful. Did you ever meet him?"

"No." Jay squatted on the edge of the quay. "Do you often go fishing at night?"

"Whenever the tide is right."

"It must be fun."

She shook her head emphatically.

"It isn't. It is often disappointing. You see I sell what I catch. We need the money."

"But surely you can't make much out of a night's fishing."

"I don't, but every little helps. My father is a cripple. He has a café in Rue Foch. It isn't a very successful café, so I have to try to add to our income."

"Do you also work in the café?"

"Of course."

"And you fish at night?"

"Yes, when the tide is right."

"It sounds as if you work very hard."

She smiled.

"I do, but I don't mind. Do you have to work hard too?"

"Sometimes."

He wondered how she would react if he told her his father was Floyd Delaney. He had an idea that it would be a mistake to tell her.

She attracted him and interested him. He liked her easy natural way of talking. She didn't pose and he felt she was sincere.

"What is your name, mademoiselle?" he asked.

She was screwing down the engine cover and she looked up, pausing in her work.

"Ginette Bereut. What is yours?"

Jay hesitated.

"Jay Mandrel," he said, giving his mother's maiden name.

"Are you down here for long?" she asked as she wound the cord around the starting wheel.

"Three or four days, then I'm going on to Venice."

"Venice? I'd love to go there. Is it to do with a film?"

"Yes. We're shooting background material."

"Well, I mustn't stay here talking. . . ."

She pulled the cord sharply and the engine fired. She made

motions to him to cast off the rope and reluctantly he pulled the end of the rope free, coiled it and tossed it into the boat.

She smiled, nodding her thanks.

Then, as the boat began to move away, Jay straightened upright. He watched her steer the boat towards the harbour entrance.

He suddenly wished he had asked her if he could have gone with her, and he was angry with himself for thinking of this too late.

He looked at his watch. The time was half-past one. He wondered when she would return. He had still two hours to wait before he need return to the Plaza. He decided to sit there a little longer in the hope of seeing her again.

As he sat on the bollard, looking across the harbour, waiting to hear the distant engine beat that would tell him the girl was returning, he began to flick the blue beads he had in his pocket far out into the water.

CHAPTER FIVE

I

FLOYD DELANEY drove his big Bentley along the Moyenne Corniche with Sophia at his side.

The dinner at the Château de Madrid had been impeccable; the *croustade de langouste*, the restaurant's speciality, delicious, the van Asters amusing, the magnificent aerial view of the harbour of Villefranche and the twinkling lights of Cap Ferrat like fairyland, and the Ausone 1947 had been the finest wine he had tasted.

Delaney told himself he should feel content and relaxed, but he didn't. He felt edgy and irritable, and the wretched little Citroën hogging the road ahead of him, preventing him from passing, infuriated him.

He drove the Bentley to within a foot of the Citroën's rear bumper, then putting the palm of his hand down hard on the button that operated the triple air-horns, he blasted the crawling car almost off the road.

He shot the Bentley past the Citroën and stormed on down the long hill into Nice.

Why wasn't he relaxed? he asked himself.

He glanced sideways at Sophia. She sat motionless, her face expressionless. Was there something wrong? Usually she was so vivacious, talkative and entertaining? To-night she had been silent and withdrawn, and whenever he had looked at her he had been disturbed to see how hard her eyes were, and there was a thrust to her chin that he hadn't noticed before, giving her an almost aggressive look.

This bothered him. He was used to her solicitous attention. His wishes were her wishes, his needs her needs, but to-night it was as if he didn't exist.

"Have you something on your mind, baby?" he asked abruptly as he slowed the car to negotiate the round-about by the harbour.

Sophia continued to stare ahead, paying no attention.

"Hey! What's the matter with you?" Delaney demanded, raising his voice. "Did you hear what I said?"

Sophia started and looked at him, then she smiled.

"Sorry, darling. I was thinking. What was it?"

Delaney frowned.

"You seem to have something on your mind. What's biting you? You've been dreamy all the evening."

All the evening Sophia's mind had been haunted by the thought of the dead girl in Jay's cupboard. The more she thought about what had happened the more angry she had become. To think that because Jay had thirsted for an exciting experience, this young, pretty girl, beginning a successful career, should now be a lifeless lump of clay in the bottom of a cupboard.

Several times during the evening, Sophia had nearly blurted out the whole story, not only to Floyd but also to the van Asters, but she had checked herself.

Floyd was like a bull at a gate. There was nothing subtle about him. Murder meant the police. It would never cross his mind not to call the police.

If she could, she was determined to save him and herself from the horror of the publicity, but that didn't mean she was going to let Jay go unpunished. Once she was sure the police didn't suspect that he had been responsible for the girl's death, and once they were out of France, she would tell Floyd. Arrangements would have to be made to put the boy in a home and they must make sure he would never get out.

He must never be allowed his liberty again. He might easily

54

be tempted to repeat the experiment later on, and some other unsuspecting girl would die at his hands.

Sophia was annoyed with herself for betraying her preoccupation. She quickly steered Floyd away from the real subject of her thoughts.

"Sorry, Floyd. I've been thinking about my silver mink. I must have the collar altered," she said lightly. "It's quite a problem. I saw Maggie in hers yesterday. It's cut like mine, and what a fright she looked!"

Delaney drew in a long breath of exasperation.

"For heaven's sake! Do you mean to tell me you've been worrying about that coat all the evening? I was beginning to think there was something seriously wrong."

"If I'm going to look the way Maggie looked, darling, then something is seriously wrong."

Delaney shook his head, helpless. He reached out and patted her knee.

"Forget it. Get another coat. I'll pay. I don't want you to worry about a thing like that. Have a look around to-morrow. You may find something you like. If you do – buy it."

Sophia leaned against him, rubbing her face against his shoulder.

"My man!" she said softly. "My lovely, kind, generous man!"

Delaney expanded his chest. This was better. This was the treatment he could absorb twenty-four hours of the day.

"Well, maybe I'm not so lousy," he said, grinning, "but that's a bet, honey." He increased the speed of the car as they got on to the broad sea road leading to Antibes. "You know, the older I get and the longer I live, the surer I am that money fixes everything. You get blue because your mink coat looks wrong. Okay, I can get you another and you're not blue any more. Take this car. I like a good car. I don't want a showy thing all chromium and yards long. I want a car that looks a million bucks, acts a million bucks and makes me feel like two million bucks. If I hadn't the money, wanting a car like that would eat my heart out. But I've got the money, so I can buy this beauty, and I don't get a frustration complex. Money fixes everything. You've just got to have enough of it."

But all Floyd's money wouldn't fix this dreadful thing that Jay had done, Sophia thought. It wouldn't fix murder. He might try to pull strings, get the smartest attorneys, even talk to the judge, but once the facts were put to the jury, Jay would be found guilty, and no money on earth could buy off the press nor hush up the horror that Floyd Delaney's son was a homicidal lunatic.

It was as they were crawling through the bottle-neck just outside Antibes, to get on to the main road to Cannes, that Delaney said suddenly: "I've decided not to take Jay to Venice. I'm going to leave him in Nice."

Sophia stiffened. She looked quickly at her husband.

"Is that such a good idea, darling?"

"Yeah. The boy doesn't know the first thing about film making. Verneuil is making a movie at the Nice Studios. He's a good technician and he knows his job inside out. I want Jay to watch him work. It'll be more useful to him than lounging about in Venice."

Sophia became alarmed. Jay wasn't fit to be left alone. There was no knowing what he might get up to. Besides, when the police began their investigation, it would be much safer to have him out of France.

"He's looking forward to Venice," she said tentatively. "Is it quite fair, Floyd? After all, he is on vacation. It may be his last chance for years to see the place and we know it is well worth seeing."

Delaney's face darkened.

"Look, honey, let me handle this. It's more important for the boy to learn his trade than to fool around in Venice. Plenty of time for him to go there. I want him to get to know something of the French technique while he is here."

By now Sophia knew Floyd well enough not to press him. Once he had made up his mind, he reacted badly to any opposition.

She thought with dismay of the danger of leaving Jay here alone, and again she was tempted to tell Floyd the truth. But she resisted the temptation to be free of the responsibility. They had still three more days before they left for Venice. She would wait and see what happened during those three days before making a decision.

She looked at the lighted clock on the dashboard of the car. It was now twenty minutes to three. She must talk to Jay when she got back to the hotel. She had to know what he intended to do with the girl's body. She felt cold and ill when she thought of that. How could Jay hope to get the girl's body out of the hotel without being seen?

What was he doing at this moment? she wondered.

It would have alarmed her if she had known just what Jay was doing as Floyd drove her along the main road to Cannes.

Jay had waited an hour and a half for Ginette's return. When he heard the steady beat of the outboard engine, he had got to his feet, aware of an undiscovered feeling of pleasure and excitement.

Ginette was surprised to find him waiting for her and for a moment she hesitated before taking his outstretched hand to help her out of the boat.

"Did you have any luck?" he asked as she stooped to tie up the boat.

"A little: better than last night. To-morrow night will be better because the tide will be earlier." She set down the basket she had got from the boat and surveyed him. "Have you been waiting here all the time?"

"Yes. It's nice here. Besides, I wanted to see you again."

She looked straight at him, smiling, and there was no coyness in her eyes.

"Did you? I wondered about you when I was fishing."

"I should have asked you to let me come with you. Could I come to-morrow?"

She nodded.

"Of course, if you want to. I shall be here about midnight."

"Then I'll meet you here."

"All right."

She picked up the basket and fishing lines and moved over to her bicycle.

"Where did you say your café was?"

"Rue Foch. It's at the corner. It is called La Boule d'Or." She laughed. "There's nothing gold about it except the gold fish in the window." She paused, looking at him. "What are you going to do now?"

"I'm going to bed."

"Where are you staying?"

He felt instinctively that it would be a mistake to tell her he was staying at the Plaza hotel. She mustn't know that he was the son of a millionaire. He was sure it would affect their association together.

"I'm staying at the Paris," he said, naming a modest hotel on the Boulevard Alsace. Then, after a moment's hesitation, he added. "I think you are beautiful. I wouldn't say it if I didn't mean it."

In the hard light of the moon, he saw the blood mount to her face.

"Do you?" She smiled and he could see she was pleased. "Thank you. I am glad you think so." She slung the basket by its strap over her shoulder and prepared to mount her cycle. "Then I will see you to-morrow night?"

Yes, you'll see me to-morrow night, Jay thought, unless I am caught carrying the body of that girl out of the suite and into the elevator. What did the Catholics say? Between the stirrup and the ground? So much could happen between this intimate moment and to-morrow night.

"I'll be here to-morrow at midnight."

She held out her hand.

"Then good night."

The feel of her firm cool flesh made his heart beat quicken. He was suddenly sure that, if he had met her sooner, he wouldn't have done what he had done.

"Good night."

He watched her cycle away, and then he began the long walk back to the Plaza hotel.

II

His head nodding, his mouth slack, Joe Kerr slept and dreamed of his wife. It was a nightmare dream that haunted his sleep. He saw himself again in his Cadillac, the horror of his wife's one blood-chilling scream ringing in his ears. He saw himself get out of the car and move to where she was pinned between the rear bumper and the garage wall. The red tail lights of the car lit up her crushed, bleeding body.

He woke with a start as Floyd Delaney and his wife came from the elevator and crossed the corridor, pausing outside the door to their suite while Delaney fumbled with the key.

Joe heard Delaney say: "Phew! I'm ready to hit the sack. How do you feel, honey?"

Sophia said: "Me too. I feel I could sleep for weeks."

Joe watched them enter the suite, and he shook his aching head, trying to clear his fuddled brain. He looked at his watch. The time was ten minutes to three o'clock.

How long had he slept?

He remembered he had looked at the time at twenty-five minutes to one. Then he must have fallen asleep. Had the Balu girl left the suite while he had been sleeping? He doubted it.

The fact that he had woken when Delaney and his wife had returned assured him that, if the girl had left, he would have known about it.

He groped for his half-pint flask of whisky, then paused as he heard the whine of the ascending elevator. A moment later the door swished back and Jay Delaney stepped into the corridor.

Joe watched him cross the corridor to the door of suite 27. He watched him tentatively turn the handle, then open the door.

Well, the family was back now. What was going to happen? Where was the Balu girl? With resigned patience, Joe prepared himself for another long wait.

In the suite, Sophia had kissed her husband good night and had gone into her room, shutting the door. She leaned against the door, listening. After a few minutes she heard the sound of the shower that told her Floyd was preparing for bed, and, cautiously, she opened her bedroom door and moved into the lounge as Jay came in.

Jay glanced quickly around, then asked softly: "Where's father?"

"He's gone to bed. I want to talk to you, Jay."

"In here?" He waved to his bedroom and she nodded. They went in together, and Jay sat on the edge of the bed while Sophia leaned against the door.

Sophia was tense and pale, but Jay was relaxed; his eyes hidden behind his dark glasses gave her no chance of knowing what his true feelings were.

She said, "Have you thought what you are going to do?"

Since leaving Ginette, Jay had been irritated to discover that he was now bored with having Lucille's body to cope with. When he had killed her, he had thought the business of disposing of her body would be an exciting test for his ingenuity and his wits, but now, his mind still full of Ginette's lovely little face, he wished he could give her his full attention and not to have to be bothered with the dead girl.

"I'm going to put her in the elevator, take the elevator to the top floor and leave it there," he said. "No one will be able to guess where she died. It's the safest way."

Sophia considered this. Her sharp wits told her that because of its simplicity it could be successful.

"But you may be seen," she said.

Jay shrugged his shoulders.

"Yes, but no plan is completely fool-proof. I must take that risk unless . . ." He paused and looked intently at her.

59

"Unless – what?" she said sharply.

"Unless you would be willing to help me."

Sophia stiffened.

"Help you? If I did, and you were caught, it would make me an accessory."

"Yes, I suppose it would." He rubbed his jaw, frowning. "It was only an idea. It would have made it fool-proof if I had someone in the corridor to warn me if anyone was coming while I got her into the elevator. That's where the risk is: carrying her across the corridor. Someone might come up the stairs. . . ."

"Are you going to do it now?" Sophia asked.

Jay looked at his watch. It was now half-past three.

"I may as well. The elevator is now on automatic. This is the best time."

"Now? This very moment?"

"Yes, when you have gone."

Sophia hesitated, then she made the decision. Everything she had gained during her struggle to fame and everything that her husband had gained was in the balance, depending on whether or not some late comer strolled up the stairs when Jay carried the girl's body into the corridor.

To take such a risk would be inviting disaster, she told herself. She had to help him.

"I'm going to the head of the stairs," she said quietly. "If anyone comes I'll call out 'good night'. You must be very quick, Jay."

He stared at her, startled.

"You mean you are going to help me? I don't understand. Why are you doing this? They could send you to prison."

"Never mind why I am doing it," she said curtly. "I'm going to do it." She looked at him, her face pale and her eyes glittering. "But don't imagine you won't have to pay for this, Jay, because you will, and you'll pay dearly."

He frowned and his hands turned into fists.

"Of course." His voice was bitter. "I was stupid enough to think for a moment you were thinking of me. You are doing it only for father and yourself, aren't you?"

"Is that so surprising?" Sophia said coldly. "Why should we suffer because of what you have done? If your father knew, he would hand you over to the police. He has the courage to face the horrible publicity of the trial and the pity of our friends, but I'm not going to let a brutal, callous act of a mentally deranged boy ruin my husband's future if I can help it. I'm prepared to take the risk of going to prison rather than see all your father's hard work go for nothing and my social life ruined. So I'm going to help you, but don't imagine you won't pay for this degenerate thing you have done."

Jay took out his cigarette case, opened it and offered it to Sophia. She hesitated, then took a cigarette. She stood motionless while he lit it for her and then one for himself.

"So you think I'm insane?" he said, sitting on the bed again. "That's interesting. You are quite wrong, of course. I'm not insane. I did it because I was bored. You don't know what it is to be really bored. For years now I have craved for something to happen that would be unusual and exciting. There can't be anything more exciting than to risk one's life. That was why I killed her." He paused and his hands moved uneasily up and down his thighs as he stared at her. "But I'll be frank with you, Sophia. This thing has misfired. It's nothing like so exciting as I had imagined it would be. There was one moment when it was worth while. It was quite a moment when you came back here unexpectedly. I got a thrill out of that, but after, it has all been flat and dull."

Sophia looked at him with loathing.

"I don't want to listen to your explanations, Jay. You have done this horrible thing, now you must try to save your father and me from the consequences."

"Of course."

His indifferent smile riled her.

"Are you ready?" she said and opened the door.

Yes."

"I'll call the elevator. Be quick."

Bracing herself, she walked into the lounge. As she went to the door leading out on to the corridor, she heard Jay cross his room and unlock the cupboard door.

She looked into the deserted corridor, then she crossed to the elevator and pushed the call button. She heard the faint whining sound as the elevator ascended. She walked quickly to the head of the stairs and peered over the banister rail. She looked down the deserted stairs, her heart hammering so violently she could scarcely breathe.

She stood there, a rigid, frightened figure, watching the stairs and listening.

Jay must have moved very quickly and silently, for she heard nothing, and, alarmed at the time he seemed to be taking, she was about to turn when she heard the swish of the elevator door as it closed, and a moment later, the whining sound that told her the elevator was in motion.

She looked around and stared down the corridor at the red indicator light that showed the elevator was climbing.

For a moment or so she remained still, then she walked unsteadily back to the suite.

She entered and closed the door, then she went into Jay's room.

The cupboard doors stood open. She looked into the cupboard, feeling a cold cramped sensation in her stomach. There was nothing in the cupboard to show that a dead girl had lain there for more than twelve hours.

Leaving the room, she went back into the lounge and sat down. She felt cold and sick and very tired. She shut her eyes, letting her head drop back against the head-rest of the chair.

She remained like that for a long five minutes, then she heard the door open and she looked up.

Jay came in. He closed the door and locked it. He was pale and his upper lip shone with sweat.

They looked at each other.

"It's all right," he said.

"Are you sure?"

He nodded as he took out his handkerchief and wiped his hands and wrists.

"Yes. No one saw me. I took the elevator to the top floor and left it there. I didn't meet anyone on the way down."

"The police will be here soon. There will be an investigation. What about your finger prints in the elevator?"

He shrugged impatiently.

"Hundreds of people use the elevator. I'm not worried about that."

"What have you done with her beads?"

"I've thrown them into the sea."

"Are you sure nothing of hers has been left here?"

"Yes, I'm sure."

"Didn't she have a handbag?"

"No."

"Are you quite sure? Girls always have handbags, Jay."

"She didn't. I'm sure."

Sophia began to relax a little. Perhaps after all it would be all right, she thought. How could the police guess the girl had died in this suite? Surely their name and reputation would put them beyond suspicion?

"Then we must hope, Jay. I'm going to bed now."

"Thank you for helping me," Jay said. "You don't have to worry. No one saw me."

But there he was wrong.

Joe Kerr had seen Sophia leave the suite and press the elevator call button. He had watched her move furtively down the corridor to the head of the stairs and look over the banister rail.

He had leaned forward, blankly surprised, wondering what she was doing when he saw Jay come unsteadily out of the suite with Lucille Balu slung limply over his shoulder.

Joe recognized the girls' blue and white dress and the colour of her hair.

He was so surprised to see Jay carrying the girl out of the suite that he remained transfixed, and it wasn't until it was too late that he groped for his camera. By then the elevator door had closed and the elevator had begun to climb.

He watched Sophia come back along the corridor, and as she passed under one of the ceiling lights, he saw how bad she looked; as if she were going to faint.

He waited.

A few minutes later, he saw Jay come down the stairs, walk across the corridor to the door of suite 27, open the door and disappear inside. He heard the key turn in the lock.

Still Joe sat motionless, staring with his frog-like, watery eyes at the door to suite 27.

His drink-sodden brain took some time before it accepted the evidence of his eyes, and even then, he was suspicious of what he had seen.

He had been waiting outside the door of Delaney's suite for a long time, and, as the hours had passed, he had become resigned to the fact that he was wasting his time, as he had wasted it so often on some hopeless assignment he had hoped would turn out to be something that would interest Manley and make him some money.

Lucille Balu had walked into the suite at four o'clock in the afternoon. This boy, Jay Delaney, had carried her out, apparently unconscious, twelve hours later and had taken her upstairs in the elevator.

Why was she unconscious? What had been happening to her during those twelve hours?

Joe grappled with this puzzle, his mind baffled.

Obviously, Floyd Delaney's high-toned wife was in the secret.

She had acted as a scout, making sure the way was clear for the boy to get the unconscious girl out of the suite.

Had the girl been drugged or made drunk so the boy could seduce her? Joe wondered. Surely a woman like Sophia Delaney wouldn't have associated herself with such a situation?

But the fact remained that the girl had been in the suite for twelve hours and had been carried out unconscious.

If he could prove that young Delaney had drugged the girl and Sophia Delaney had assisted in such an act, what a story it would make!

Unsteadily he got to his feet.

Where had the boy taken her? he wondered. He was pretty sure the girl wasn't staying at the hotel. Where had she been dumped to sleep off the effects of the drug or drink the boy had plied her with?

Joe moved out of his hiding place and walked softly down the corridor to the elevator, then, deciding it might be dangerous to bring the elevator down to that floor, he started up the stairs to the floor above.

He was breathing heavily by the time he reached the third floor. Stair climbing and a diet of two bottles of whisky a day didn't agree with him.

He thumbed the elevator button and, leaning against the wall, he waited for the elevator to descend, planning to start on the top floor and search any empty room he found until he discovered the girl.

A few seconds later, he was standing rigid, sweat on his face, as he stared down at Lucille Balu's dead body.

She lay on her back, her legs bent, her skirts above her knees. There was a look of frozen terror on her blood-congested face that sent a chill up Joe's spine. Around her throat was the mark of a cord that had been pulled brutally tight, leaving a deep impression on her brown, tender skin. Her long slim fingers were hooked in agony: her eyes, starting out of her head, were fixed in the impersonal stare of death.

Joe felt a sudden thump of pain at his heart as he looked at the dead girl. The pain made him giddy and faint. He took a step back, grimacing. For some moments he stood motionless, aware that the shock had been a dangerous one and that his heart, which he had suspected for some time, had reacted badly. Then, making an effort, he turned and started a slow, shambling retreat down the corridor to the stairs.

The night clerk who sat the reception desk, idly turning the pages of *Paris-Match*, was surprised to see Joe lurch down the stairs and cross unsteadily to the revolving doors that led out to the Croisette.

He recognized Joe and grimaced. He supposed that Joe had been somewhere upstairs sleeping off a bout of drinking, and he watched him manoeuvre himself through the revolving doors with a feeling of relief that Joe wasn't going to make a nuisance of himself.

Joe kept walking: his brain frozen and numbed.

It wasn't until he had reached the Beau Rivage hotel, a fifth-rate hotel in Rue Foch, where he was staying and had got up to his bedroom that he recovered sufficiently from the shock to begin to analyse what he had seen.

Twenty years ago, Joe had been the crime reporter on the *New York Inquirer*. During the four years he had worked on the paper, he had photographed innumerable bodies, murdered violently. He had become hardened to the horrors he had had to see. Also, he had been able to tell at a glance how the unfortunates he had had to photograph had died.

He knew that Lucille Balu had been strangled by a cord that had been looped around her throat and then pulled tight. From her congested face, the marks around her throat and her expression of agony, he had no doubt that she had been murdered.

His first and immediate reaction was to talk to Manley. A story as big as this needed co-operation, and he was about to reach for the telephone to put through an unheard-of-expensive call to Hollywood, when he paused. An idea dropped into his mind and he leaned back to consider it.

Floyd Delaney was a millionaire four or five times over. In Joe's Rolliflex was incontestable evidence that Lucille Balu had entered Delaney's suite at four o'clock. Any police surgeon worth a damn could tell within a half an hour when she had died, and Joe was pretty sure the girl had been murdered between four and four forty-five, when Jay Delaney had been in the suite.

That meant either young Delaney or Sophia Delaney had murdered her, and Joe thought it wasn't likely that Sophia had done it, but obviously she was an accessory.

Here then was a situation that could be turned into profit. Why call Manley? Why bother to write the story? All Joe had to do was to talk to Delaney, come to a financial understanding with him to keep his mouth shut, and he would be on easy street for the rest of his life.

65

Joe's raddled face lit up at the thought, and he shifted the grimy pillow at his head, making himself more comfortable.

Delaney might be persuaded to part with half a million. With that Joe could retire and settle somewhere on the French Riviera. He could buy a small villa, get a housekeeper to look after him and give up the struggle of competing with the smart young punks who were trying to push him out of his job. What a terrific kick he would get out of telling Manley to go jump in a lake!

He frowned, stroking his red, raddled nose.

A half a million! With that money, he could get a villa with a view of the sea; he could afford a comfortable armchair, a good radio and a continuous flow of whisky. Pretty good, he thought, and no more work.

As he lay thinking about this, a sudden uneasy thought came into his mind.

Technically speaking, if he went to Delaney and asked him for half a million in return for his silence, he would be committing blackmail. If Delaney wasn't prepared to make a deal with him, he might find himself in the hands of the police. Also, by keeping silent, even if Delaney parted with the money, he would be making himself an accessory to murder, and if he were found out, he could be faced with a stiff prison sentence.

Joe flinched at the thought of getting into trouble with the police, and again he was tempted to call Manley, to give him the story and let him handle it, but, as his hand moved to the telephone, he again hesitated.

"Take it easy," he said aloud. "Wait and see how this thing develops. You've got the pictures. You mustn't rush this. If the police get a lead on the boy, Delaney might jump at the chance of buying the pictures off me. The thing to do is to take it nice and easy and wait. It'll be tricky, but you can cope with it. This could be the biggest thing that has ever happened to you if you don't make a mess of it."

He reached up and turned off the light. The time was now twenty minutes past four. His body ached for sleep, and, as soon as the sordid little room turned dark, he closed his eyes and slept. He dreamed he was carrying his wife's crushed and bleeding body along a corridor in the Plaza hotel.

Lucille Balu, giggling excitedly, walked by his side.

CHAPTER SIX

I

At 6.15 a.m., a waiter making his way to the Service room on the third floor of the hotel noticed the elevator door was standing open, and he went over to close it.

A few minutes later, in response to his frantic telephone call, Vesperini, the assistant manager, and Cadot, the hotel detective, came hurriedly upon the scene.

Vesperini had been about to leave the hotel for the flower market. He was freshly shaven and immaculate, wearing a dark, well-cut suit and a carnation in his button hole.

Cadot, roused out of his bed, wore jacket and trousers, hastily pulled over his pyjamas. His fat face was unshaven and still puffy from sleep.

The two men looked at the dead girl and reacted in different ways. Vesperini immediately thought of the hotel's reputation, and what must be done to cause the hotel's clients the least inconvenience.

Cadot, on the other hand, had difficulty in concealing his pleased excitement. Nothing had happened in the hotel since his appointment to give him a chance to exercise his talents as a detective. Here was his big chance, and he was already visualizing his photograph in all the newspapers.

Cadot said: "If Monsieur would be good enough to notify Inspector Devereaux, I will remain here. It would be better to arrange to have 'out of order' signs put on the elevator doors on all floors in case someone wishes to use this elevator."

Vesperini instructed the staring waiter to get this done, and then, leaving Cadot, he hurried away to call the police and inform the management.

Left on his own, Cadot examined the girl, being careful not to move her. He recognized her, and he thought how fortunate it was that she was not without some fame. The murder, when the news broke, would cause a major sensation.

He lightly touched the girl's arm. From the hard, boardlike feel of her flesh, he judged she had been dead for at least twelve hours.

Had she been strangled in the elevator? This seemed un-

67

likely. As she wasn't a resident of the hotel, she must have come here to visit someone.

He closed the elevator door and leaning his fat back against it he speculated on whom the girl could have visited and why she had been strangled.

He was still cogitating ten minutes later when Inspector Devereaux of the Cannes Homicide hurried out of the elevator at the far end of the corridor with four plain-clothes men at his heels.

There was a brief consultation, then Cadot asked for permission to dress and shave while the Inspector made his preliminary investigation.

The inspector agreed to this, and Cadot hurried away to his quarters in the basement.

Inspector Devereaux was a short, thickset man, in his late forties. He had a round face with a small beaky nose, a thin, hard mouth and bright, small black eyes. He was an efficient police officer with a reputation for thoroughness. As he looked down at the dead girl, recognizing her from the photographs he had seen in *Jours de France* and *Paris-Match*, he realized that this case would receive enormous publicity, and it was going to be difficult to solve.

He realized that the girl couldn't have met her death in the elevator. She had been murdered in one of the hotel's five hundred bedrooms. Since all these bedrooms were occupied by people of wealth and importance, the investigation would have to be handled with extreme tact and caution.

It was necessary that the girl's body should be removed from the elevator as quickly as possible, and he gave orders for the body to be immediately photographed and then, walking over to Vesperini, who was hovering in the background, he asked him if there was an unoccupied room where the body could be removed as soon as the police photographer had completed his task.

Vesperini suggested one of the bathrooms since all the bedrooms were occupied, and Devereaux agreed to this.

Within ten minutes, the girl's body had been photographed, and then carried into a bathroom and laid on the floor. By this time the police surgeon had arrived and Devereaux left him to his examination.

His men were examining the cage of the elevator, dusting the surfaces for finger prints.

"I want every print you find recorded," Devereaux told them.

Then, leaving them to work on this, he and Henri Guidet, his assistant, went down to the lobby with Vesperini.

Vesperini put his office at the inspector's disposal, and as soon as the Inspector had seated himself behind the big mahogany desk he asked for the hall porter.

From experience Devereaux knew that the most observant member of any hotel staff was the hall porter. He had found they made excellent witnesses, and many a hotel case had been solved because of information supplied by these observant men.

The hall porter had just come on duty, and he entered the office and shook hands with Devereaux, with whom he occasionally played boule when the Inspector had an hour to himself.

The hall porter had already heard the news so it wasn't necessary for Devereaux to waste time explaining what had happened. He immediately launched into his interrogation.

"Can you tell me when this girl came into the hotel?"

The hall porter screwed up his eyes while he thought.

"It would be about four o'clock in the afternoon," he said finally.

This surprised Devereaux.

"Four o'clock in the afternoon? So she had been in the hotel for over fourteen hours. Did she ask for anyone?"

"No. She crossed the lobby and made for the stairs as if she knew exactly where to go."

"She didn't use the elevator?"

"No."

"Then it is possible the room she visited was on the first or second floor? If it had been on the third floor she would have used the elevator."

The hall porter nodded.

"I agree."

"Did anyone inquire for her?"

"At about half-past six; one of the press photographers asked if she had left the hotel," the hall porter said after another long pause for thought. "I told him she hadn't."

"Who was this man?"

"Monsieur Joe Kerr," the hall porter said, and from the tone of his voice the Inspector gathered that he thought nothing of him. "He represents an American scandal sheet called *Peep*: a man I don't care to see in the hotel. He is a drunkard, and his appearance is distasteful."

Devereaux made his first note on the sheet of paper he had

laid before him. He wrote in his neat hand: *Joe Kerr, drunkard, pressman,* Peep. *Asked information re L.B.* 6.30 *p.m.*

"He didn't say why he was interested in the girl?"

"No. Before then he had given me a thousand franc note to tell him when any of the Delaneys returned to their suite on the second floor. Knowing the man, I was surprised that he should give me as much as a thousand francs."

"The Delaneys?" Devereaux was a rabid film fan and his knowledge of film stars and producers was extensive. "Would that be the American producer?"

"Of course. Monsieur Delaney, his wife and his son have a suite on the second floor."

Again Devereaux made a note.

"No one else inquired for the girl?"

"No."

Devereaux frowned, fiddling with his pencil. He was a little disappointed. He had hoped for more useful information from the hall porter. At least he had something to work on, but he was pretty sure this Joe Kerr had only been interested in Lucille Balu from a professional point of view. After all, Kerr had made his inquiry at six-thirty, and the girl had been in the hotel apparently for two and a half hours.

He thanked the hall porter and said that if he could think of any way he could be of further help, he would consult him again.

When the hall porter had gone, Devereaux picked up the telephone and asked to be connected with the bathroom on the third floor where the police surgeon was making his examination.

The girl on the switchboard, who had heard the news and had kept herself informed of what was going on, immediately connected him.

"Have you anything for me yet?" the Inspector asked when the police surgeon came on the line.

"You are always in such a hurry," the police surgeon grumbled. "However, I can tell you when she died. It would be between half-past three and half-past four in the afternoon: not later and not earlier."

"She arrived at the hotel a few minutes to four."

"Then she was killed between four and half-past."

"Anything else?"

"She was strangled by a brocaded cord – almost certainly a curtain cord. The pattern of the cord has made an impression on her skin. The cord shouldn't be difficult to trace."

"Tell Benoit to photograph it immediately. See if he can

develop the plate and let me have a print at once. Tell him it doesn't matter if it isn't dry."

"I'll tell him, but it will delay my examination."

"The print is important. Anything else to tell me?"

"There are some fragments of skin under the finger nails of the girl's right hand. She must have scratched her assailant while he was killing her. From the amount of skin, I'd say he would have three pretty deep scratches either on his wrist or his arm."

Devereaux's eyes half closed as he nodded.

"That is very good," he said and hung up. Turning to Guidet, who had been sitting on the edge of the desk, listening, he said: "This may be less difficult than I had thought. I want you to find out where the girl was staying. She worked for the Paris Film Company. They should know. Find out what she was doing yesterday. I want her complete movements, especially between two and four o'clock. Put as many men as you need on the job, but do it thoroughly. I want all the boatmen, the beach attendants, the shop people questioned. They will know her, and if she has been seen, they will be able to tell us. Find out where this man Kerr is staying and bring him here. As you go out, tell Cadot I want him."

Guidet nodded and went quickly from the office.

A few minutes later, Cadot, freshly shaved and wearing his best suit, came in.

"Did you see this girl come into the hotel?" Devereaux asked as soon as Cadot had sat down.

"No. I was patrolling the corridors at four o'clock. It is my usual routine," Cadot said. "At that hour, very few people remain in their rooms, and I take the precaution to have a walk around. With so many strangers in the hotel because of the Festival, it is easy for a thief to slip upstairs."

Devereaux pulled a face.

"Then it would be easy for a non-resident to use one of the bedrooms in which to kill this girl?"

"I wouldn't say it would be easy, but some of our clients are careless and leave their keys in the doors. It is possible to use an unoccupied room, but it would be very risky."

"It is a possibility that we mustn't overlook, but I don't think it happened like that. I think the girl was killed by someone staying in the hotel. As she died between four and half-past, her body must have been kept hidden until the killer felt it safe to put her in the elevator. That was a clever move. You can be sure

71

she wasn't killed on the third floor. The fact she walked up the stairs makes me think it happened on the first or second floors. Can we find out when the elevator was last used before the girl was found?"

Cadot smirked modestly.

"I have already found that out for you, Inspector. The elevator goes on automatic at three o'clock. It was standing on the ground level within sight of the night clerk at that time. Between half-past three and four – he doesn't remember to the minute – the night clerk says he saw the red light flash up, indicating that someone was calling the elevator from upstairs. Some ten minutes later, the red light again flashed up, showing that the elevator had again been moved between the floors. It is safe to assume I think that the murderer was using the elevator at that time. The elevator didn't move after that."

Devereaux made a note.

"During your patrol, did you see anyone in any of the corridors who had no business to be there?"

Cadot nodded.

"Yes. There was a pressman on the second floor. I caught him listening outside Mr. Delaney's suite."

"And who was he?" Devereaux asked, pencil poised.

"His name is Joe Kerr. He . . ."

"Ah, yes. I have information about this man already," Devereaux said. "He begins to interest me. What was he doing outside Monsieur Delaney's door?"

"He said he had been told at the desk that Monsieur Delaney was in."

"And was he?"

"No. His son was, but he left a few minutes before I caught Kerr outside the door."

"So no one was in the suite?"

"That's right."

"You say Kerr was listening outside the door?"

"That's what it looked like. He may have knocked and was waiting for the door to be opened."

"What time was this?"

"Quarter to five."

Devereaux scratched the side of his nose with the end of his pencil.

"Soon after the girl was killed," he said as if talking to himself. "So this man Kerr was in the hotel around the time of her death."

"It looks like it."

"Can you find out for me when he left the hotel?"

"It's possible. I will ask the night clerk, who is waiting to see if he can be of help."

While Devereaux waited, he turned over in his mind what he had learned. He glanced at the desk clock. The time was now twenty minutes to eight.

Cadot returned in a few minutes.

"The night clerk says he saw Kerr leave at three fifty-five this morning."

Devereaux, who was tapping with his pencil on the blotter, stiffened and looked up.

"Did he say what he was doing in the hotel at such an hour?"

"No. He came down the stairs and the night clerk said he thought he was drunk – anyway, he was walking very unsteadily. He went out without saying anything."

"This becomes interesting. This was the time about when the girls' body must have been put in the elevator." Devereaux consulted his notes. "The girl was strangled with a curtain cord. Are there such cords in every room in the hotel?"

Cadot shrugged his shoulders apologetically.

"I don't know, but it is easy to find out."

"Find out for me," Devereaux said. "If the cords are different on the various floors let me have samples."

Cadot said he would do what he could and left the office.

Devereaux relaxed back in the leather desk chair. He lit a cigarette and puffed at it while he frowned at the opposite wall.

Benoit, the police photographer, came in. He laid a damp print on the blotter in front of Devereaux.

"Here it is, Inspector," he said. "It's the best I can do until I get back to the lab."

Devereaux studied the photograph. He took a magnifying glass from his pocket and bent close. Then he straightened and laid down the magnifying glass.

"It's not bad. The cord is brocaded: the pattern is quite distinct. I don't think it will be difficult to identify the cord if it is found."

He was still studying the photograph when Cadot returned. He carried two silk curtain cords: one of them was scarlet and the other green.

He laid them on the desk.

"Only the first- and second-floor rooms have brocaded cords," he said. "Are these what you want?"

73

Devereaux examined the two cords, then he pushed aside the green cord, examined the scarlet cord again, then sat back, smiling at Cadot.

"This cord comes from – where?"

"The second floor."

"We are getting warm. We now know she was strangled by a cord similar to this one, and that means she was strangled in a room on the second floor. I would now like a list of everyone who is staying on this floor."

At this moment the telephone bell on the desk rang.

Cadot answered it and then held the receiver out to the Inspector.

"It is for you."

It was Guidet calling.

"I am at the girl's hotel," he said. "Her agent, Jean Thiry, is coming over to see you. The girl was seen talking to a young fellow on the beach at three thirty yesterday afternoon. He has been identified by two witnesses. He is Jay Delaney: the son of the producer."

Devereaux remained silent for so long that Guidet said, "Are you there, Inspector?"

"Yes. I was thinking. I want this man Joe Kerr. It is now urgent. Concentrate on finding him. Use as many men as you need," Devereaux said and hung up.

He looked at Cadot.

"Jay Delaney," he said. "What can you tell me about him?"

Cadot lifted his shoulders.

"He is about twenty-one or -two. He seems a nice, quiet, well behaved young fellow. All the Delaneys are nice people. Monsieur Delaney is, of course, very rich."

"Can you find out if this young man was in the hotel at the time the girl died?"

"I'll ask," Cadot said and went out of the office.

Devereaux picked up his pencil and began to draw aimlessly on the blotter. He was still drawing and puffing at his cigarette when Cadot returned.

"Young Delaney returned to the suite a few minutes to four o'clock," Cadot said. "Mrs. Delaney joined him immediately afterwards."

"Mrs. Delaney?"

"Yes. The clerk remembers her asking for the key and he told her Mr. Delaney junior had just gone up to the suite."

Devereaux pushed out his lower lip and tapped it gently with his pencil.

"So Mrs. Delaney was with her step-son at the time the girl died?"

Cadot looked sharply at him.

"It sounds as if you thought he had something to do with it. . . ."

Devereaux shrugged his shoulders.

"One has to think of everything, but obviously he couldn't have. Well, we must see what Kerr has to say for himself. A drunkard." He frowned. "What puzzles me is why the girl should have been killed." He reached for the telephone and called the police surgeon. "Are there any signs that the girl was sexually interfered with?" he asked when the police surgeon came on the line.

He listened for a moment or so, then grunted and hung up.

"There was no assault and no attempt at assault. Then why was she killed?"

Frowning, he began again to make aimless patterns on his blotter.

II

A little after eight o'clock, Jay woke out of a heavy sleep. He lifted his head to look at the bedside clock, then, grimacing, he slid further down in the bed and shut his eyes.

He lay for some minutes, thinking of Ginette, and then, abruptly, he remembered Lucille Balu.

For a brief moment, a chill of uneasiness ran through him, then, with an impatient shrug, he told himself he had nothing to worry about.

It was unfortunate that he had given way to the stupid impulse, and had killed the girl. But he had got rid of the body, and the police couldn't possibly trace the murder to him. There was no more difficult murder to solve than the murder without motive.

He wondered if she had been found, and, impelled by a sudden urgent curiosity, he lifted the telephone receiver by his bedside and ordered *café complet* to be sent to his room.

He got out of bed and took a shower. As he was combing his hair the waiter came in and put the breakfast tray on the table.

Jay eyed the man curiously, but the stolid fat face told him nothing.

75

"What is all the excitement about?" Jay asked casually as he slipped on his dressing gown.

"Pardon, monsieur?"

"I thought I heard some sort of commotion just now. Is someone ill?"

"Not that I know of, monsieur."

Impatiently, Jay waved him away, and, when the waiter had gone, Jay walked over to the open window and looked out.

Although it was still early, there were a number of people bathing, and also a larger number of people wandering along the promenade.

Parked opposite the hotel were two police vans, and Jay smiled uneasily, stepping back and letting the curtain fall into place.

So they had found her.

A cold knot of excitement coiled into a tight ball in his stomach as he poured coffee and drank it thirstily. Then he went into the bathroom and rapidly shaved with his electric razor.

It would be interesting to go down and see what was happening, he thought. After all it would be a pity to miss any possible excitement after he had set the stage for the actors to strut on.

Finishing his second cup of coffee, he slipped on a singlet, a pair of cotton trousers and, pushing his feet into a pair of espadrilles, he moved to the door, then paused.

He remembered the three scratches on his arm and he examined them. They were slightly inflamed and startlingly red against his heavily tanned skin. It would be safer to wear a coat, he thought, and going to his cupboard he took out a cotton jacket and slipped it on.

The first thing he noticed when he reached the corridor was the "out-of-order" sign on the elevator. So they had begun the investigation, he thought, and he was aware of a growing feeling of excitement. Perhaps, after all, this thing he had done wasn't going to be such a bore. It had been the waiting that had bored him. Now the police were active, this might turn out more exciting than he had imagined.

Casually, he walked down the stairs. As he reached the head of the stairs leading into the lobby, he paused to look around.

The smooth machinery of the hotel appeared to be working with its usual efficiency. The hall porter was checking through a pile of letters. The reception clerk was writing at his desk. Vesperini, the assistant manager, stood by the revolving doors, apparently admiring the hydrangeas that stood either side of the entrance.

Jay took a few steps that brought him past the telephone booths and where he could have an uninterrupted view of the whole lobby.

There were no signs of any uniformed policemen and Jay felt vaguely disappointed. The hotel seemed to be taking the discovery of a dead girl in one of their elevators with extraordinary calm.

He crossed over to the hotel porter and bought a copy of the *New York Times*, then, choosing a chair that would give him a good view of the entrance to the hotel, he sat down.

He sat there, glancing at the newspaper, for some fifteen minutes before he saw a tall man, broad shouldered, with a hard face and alert eyes come into the lobby. He nodded to Vesperini who inclined his head in acknowledgement, then walked into the office behind the reception desk.

So that's it, Jay thought. They're in there having a conference. I bet they're absolutely foxed. I wonder what line they are working on.

He took his gold cigarette case from his pocket and lit a cigarette. As he was putting the case away, one of the elevator doors opened and Jean Thiry and Guidet came out.

Guidet had taken Thiry up to identify the girl's body. The shock of having to see her made Thiry walk a little unsteadily. His face was pale, and there was a stunned expression in his eyes.

Jay watched the two men disappear into the office behind the reception desk. He guessed Thiry had been up to identify the body, and he felt a morbid curiosity to see how pale the man was. This was becoming interesting, he thought. It was a pity he couldn't hear what was going on from this chair in the lobby, but at least he was keeping track of the developing drama.

Thiry was being questioned again by Inspector Devereaux, who handled him gently, seeing the shock Thiry had had. Thiry had already told him about the message he had received telling him that the girl had gone to Monte Carlo for the evening. Devereaux had got Guidet to question the message clerks, but neither of them could recall who had given the message except that it had come over the telephone.

Devereaux said: "Of course the girl didn't send the message. It was sent by the killer to gain time. You can make no suggestions as why she was killed?"

Thiry shook his head.

"No. It must have been the work of a lunatic. Who would want to kill her? She was just a kid," and he blew his nose violently to conceal his emotion.

"So Monsieur Delaney was interested in her future as a star?" Devereaux said, consulting his notes, "and you had an appointment with him at nine?"

"Yes. He wanted to meet her. I had already arranged to meet her in the bar here at six, and then I got this message. Feeling Delaney was going to make her an offer, I went at once to Monte Carlo to bring her back, but I couldn't find her."

"Naturally. She was dead by then. You left the girl by herself on the beach at around half-past three, and you went to the cinema, where you met Monsieur Delaney. That's correct, isn't it?"

"Yes."

"You saw Monsieur Delaney at nine and explained the girl had gone to Monte Carlo and you couldn't find her?"

"Yes."

"This is a very unfortunate thing for you, monsieur."

"Yes." Thiry's face was bitter. "It was her great chance and mine too. The man who did this must be caught and punished."

"Certainly, but I must have as much help as possible," Devereaux said. "First, can you tell me if she made a practice of carrying a handbag with her? When she was found in the elevator she had no handbag, and this strikes me as curious. Usually, a girl never moves without some kind of handbag."

"Yes, she had one. It was one I gave her. It was small. She only carried a powder compact, handkerchief and lipstick in it. It was a narrow, lizard-skin bag with her initials on it."

"She could have left it at her hotel, of course. I must have a search made for it."

"She wouldn't have left it at her hotel. I've never seen her without some bag or other."

Devereaux made a note on the sheet of paper lying in front of him.

"There is another thing also," Thiry went on. "She had a habit of wearing bead necklaces. I suppose the doctor removed her necklace when making his examination. I didn't notice it when I saw her."

"A bead necklace? She wasn't wearing any necklace when she was found in the elevator. I'll check that. There is nothing else you can tell me? She had no lover?"

"No. She was a serious girl. All she thought about was her career. She knew it was too soon to think of getting married."

When Thiry had gone, Devereaux gave instructions that a search should be made for the handbag, and then he went out into the lobby and crossed over to the hall-porter's desk.

"Do you remember if Mademoiselle Balu was wearing a bead necklace when you saw her come into the hotel?"

The hall porter thought for a long moment, his face tight with concentration, then he nodded.

"Yes, she was. I remember I thought how well the blue beads looked against her tan: a necklace of big sapphire blue beads, about the size of walnuts."

"Your memory is remarkable," Devereaux said. "I congratulate you."

The hall porter inclined his head, gratified.

Watching, Jay wondered who this man who had come out of the office and was now speaking to the hall porter could be. It was obvious that he was a police officer, and there was an air of importance and authority about him. Perhaps he was the man in charge of the investigation.

He studied him.

A hard, shrewd man, he decided, and again he felt the chill of excitement run through him.

He became aware that the hotel detective whom he recognized had come into the lobby and had given him a quick, hard stare. Then the hotel detective crossed over to the police officer. Jay, interested, watched the men talk together in low tones, then both of them suddenly turned their heads and looked directly at him.

Jay had been so curious and interested in what had been going on that it hadn't occurred to him that he was the only non-member of the hotel staff in the lobby nor had it occurred to him that he was in any way conspicuous. Until these two men suddenly turned to stare at him he had considered himself as an invisible spectator, enjoying what was going on without being noticed himself.

With a sudden quickening of fear, he glanced away from the two men and, as casually as he could, he pretended to be reading the newspaper he was holding.

Perhaps he had been rash to come here so early in the morning, he thought, his heart-beat quickening. Perhaps he was drawing attention to himself; not, of course, that it could matter. The police had no reason at all to connect him with the dead girl. All the same it might be safer to leave now. He would take a stroll along the promenade and return when there were more people in the lobby.

Casually, he folded the newspaper, and, behind the screen of his dark glasses, he glanced quickly at the two men, then his heart skipped a beat and he stiffened as the police officer suddenly moved away from the hotel detective and came directly towards where he was sitting.

Jay watched him come, sudden panic gripping him. He remained motionless, his cigarette burning between his fingers, aware of a cold dampness breaking out all over his body.

The police officer's face was expressionless, his small black eyes probing as he stopped in front of Jay.

"Monsieur Delaney?"

"That's right," Jay said, and his voice was husky.

"I am Inspector Devereaux, Cannes police. I would like you to give me a few minutes of your time, if you please."

Jay found it necessary to touch his lips with the tip of his tongue before saying, "Why? What is it?"

"Will you be good enough to come with me where we won't be interrupted?" Devereaux said. "In this office, over here."

Turning, he started across the lobby, not looking to see if Jay was following him.

For perhaps ten seconds, Jay remained in the chair. What did this mean? Fear tugged at his heart. Had something gone wrong? Had he done something unbelievably stupid, and they were now on his track already? Was this man going to arrest him?

Then, pulling himself together, he got to his feet and sauntered across the lobby.

This was the test he had deliberately invited, he was thinking. How can they prove anything?

But the cold fear that gripped him made him feel slightly sick. He didn't like the feeling, and his heart was hammering as he walked into the office where the Inspector waited for him.

CHAPTER SEVEN

WHENEVER Joe Kerr came to report on the Cannes Film Festival, and this was his third visit, he stayed at the Beau Rivage hotel because it was extremely cheap, because he was allowed to use the bathroom to develop his films, and because the owner, Madame Brossette, allowed him from time to time to share her bed.

After so many years as a widower, Joe grasped at any crumb of feminine kindness, and although he was a little frightened of this woman because of her size, strength and outbursts of temper, he eagerly looked forward to his yearly visits.

A few minutes after half-past nine a.m., he slid the prints he had finished into the toilet basin for their final wash.

He bent over the toilet basin and examined the prints. There were three of them. One showed Jay Delaney unlocking the door to suite 27; the second one showed Lucille Balu knocking on the same door, and the third one showed Sophia Delaney, her hand on the door handle, an impatient frown on her face. The three pictures were linked together by the wall clock that showed plainly in each print. It showed that Jay Delaney had arrived at the door a few minutes to four, that the girl had arrived exactly at four, and Sophia had arrived at seven and a half minutes past four.

Joe blew out his cheeks as he studied the prints. If they got into the hands of the public prosecutor, the boy would be a dead duck, he thought, and what was more, Delaney's wife would face an accessory rap.

He changed the water, then, lighting the butt-end of a cigarette, he began to clear up the mess he had made in the bathroom.

As he was tipping the hypo down the W.C., he heard a tap on the door.

A little startled, he went to the door, unlocked it and opened it a few inches.

Madame Brossette stood in the narrow passage, her arms akimbo, and looked at him, her green eyes probing, her small red mouth set in a hard line.

Madame Brossette was forty-five. She had buried two hus-
bands, and wasn't anxious now to take on a third. Her last husband had left her the hotel, the main business of which was to
let out rooms by the hour to the girls who walked the back streets
of Cannes during the early afternoon and far into the night.
Apart from this source of income, Madame Brossette worked
hand-in-glove with the tobacco smugglers of Tangiers, and also
she had important connections in Paris for the disposal of stolen
jewellery.

Her appearance was impressive. Close on six feet tall and
massively built, she always reminded Joe of a character out of a
gangster picture. Her face was heart-shaped, her hair was the
colour of rust, and she was enormously fat.

"Hello," Joe said feebly. "Did you want me?"

Madame Brossette moved forward like a steam roller, and Joe
hastily gave ground. She came into the bathroom, closed the door,
then settled herself with ominous composure on the toilet seat.

"What have you been up to, Joe?" she demanded, her eyes as
hard as emeralds.

"Up to? What do you mean?" Joe said, leaning his back
against the toilet basin to hide the prints from her sight. "I've
been up to nothing. What's wrong?"

"So long as you haven't been up to anything, then it's all
right," she said, settling her massive buttocks more comfort-
ably on the toilet seat. "I'll tell them you're here, and they can
talk to you."

Joe felt a tug at his heart. His raddled face lost some of its
colour.

"They? Who?"

"Who do you think? The police have just been here asking
for you."

"For me?"

Joe suddenly felt so bad he sat down abruptly on the side of
the bath.

"The police? For me?"

"Don't keep saying that!" There was an impatient note in her
voice. She had never been afraid of the police, and she had no
patience with those who were afraid of them. "I told them you
weren't here, because I thought you might have got yourself into
some kind of trouble last night." Her eyes were accusing. "You
were late enough back here."

Joe ran his fingers through his thinning hair and opened and
shut his mouth without saying anything.

"It's the homicide men on the job," Madame Brossette went on, watching him closely. "They told me if you did come here, I was to call them. What have you been up to?"

Joe hadn't been a crime reporter for nothing. He suddenly realized the danger he was in. That damned hotel detective must have told the police he had seen him in the corridor around the time the girl had died. The night clerk must have told them the time he had left the hotel. They would want to know what he had been doing in the hotel all those hours and what he had seen. He felt another tug at his heart. They might be crazy enough to imagine he had killed the girl!

Madame Brossette, watching him, saw his raddled face turn slightly green.

So he had been up to something, she thought, and she began to grow anxious, for she liked Joe.

She was a woman who needed a lover. When Joe wasn't in Cannes, she found a variety of substitutes, but Joe's love-making was something special. He was the only man who was tender with her, and to a woman who had lived hard, who trusted no one and who was becoming sharply aware of her advancing years, tenderness from a man meant a great deal.

"You'd better tell me, Joe," she said, her harsh voice softening. "Come on: get it off your chest. You know you can trust me. What have you done?"

"I haven't done a thing," Joe protested violently. "Don't look at me like that! I swear I haven't done a thing!"

She lifted her massive shoulders.

"All right, don't get so excited. Then it's all right for me to call the police and tell them you're here?"

Joe winced.

No, it wouldn't be all right to tell them he was here. Once they got him down to headquarters and that cold fish Devereaux started to work on him he would either have to tell them the truth and give up the idea of putting the bite on Delaney or he would have to lie and that would make him an accessory to murder.

He had to see Delaney before the police got at him. If Delaney refused to part with the money, then he would go to the police and tell them what he had seen. If Delaney gave him the money, then he would have to risk lying to the police: to have that amount of money would be worth any risk.

He had hoped to have handled this thing himself. He knew that, once Madame Brossette knew about it, she would take charge. She would control the money he got from Delaney. She would buy the villa for him, and heaven help him if he invited any other woman to the villa and she got to hear about it.

But he knew enough of her background to be satisfied that she was much more capable of handling this thing than he was, and, weakly, he decided to shift the responsibility onto her fat, massive shoulders.

"There's nothing wrong," he said, leaning forward and lowering his voice, "but . . ."

Then the whole story poured out of him.

Her big red hands in her lap, her emerald-green eyes fixed in a stare of concentration, Madame Brossette listened.

The story told to her made her breathe quickly, and when she breathed quickly her enormous bosom was agitated.

She said nothing until he had finished, then she held out her hand and said briefly: "Let's have a look."

He gave her the wet prints and watched her examine them. She handed them back, then, scratching the side of her neck, she said: "Give me a cigarette, Joe."

He gave her one and lit it and one for himself.

"What do you think?" he asked anxiously.

"What do I think?" she repeated, and her small, red mouth moved into a smile. "I think we have a gold mine here, Joe. What were you going to take for the negatives – five million francs?"

"Something like that," Joe said. "He can afford it."

"So you were going to Delaney?"

"Of course. Who else has the money? Of course he's the one to go to."

"You're wrong, Joe. I've seen him. A man with a face like his doesn't pay blackmail. He'd hand you over to the police before you knew where you were. The one we'll go to is the woman. I know something about her. Do you know where she was born?"

Joe stared at her.

"Born? What does it matter where she was born?"

Madame Brossette showed her even white teeth in a humourless smile.

"A lot, Joe. She was dragged up in the back streets of Naples. She's not going to lose what she's gained. She's the one we'll deal with. Maybe she hasn't much cash, but she's got plenty of jewels. Her diamonds alone are worth fifty million francs. I took a look at them when she wore them at the opening night. We've got a steady income for life here, Joe. We'll let her down gently at first. I'll get her to part with some small stuff around twenty million first, then gradually we'll put on the pressure. This could be a gold mine if we handle it right."

Joe moved uneasily.

"I'd rather settle for an outright payment. I don't like this steady income idea. It's too much like blackmail."

Madame Brossette patted his knee.

"You leave this to me, Joe. I'll handle it. You're going to keep out of it. You'll have to stay in your room, out of sight, until I've come to terms with her, then you'll be able to show yourself. I'll arrange for you to have a room at a hotel of a friend of mine in Antibes. That way you can explain to the police why they didn't find you in Cannes. As soon as we know she's going to part, you'll have to go to the police and tell them a story. We'll work that out together later."

"It'll make me an accessory," Joe said feebly.

Madame Brossette continued to smile.

"Just relax, Joe. You can't make an omelette without breaking a few eggs. If they find out you've told them a lie or two, they'll also find out I've made some money out of her." Her smile widened. "I don't look worried, do I? For the money we're going to collect, the risk is worth it. At least they can't kill us, and that's more than young Delaney can say." She stood up. "I'll go down and telephone her. You get back to your room."

Ten minutes later, Joe heard her coming slowly up the steep stairs and went to his door, expectant and uneasy.

Madame Brossette smiled reassuringly at him.

"It's all right. She's coming to see me. She'll be round here in half an hour."

"Coming here?" Joe said, his voice shooting up. "That's not a good idea, is it?"

"You don't imagine I want to talk to her at the Plaza, do you, Joe? Here I can get a little rough with her if it is necessary. She's not a weak one, Joe, I can tell you. She'll need handling."

Joe fingered his chin uneasily. He suddenly wished he hadn't brought her into this, and he felt an urgent need for a drink.

"Well, all right. I'll leave it to you." He began to back into his tiny bedroom. "You let me know."

"Don't worry about anything. Just give me the photographs and I'll do the rest."

Joe got the damp prints and handed them to her. He watched her walk heavily down the stairs, then he turned quickly, shut the door of his room and reached for the whisky bottle.

II

Inspector Devereaux waved Jay to a chair and then sat down behind the desk.

He looked searchingly at Jay.

A good-looking young fellow, he thought. He seems nervous. Well, that's understandable. Everyone is nervous when I talk to them. Possibly he has something on his conscience. Most people have, and they usually discover it when they meet me. I don't want to frighten him.

"I'm sorry to be taking up your time, monsieur," he said, leaning forward and resting his hands on the blotter, "but I believe you may be able to help me. Let me explain. This morning, a young woman's body was discovered in an elevator here. She had been murdered. I have reason to believe you are one of the last people to see her alive."

Jay sank lower in his chair. He was thankful for his dark glasses. They gave him a feeling of protection. He was slightly relieved that Devereaux's voice and manner seemed suddenly friendly, but he warned himself to be on his guard. This man might be laying a trap for him.

"Murdered?" he said. "Who is she?"

"Lucille Balu," Devereaux said, and picking up his pencil he began to make patterns on the blotter. "I believe you talked to her about half-past three yesterday afternoon?"

"Lucille Balu?" Somehow Jay managed to instil shocked surprise into his voice. "She has been murdered? Who did it?"

Devereaux smiled patiently.

"That is what I am trying to discover, monsieur. You talked to her yesterday afternoon?"

"Yes, that's right. She had been posing for photographers. I was on the beach. My father was interested in her, and I made casual conversation." He was wondering who had told the police that they had been seen talking together. They certainly found that out fast enough. "I can't really remember what we talked about. We only talked for a few minutes."

"She didn't say where she was going when she left the beach?"

"No. I think I said I hoped my father would give her a contract, and I believe I asked her if she wanted to live in Hollywood. It was that kind of conversation," Jay said, gaining confidence.

It was only because he had been rash enough to come down to

86

the hotel lobby that he had been caught up in this interrogation, he told himself. But he must still be on his guard, although now he was sure this police officer was merely making routine inquiries.

Devereaux tapped with his pencil on the desk as he asked, "You returned to the hotel about four o'clock?"

"Yes. I had been on the beach for some time, and I decided to have a swim. I returned to the hotel for my swimming trunks."

"Mademoiselle Balu wasn't visiting your father, by any chance?" Devereaux asked.

Jay felt his heart give a little kick against his side.

"My father? Why, no. My father was in the cinema at that time."

"Perhaps she didn't know that. She didn't mention that she intended to visit him?"

"Of course not." Jay was aware that his voice was unnecessarily loud and he controlled it. "There was no question of her visiting my father."

Devereaux laid down his pencil.

"The reason why I asked, Mr. Delaney, is because we know for certain that she was visiting someone who had a suite on the second floor. You didn't see her when you went up to your suite?"

Jay's mouth suddenly turned dry. How on earth had they discovered she had come to the second floor? Had someone seen her? Was it possible someone had seen her rapping on the door of the suite?

"No, I didn't. I would have told you if I had."

"Of course. So you went up to the suite, got your swim-suit and left: is that correct?"

Jay saw the trap. It was possible this man knew more than he was making out.

"I was about to leave when my step-mother came in. We talked. She also had the idea of taking a swim. She collected her costume, and then left. I left later. I had a letter to write."

Devereaux nodded.

"And at no time after you had spoken to the girl on the beach did you see her in the hotel?"

"That's right."

"Did you see anyone, apart from Mademoiselle Balu, when you walked down the corridor to your suite, monsieur?"

"No. At that time most of the suites are empty."

"You didn't notice a man hanging about in the corridor: a man with a camera?"

"A man with a camera?" Jay stiffened. "Why, no. I didn't see anyone. Was there a man up there?"

Devereaux nodded.

"Yes. He was seen by the hotel detective knocking on the door of your suite after you had left. He is a press photographer. His name is Joe Kerr. We are looking for him now."

Joe Kerr. . . .

The name sounded familiar, then Jay remembered the red, raddled face: the man who had asked him if he could arrange an interview with his father. He must have come up to the suite in the hope of catching Floyd Delaney after Jay had left.

Jay told Devereaux how he had spoken to Kerr on the beach, and how Kerr had asked him to arrange a meeting with his father.

Devereaux listened, disappointment clearly showing on his face.

"So he had a reason to be knocking on your door?"

"I suppose he had. No doubt he wanted to talk to my father."

Devereaux thought for a moment, then laid down his pencil.

"Well, I think that is all, Mr. Delaney. I'm sorry to have taken up your time."

With a feeling of acute relief, Jay got to his feet.

"That's all right. I'm sorry I couldn't be more helpful."

"Every scrap of information helps, monsieur," Devereaux said, standing up. "I wonder if you could describe the bead necklace the girl was wearing?"

"Why, yes," Jay said, without thinking. "They were big sapphire blue beads . . ." Then he could have bitten his tongue out for he remembered that the girl hadn't been wearing a necklace when she had been on the beach. She had put the necklace on when she had come to the suite!

Deveraux was saying casually: "Sapphire blue? Yes, that was what the hall porter said. The beads must be very distinctive for you to remember them." He walked round the desk and opened the door. "The necklace is missing. We're trying to find it. Well, thank you, monsieur."

Jay walked out of the office and started across the lobby towards the exit. He was feeling cold. What a stupid blunder to have made! he thought. Luckily the police officer hadn't noticed it. The chances were that he wouldn't think to check if the girl was wearing the necklace or not when she had been on the beach.

If he did he would probably have forgotten that Jay had said he had seen her wearing it. But it was dangerous. By admitting having seen the necklace, he was also admitting having seen the girl when she came to the hotel, and this he had denied. A stupid mistake like that could lose a man his life!

"Jay!"

Startled, he looked around.

Sophia was crossing the lobby. She had on a pair of white slacks, a red beach coat and her hair was caught back by a white silk scarf. There was a bony, scraped look about her face that Jay hadn't seen before. For the first time since he had known her, he realized with a sense of shock, that this girl was as hard as a diamond.

"Why, hello, Sophia," he said uneasily. "Where are you going?"

"Come with me," she said curtly and continued across the lobby to the revolving doors.

Then he knew something must be badly wrong, and again panic edged into his mind. He followed her out into the hot sunshine.

"Where's father?" he asked as he fell into step beside her.

"Still sleeping," she said curtly.

She crossed the road and went down into the Plaza beach enclosure.

At that hour – it was now a few minutes after ten – the enclosure was deserted.

She sat down at one of the tables and waved the waiter who had appeared impatiently away.

Jay sat opposite her. He put his clenched fists between his knees and squeezed them.

"What's wrong?" he asked huskily.

Sophia opened her bag and took out her cigarette case. She lit a cigarette while she stared at Jay, her dark eyes glittering.

"You might well ask that!" There was a cold fury in her voice that made him flinch. "You contemptible, degenerate fool! You might well ask what's wrong!"

"Don't talk to me like that!" Jay said, feeling blood mount to his face. "What has happened?"

"A woman telephoned," Sophia said, keeping her voice down with an effort. "She said she wanted to see me, and she's given me the address of some little hotel in Rue Foch. She knows you did it!"

Jay sat very still.

"What do you mean?" he managed to say. "Who is she? How could she know?"

"She said her name was Brossette and she was the owner of the Beau Rivage hotel. She said I would be interested to see some photographs connected with the affair that happened yesterday afternoon in the Plaza hotel. She said she expected me to come to her place within an hour, and she hung up."

"Photographs? What photographs? What are they of?" Jay said, trying to control the panic that seized him.

"That's all she said, and keep your voice down! Could anyone have photographed you as you took the girl to the elevator?"

"Of course not! Not in that light! They would have had to use a flashlight . . ." Then he broke off, remembering what Devereaux had said.

You didn't notice a man hanging about in the corridor: a man with a camera? He was seen by the hotel detective knocking on the door of your suite. He is a press photographer. His name is Joe Kerr.

Jay recalled the shabby, down-at-heel man with his drink-ruined face: a man capable of anything. He remembered the Rolliflex camera that had hung from a strap around his neck.

"I think I know. . . ." He took out his handkerchief and wiped his face and hands. "There was a press photographer seen up there. The police told me."

"The police?" Sophia stiffened. "Have you been talking to the police?"

"They found out that I had spoken to the girl on the beach. They wanted to know if I could help them," Jay said. "The Inspector mentioned this man. His name is Joe Kerr. The police are looking for him now."

Sophia's hands gripped her handbag until her knuckles turned white.

"You should have persevered with your Russian roulette game, Jay," she said, her voice seething with anger. "If you had blown your horrible, insane brains out, I wouldn't be in this position now. How are you enjoying the excitement? You planned to put your life in danger, didn't you? Well, it certainly is in danger now. You don't appear to be wildly excited about the prospect. In fact you look like a badly frightened rabbit!"

Jay made an angry gesture.

"You must talk to her. The photographs may be harmless."

"Do you think so?" She got to her feet. "We'll soon see. You realize your father will have to know now?"

"That may not be necessary," Jay said, shifting uneasily. "Find out first what these photographs are and how much she wants for them. Then we can see what to do."

"It doesn't bother you, Jay, that you have drawn me into this ghastly thing?" Sophia asked, leaning forward and staring at him.

Jay shrugged his shoulders.

"I didn't draw you into it, Sophia. You were thinking of yourself. You could have called the police. You preferred taking a risk than facing the publicity. You said so. You had the choice so don't try to make out I've drawn you into anything."

Sophia made a resigned movement with her hands.

"Yes, I should have told the police." She got to her feet. "I don't know how long this will take. You'd better go back to the hotel and tell your father I've gone for a swim. He'll be wondering where I am."

"All right," Jay said. "I'll wait for you in the suite."

He watched her leave the enclosure, cross to where her Cadillac convertible stood and drive away.

He sat for some minutes, thinking.

He had got over his first feeling of fear, and now he began to look for a way out. Before he could solve that problem, he had to know how dangerous the photographs were. They must be pretty dangerous, otherwise this woman wouldn't have dared to get into touch with Sophia. Obviously, he would have to try to get hold of the photographs and the negatives, then he would have to think of a way to make sure the woman didn't bother him again.

Where was Kerr? He also had to be taken care of. The chances were he was at this hotel and the woman was acting as his mouth-piece.

The police were hunting for Kerr. It was possible they suspected that he had killed the girl.

Jay suddenly smiled.

Perhaps here was the way out. If he could strengthen this suspicion in some way, if he could convince the police that Kerr was the man they were looking for. . . .

This needed thought.

He got to his feet and walked back to the hotel. By now it was after half-past ten and the activity of the day had begun.

Press photographers had taken up their positions, waiting for someone worth while to photograph. Starlets were beginning to show themselves off in their brief beach shorts and halters, moving about the lobby on the off-chance that some producer or casting director would spot them. The hall-porter's desk was surrounded by people collecting letters, newspapers and asking for information.

Jay paused just inside the entrance and looked quickly around. There was no sign of any detective. He saw his father come out of the elevator with Harry Stone and he went over to him.

"Sophia's gone for a swim," he said, after his father had greeted him. "She'll be back in an hour."

Delaney nodded.

"I'm going over to Nice. I'll be at the Studios. If she wants to come, tell her I'll be free about midday." He started to move away, then paused. "What are you doing?"

"I said I'd keep her company. I'm just going up for my swim-suit."

Delaney frowned, then shrugged his shoulders.

"Well, okay. See you," and beckoning to Harry Stone, he went out of the hotel with Stone hurrying after him.

Jay walked up the stairs to the second floor. He paused at the head of the stairs and looked along the deserted corridor, then, moving slowly, he walked towards his suite, paused for a moment outside the door, then continued on down the corridor. He had only taken fifty or so paces when he came upon the concealed alcove and he stopped. He realized then that the alcove he had thought was an entrance to another corridor was a bay window and it offered a convenient hiding place. He guessed this was where Joe Kerr had hidden himself.

His face set in concentrated thought, Jay walked back slowly to the door of suite 27, turned the handle and entered.

He moved over to a lounging chair and sat down.

For an hour he remained motionless, his mind active. He was still sitting there when he heard the door handle turn and he looked up to see Sophia come in.

She shut the door and leaned against it.

Jay saw that she looked pale under her tan and her eyes were very hard.

"Where's your father?" she asked, keeping her voice down.

"He's gone to Nice. There's no one here." Jay got to his feet. "Well?"

She moved away from the door, opened her handbag and took out a soiled envelope. She handed it to Jay and then walked across the room to the window, turning her back on him.

Jay's hands were unsteady as he took the three photographs from the envelope.

He studied them for some moments, then laid them on the table.

He had been expecting something much worse than this. Looking at the photographs, he thought they didn't appear to be anything like as dangerous as he had feared.

Of course the clock told the story, but that wasn't proof that he had murdered the girl. It was unfortunate that he had had the interview with the Inspector before he had seen these pictures. He would have told the Inspector a different story had he known there was a photograph showing the arrival of the girl at his father's suite. Now, he was saddled with a lie, and if the Inspector obtained further evidence against him, the lie might prove fatal.

On the other hand, he could still withdraw his statement about not seeing the girl after she had left the beach. He could tell the Inspector the same story that he had told Sophia – that the girl invited herself to the suite, that he had been weak enough to agree, and then, at the psychological moment, Sophia had walked in. When she had gone, he had got rid of the girl, and that was the last he had seen of her. He would hint that Kerr, hanging about outside, in a drunken frenzy, had dragged the girl into an empty room and had strangled her. But before his story made sense, he would have to strengthen the evidence against Kerr.

Turning, Sophia said, "Well?"

"These aren't so alarming, are they?" Jay said. "Of course the clock establishes that you and the girl and I were together in the suite around the time she was killed. But I should have thought it made things a little safer. No one would imagine that you would assist in a murder, surely?"

Sophia made an impatient movement with her hands.

"That's interesting," she said and moved over to a chair and sat down. "I think I would like a drink, Jay. Would you make me a very large martini?"

As Jay crossed over to the cocktail cabinet, he asked, "Who is this woman?"

Sophia rested her head against the chair back and closed her eyes.

The shabby, sordid little hotel made a vivid picture in her mind. It was the kind of hotel she used to take men to when she had been walking the streets in Rome.

Her suspicions had been confirmed when she entered the tiny, evil-smelling lobby and saw the enormously fat woman with rust-coloured hair sitting behind the reception desk: a woman Sophia recognized as a brothel-keeper.

"Madame Delaney?" the woman had said, and her thick, glistening red lips had parted to show white teeth. Her eyes had moved over Sophia's face, probing and curious and her smile had widened. "I thought it would be more convenient for you to come here than for me to come to the Plaza. What a magnificent hotel! How fortunate you are to be able to stay there!" Her great fat evil face seemed to hover before Sophia's eyes. "You like it there, *cherie?*"

"You have something to show me?" Sophia said, her voice flat and cold.

"Yes, I have something to show you." Madame Brossette got to her feet and she walked with heavy, creaking steps to a door which she opened. "Come with me. In here, we won't be disturbed."

Sophia followed her into a small, dingy office. She could smell the rancid smell of stale perspiration on the woman now she was close and she could even feel the heat that came from her great body.

Sophia had reacted to this situation as very few women would have done. Her experience in the past stood her now in good stead. She had dealt with women like Madame Brossette in her past, and she wasn't sickened, as most women would have been.

She sat down and watched Madame Brossette heave her body around the small desk, open a drawer and take out three photographs. These she laid in front of Sophia, then she sat down, showing her white teeth in a grin of triumph.

Aware that her heart was beating quickly, Sophia examined the photographs. Her shrewd, quick mind saw that the clock in each photograph was the story-teller.

Her face was expressionless as she looked at Madame Brossette.

"You want to sell these?"

"Yes. The man who took them was curious that the girl didn't leave your apartment," Madame Brossette said. "Anything odd interests him. He sat outside the door of your apartment until half-past three in the morning. Then he saw this young man carry the girl to the elevator. She was dead. With these pictures and his evidence, both of you could go for trial. Yes, I would be willing to sell them, providing the price is fair."

"How much?" Sophia asked as she arranged a loose strand of hair that had escaped from the ribbon around her head.

Madame Brossette regarded her with unconcealed admiration.

"You will appreciate that if my friend doesn't tell the police what he knows, he will become an accessory to murder?"

Sophia deliberately took out her cigarette case, selected a cigarette and then lit it. Her movements were unhurried, so that Madame Brossette could observe how steady her hands were.

"How much?" she asked, blowing a cloud of smoke into Madame Brossette's face.

"Shall we say ten million francs now as an immediate payment?"

"And after?"

Madame Brossette lifted her dyed eyebrows.

"For an immediate payment of ten million francs you would have my word of honour that the police wouldn't be shown the photographs. Later, my friend might need a little more money, but I assure you he isn't interested in great wealth. He is a man of very simple tastes."

"How much for the negatives?" Sophia asked.

Madame Brossette shook her rust-coloured hair.

"The negatives are not for sale. I'm sorry, but my friend is anxious to have a sense of security. One never knows: money can be useful from time to time."

Sophia leaned forward and tapped the ash off her cigarette into the glass bowl on Madame Brossette's desk.

"I haven't ten million francs," she said.

Madame Brossette lifted her fat, massive shoulders.

"That I can understand. You have a very rich husband, but he doesn't give you much money. The diamond necklace you wore at the opening night of the Festival would do very well. Your husband wouldn't miss it, and I could make use of it. Suppose we agree that the first payment should be the necklace?"

Sophia drew in a lungful of smoke and let the smoke drift down her small, beautifully shaped nostrils.

"That might be arranged."

Madame Brossette's smile widened.

"You are not without experience, *ma cherie*," she said. "In the past, you have had a hard life. Girls in trouble come to me from time to time. I deal lightly with them because I am sorry for them. I too have been in trouble. I'm willing to wait until to-morrow, but after to-morrow the photographs will go to the police. From now until nine o'clock to-morrow morning I will wait. After then, I must go to the police. Is that understood?"

Sophia got to her feet. She placed her small, beautiful hands on the desk and leaned forward so that her glittering eyes stared fixedly into the small, greedy eyes that looked up into hers.

"Don't confuse me with the other women you have had to deal with," she said softly, and the viciousness in her voice would have shocked her husband could he have heard it. "Don't make the mistake that you can dictate to me, you fat old cow! Don't imagine that, if I get the chance, I won't make you pay for this!"

Madame Brossette smiled. She had been often threatened in the past, threats had become meaningless.

"I appreciate how you feel," she said. "I'd feel the same way. Bring the necklace before nine to-morrow morning." Her white teeth glistened in the sunlight. "After the luxury you have found, you would not like to spend years in prison." She pushed the photographs across the desk. "Take them and show them to the boy. I have plenty more."

Sophia picked up the photographs, put them into the soiled envelope and the envelope into her bag. She stared for a long moment at the fat, evil face, then she walked out of the room, through the tiny lobby and into the sunshine.

Without looking at Jay she recounted the story of her meeting with Madame Brossette.

Jay sat opposite her, his hands folded in his lap, his face set and pale.

When she had finished, she said quietly: "Well? This is only the beginning. If I give her the necklace, she will ask for something else. What are you going to do, Jay?"

"We have until nine o'clock to-morrow morning," Jay said. "I don't think you will have to give her the necklace." His pale lips curved into a meaningless smile. "Between now and nine o'clock to-morrow morning I will have arranged something."

"What?"

Sophia's voice was suddenly sharp.

"Something. Try not to think about this, Sophia. Don't worry about it. Thank you for seeing this woman. It was kind of you."

He made a move to the door.

"Jay!"

He paused, looking at her.

"Wait a moment," Sophia said. "I must know what you are planning to do."

He shook his head.

"I don't think so, Sophia. It is best that no one knows that except myself."

He opened the door and went out, closing the door behind him.

Sophia sat motionless, her heart beating fast, a sudden sick feeling of fear gripping her.

CHAPTER EIGHT

I

WITH the sun burning on his back, Jay walked slowly down Rue d'Antibes. The principal shopping street of Cannes was crowded. In his beach wear he blended with the crowd of tourists in their gay holiday clothes.

He walked slowly, his hands deep in the pockets of his pale blue and white striped cotton trousers, his eyes hidden behind the dark lenses of his sun-glasses.

He reached Rue Foch and paused.

La Boule d'Or stood at the corner, as Ginette had described, and a little way down the narrow street was the hotel Beau Rivage, Madame Brossette's establishment.

Jay took out his cigarette case and lit a cigarette whilst he looked beyond the café at the small hotel.

It was as Sophia had described it: small, sordid and dirty. The lace curtains, grey-white with age and dirt, that screened the windows gave it a poverty-stricken look.

As he stood at the corner, feeling the hot sun burning down on his head, a girl in a clinging flowered patterned dress, a big handbag slung over her arm, a dark flashily dressed man at her heels, walked into the hotel.

Jay crossed the street and paused outside La Boule d'Or. This was a gay, clean little café with five tables set out on the street, and a blue and white sun awning, offering welcome shade.

Four of the tables were occupied by young holiday makers, sipping orange juice and eating ices. They glanced casually at Jay as he took the vacant table.

He looked into the dim cool interior of the bar.

Behind the bar sat a thickset man, around fifty years of age. His general appearance, with his big fleshy face, heavily tanned, his close-cropped white hair, his pale bright blue eyes, suggested that for most of his life he had been at sea, and this was true.

Jean Bereut had been a master mariner until an accident had deprived him of both his legs. Now, he was forced to sit behind the bar of La Boule d'Or and serve drinks while his mind drifted away from time to time to the far oceans where he had spent the best years of his life.

Seeing Jay seat himself, Bereut reached forward and struck a bell that hung within reach. A moment or so later, Ginette came out from the rear room and looked inquiringly at her father. He gave her a friendly grin and he jerked his thumb towards Jay.

She came across the room and paused at Jay's side, her back turned to her father. Jay looked up and he felt a surge of pleasure run through him to see the flush that mounted to her face as she recognized him.

"Hello," he said. "I was passing . . ."

"Father mustn't know," she said, her voice an anxious whisper.

He understood that. He wouldn't want his father to know either. His eyes moved over her. She was wearing a simple light blue dress and her hair was caught back by a strip of blue ribbon. He thought she looked lovely, and he felt blood mount to his own face.

"Can I have a Vermouth, dry, with ice?" he said, then added quickly, "I'll be down at the harbour at midnight. You will be there?"

"Yes, I'll be there."

She gave him a quick smile, then she went into the bar and he heard her ask her father for a Vermouth.

Jay looked across at the Beau Rivage hotel. The place stood inactive in its dingy sordidness. Then, as Ginette brought the Vermouth to his table, a girl with dyed red hair, wearing a shabby grey coat and skirt, accompanied by a red-faced, anxious-looking man in shorts and a flowered patterned shirt that proclaimed him to be an American on holiday, entered the hotel.

"I'm looking for another hotel," Jay said. He nodded across to the Beau Rivage. "Is that any good?"

"The Beau Rivage?" Ginette's eyes opened wide. "You mustn't go there. It is a horrible place. All the street girls use it."

"I didn't know." Jay leaned back in his chair, looking up at her. He saw she had a tiny mole just under her chin and he felt an urge to kiss it. "Do you know of any place – that's cheap?"

"Well. . . ." She hesitated. "We have a few rooms. They're clean, but I don't suppose they are what you are used to."

Jay laughed.

"You want to see the place where I am staying now. It's clean, of course, but it isn't very exciting. I may need to make a change. If I could have a room . . ."

"Yes. It would be five hundred francs a day." Ginette looked anxiously at him. "Would that be too much?"

"No, that would be fine. Well, if I have to leave the other place I'll come here and discuss it with your father." Jay had no idea why he was talking like this. He wanted to keep her at his side and he knew she wouldn't remain there unless he held her on the legitimate excuse of business.

"Would you be staying long?" she asked.

"No, not for long. I shall be leaving for Venice some time next week."

He was glad to see her expression of disappointment.

"I see," She moved back. "Well, I must go."

"To-night," he said. "I'll be waiting for you."

She nodded and went back into the rear room.

Jay finished the Vermouth, lit another cigarette, and after a moment or so, he got up, went into the bar and laid a five hundred franc note on the counter.

Bereut put aside his paper and gave change, nodding genially to Jay.

"Come again, monsieur," he said. "You will always be welcome."

Jay thanked him. As he moved out into the sun-baked street, he had a feeling he was being watched, and he looked back.

Ginette was standing in the doorway of the inner room. She raised her hand and smiled at him. Looking quickly at the bar and making sure her father was intent on his newspaper, Jay returned her smile and her signal, then he walked out of the café and strolled past the Beau Rivage hotel.

He caught a glimpse of an enormous woman sitting behind the reception desk: a woman with rust-coloured hair, and whose bodice seemed to be about to burst in its effort to contain the grossness of her bosom.

So this was Madame Brossette, Jay thought. She looked imposing enough and terribly strong. He flinched at the thought of having to kill her. She wouldn't be easy to kill: not like the slight, beautifully proportioned Lucille Balu.

He walked on through the dark shadows and the patches of hard, white sunlight, then suddenly he paused before the window of a jeweller's shop, stopping abruptly as if he had been caught hold of by an invisible hand and had been jerked to a standstill.

In the centre of the shop window was a necklace of sapphire blue beads, the size of small walnuts. They were the exact replica of the beads that Lucille Balu had worn and which he had dropped one by one into the harbour.

He stood staring at the beads. Providence, he was thinking. Luck seems to be favouring me.

He walked into the jeweller's shop and bought the necklace. It cost four thousand five hundred francs.

When the assistant wanted to wrap the beads in tissue paper Jay stopped him.

"It's all right. I'll take them as they are," he said, and, picking up the necklace, he dropped it into his hip pocket and laid on the counter a five thousand franc note.

Taking his change, he left the shop, and a few yards further on, he came to a hairdresser's shop. He entered and asked for a razor.

The assistant showed his surprise at the request. He tried to interest Jay in an electric razor, but Jay, shaking his head, and smiling his meaningless smile, said: "No. I want a razor. The old-fashioned kind. After all, they do give the best shave. Haven't you one?"

Yes, they had one, but it took several minutes for the assistant to find it. He laid the razor, its blade glittering in the sunshine, on the counter.

"Yes, that's what I want," Jay said.

He paid and let the assistant put the razor into its leather case, then, taking it from the man's hand, he slid it into his hip pocket.

Moving slowly, he again passed the Beau Rivage hotel. This time he noticed there was a young girl behind the reception desk: a thin slattern who was yawning over a newspaper, scratching her head as she read with a bored expression on her thin, sun-tanned face.

It would be unwise, he thought as he passed the entrance and headed once more up the Rue d'Antibes, to do anything until it was dark. The back streets would be deserted soon after ten o'clock: then would be the time, and he felt a quickening of his pulse as he thought what he had to do.

While he was walking back to the Plaza hotel, the news of the murder exploded like a hand grenade among the pressmen haunting the Plaza lobby.

For more than half an hour Inspector Devereaux was besieged in the assistant-manager's office. Then when the pressmen were satisfied that they had all the information he could give them, there was a mad rush to the telephones.

Left alone with Guidet, Devereaux sat back and mopped his perspiring face.

He had said nothing about Joe Kerr to the pressmen. He had given them the details of the girl's death. He had given them permission to visit the morgue where she had now been taken. He had said that the investigation was proceeding but so far there were no clues.

This was all very well for a few hours, but he knew before long pressure would be brought to bear on him for further information and a demand made for an arrest.

"Still no sign of Kerr?" he asked Guidet.

"Not yet. He's not staying at any of the hotels here," Guidet said. "We are extending the search further afield, and I have every available man on the job. It looks suspicious. The hall porter tells me that Kerr always arrives before eleven in the morning and hangs about up to midnight. To-day, so far, there has been no sign of him."

Devereaux dug his pencil viciously into the much-marked blotter.

"He was up there at the time the girl died; he left at the time she was put in the elevator. Now he has vanished. It looks like he is our man. He's got to be found!"

"He will be," Guidet said soothingly. "With a face like that. . . ."

"We still don't know why the girl was up there. Who could she be visiting?" Devereaux picked up a typewritten list of the names of the occupants staying on the second floor. "There were only five suites occupied at the time of the girl's death. The rest of the people were out. The fact she didn't ask at the reception desk but went straight up, looks as if she knew where she was going and the room number. Then who was she going to see?"

Guidet shrugged his shoulders. He had puzzled his head about this point for the past half hour and had come to no conclusion.

"It is possible," Devereaux said, tapping on the desk with his pencil, "that she knew most of the important film executives have suites on this floor. She may have gone up there on the off-chance of meeting one of them with the view of getting herself noticed. So many young stars are doing that in the lobby. She may have thought there would be less competition up there."

Guidet grimaced. He didn't think much of this idea.

"Then she chose an odd time. There was scarcely anyone up there."

Devereaux consulted his list.

"There's this man from the London Studios: Monsieur Hamilton. He is a casting director. She may have been trying to see him."

"How did she know he was in? How did she know his room number?"

"He may have told her."

"And you think Kerr was up there to see Delaney, and, finding himself alone in the corridor with a pretty girl, attacked her? She wasn't assaulted."

"He didn't mean to kill her," Devereaux said. "When he found she was dead, he became frightened and ran away."

"There's the curtain cord. If he had strangled her with his hands I might agree with you, but the cord makes it premeditated."

Devereaux nodded, frowning.

"Yes, He would have had to entice her into an empty suite. If she saw him undo the cord she would know he meant harm and she would have had time to scream. Yes, you're right, he must have had the cord ready. Then why did he kill her?" He dropped the pencil on the desk. "We must find him." He again picked up the sheet of paper and studied it. "Take some men with you and examine all the suites that were unoccupied at the time of the girl's death. Monsieur Vesperini will tell you if they are occupied now or not. We must work with him. His position is difficult. We mustn't disturb his clients if we can help it."

While they were talking Jay had entered the hotel lobby. He could tell immediately from the buzz of excited conversation that the news had broken.

No one paid any attention to him as he made his way through the crowd to the elevator.

As the elevator took him to the second floor, he slid his hand into his hip pocket and with his thumb nail he broke the string of the necklace so the beads rolled free in his pocket.

At the second floor, he left the elevator and began to walk slowly down the corridor.

When he was near the door to suite 27, he paused and took out his cigarette case and casually glanced behind him.

A big, heavily-built man was standing at the head of the stairs looking down the corridor at him.

Jay wasn't surprised. He had been prepared to find a detective up here by now.

Having lit his cigarette, he moved on to suite 30. The occupant of this suite was Merril Ackroyd, one of his father's top directors. Jay knew Ackroyd had been to Paris for the past two days. He knew also that he was due to return this morning. He paused outside the suite and rapped on the door, aware that the detective was watching him.

This was an exciting moment, and Jay felt his heart beating fast. He heard footsteps cross the room, then the door jerked open.

Ackroyd, a small, thin man with a crew-cut and a tanned, handsome face, stared at Jay, surprised, then he grinned.

"Hello there, Jay! Come on in! I've just this minute got back."

Jay followed him into the big sitting-room and closed the door.

"I was passing," he said, wandering away from Ackroyd. "I wondered if you were back. Did you have a good trip?"

"Yeah, swell." Ackroyd was puzzled to have this visit from Jay, but, as Jay was Floyd Delaney's son, he was prepared to waste a little time in being sociable. "Have a drink? What's all this I hear about a murder here last night? Is it right the girl was Lucille Balu?"

"Yes." Jay said. He was now standing by the window. He saw the drapes hadn't been caught back and were hanging loose. "The police are swarming all over the hotel."

Ackroyd said: "Well, what do you know! Hang on a second, Jay. I haven't unpacked yet. I've got a bottle of White Label in my grip. I'll get it."

He went into his bedroom.

Jay took the scarlet cord off its hook, twisted it into a coil and slid it inside his shirt. Then, taking out two of the blue beads, he flicked them under the settee.

He was sitting in a lounging chair by the time Ackroyd came back with the whisky.

"That kid!" Ackroyd said as he poured two big shots into glasses. "For heavens sake! Who would want to kill her? What's your father think? He was going to get her under contract."

103

"I don't think he knows yet," Jay said mildly. "He left for the Nice Studios before the news broke." He took the whisky, noticing with a sense of pride how steady his hand was.

"Must have been some lunatic, I guess. Well, I sure hope they catch the sonofabitch." Ackroyd finished his drink. "A kid like that! I'm sorry for Thiry. She was the only string in his stable worth a damn."

"Did you see any good shows in Paris?" Jay asked abruptly, changing the subject. The reference to a lunatic sent a wave of irritation through him. Why must everyone jump to the conclusion that the girl had been killed by a lunatic?

"Nothing worth getting excited about," Ackroyd said. He talked about this Paris trip for a few minutes, then pointedly asked Jay if he would like another drink.

"No, thanks. I must be getting along," Jay said and got to his feet. "Are you going to Nice?"

"Yup." Ackroyd pushed himself out of the lounging chair. "I promised your father to have lunch with him." He looked at his wrist watch. "Suffering cats! It's after twelve!"

They walked to the door together, and as Jay stepped into the corridor, he saw Guidet and three police officers entering a suite further down the corridor. The assistant manager of the hotel was with them. They didn't notice Jay.

"Looks like business," Ackroyd said, watching the detectives disappear into the suite. "Well, see you," he said, and waving his hand, he shut the door.

Jay walked down the corridor and entered his suite.

Well, he had set the stage, now there was nothing he could do until nightfall. He must hope that the police wouldn't find Joe Kerr before then. It was a risk he had to take.

He went into his bedroom, took the silk curtain cord from inside his shirt and put it in the top drawer of the chest. He put by its side the razor and the rest of the beads. Then he locked the drawer and pocketed the key.

Taking his swimming-trunks and a towel, he left the suite.

The detective at the head of the stairs glanced at him casually, then looked away.

Jay had difficulty in suppressing a giggle of excitement. If this man only knew what he had been doing, he thought, as he pressed the button for the elevator.

This was developing into an experience as exciting as he imagined it would be.

II

A little after three o'clock in the afternoon the telephone bell on Devereaux's borrowed desk started into life.

For the past hour, the Inspector had been rearranging the notes he had taken during the morning and had been busy studying them. The more he studied them the more he became convinced that Joe Kerr was the man he was after, and it irked him that Kerr hadn't as yet been found.

So, with an impatient frown, he lifted the receiver and barked, "Yes? Who is it?"

"Will you come up to the second floor, Inspector?" Guidet said, excitement in his voice. "We have found the suite where she was killed."

"You have?" Devereaux got hastily to his feet. "I'm coming."

He left the office, pushed his way through the crowded, excited lobby, and, not waiting for the elevator, he ran up the stairs to the second floor.

He was immediately pursued by a group of pressmen and four or five photographers.

Guidet must have anticipated trouble, for he had posted four gendarmes at the head of the stairs who stopped the pressmen entering the corridor.

There was an immediate uproar and, impatiently, Devereaux told them that he would make a statement as soon as he could; then he hurried down the corridor to where Guidet stood outside the door of suite 30.

"Well?" Devereaux demanded.

"There's a curtain cord missing in here, and I've found two of the beads from the girl's necklace on the floor."

Devereaux's face lit up with a triumphant smile.

"Now we're getting somewhere. Who owns the suite?"

Vesperini came forward.

"It belongs to Monsieur Merril Ackroyd. He is an important American film director. He was in Paris last night, and has only just returned. He got back at ten-fifteen this morning."

"So the suite was empty last night?"

"That is right."

Devereaux entered the suite and stood looking around.

"The beads?"

"They are under the settee. I left them where I found them for you to see."

Two of the police officers picked up the settee and moved it out of the way. On the carpet lay two blue beads.

Devereaux bent over them and examined them without touching them.

"No more of them?"

"No."

"In the struggle, the necklace must have broken. The beads would have shot all over the room. He missed these two. And a curtain cord is missing?"

"Yes." Guidet pulled aside the drapes. "There's one on the left, but the right one is missing."

"Have the beads photographed as they lie," Devereaux said. "Then test them for prints." He turned to Vesperini. "The suite was locked, of course, when Monsieur Ackroyd left for Paris?"

"Yes."

"And yet someone got in here. How was that possible?"

Vesperini shrugged his shoulders.

"Although it is unlikely, someone could have got hold of a pass-key. The maids do sometimes leave their keys in the doors while they are cleaning."

"Test the room for prints," Devereaux said. "It'll be a job, but I want every print you find." He turned to Vesperini. "Can you move Monsieur Ackroyd to another suite? It will be necessary for my men to seal this one after they have finished working."

Vesperini nodded.

"I'll arrange something."

Signing to Guidet, Devereaux left the room.

"Kerr must now be found at once," he said. "I am going to give the press his description with permission to print in the evening papers if we don't find him by late this afternoon."

"All right," Guidet said. "The usual formula about believing he can help us in the investigation?"

"That's it," Devereaux said. "A description of him, but no photograph. While I'm talking to the boys, find Thiry and get him to identify the beads. Show them to the hall porter, too," and, leaving Guidet to take the elevator, Devereaux marched down the corridor to where the pressmen were impatiently waiting.

After he had told them that they now knew where the girl had been murdered and had promised the photographers access to the room the moment the police had finished examining it, he went on: "Do any of you gentlemen know a photographer whose name is Joe Kerr?"

There was a roar of laughter from the pressmen and the *New York Tribune* photographer said sarcastically, "Is there anyone who doesn't know him? Why, Inspector?"

"He may be able to help us in the investigation," Devereaux said cautiously. "He was up on this floor about the time the girl met her death."

The *Tribune* photographer looked around, frowning.

"Anyone seen Joe this morning?"

No one had.

"Perhaps one of you knows where he is staying?" Devereaux asked.

The *Nice Matin* reporter said Joe was staying in some hotel off Rue d'Antibes.

Devereaux stiffened to attention.

"There are a great many hotels off Rue d'Antibes," he said. "Do you remember the street or the name of the hotel?"

The *Nice Matin* reporter shook his head.

"Can't say I do. A couple of nights ago I dropped the old soak off by the Casino. He had asked me for a lift. I remember he said he was staying off the Rue d'Antibes."

"He could be an important help," Devereaux said, trying to appear casual. "If any of you see him you might tell him I'd like to talk to him." He paused, then went on, "If we don't trace him by five o'clock tonight, I'll get you to put a paragraph in your paper. Just a description, saying we would like to interview him."

"Hey! Just a moment." Lancing of the Associated Press pushed forward. "Do you think the old buzzard killed the girl?"

Devereaux shook his head.

"I don't know who killed her," he said. "I know Kerr was on the second floor at the time she died. I'm hoping he might have seen the killer."

"Yeah?" Lancing's red, aggressive face sneered. "I bet! Let me tell you something: that old vulture was always making passes at the girls. Why, only last week he had the nerve to goose Hilda Goodman as she was passing through the lobby, and Hilda took a swipe at him. She bust his bridgework. Maybe he tried the same stunt with the Balu girl and, when she socked him, he strangled her."

"Pipe down!" the *Tribune* reporter said curtly. "Joe may be a soak, but he isn't a killer. And let me tell you, if you had the nerve, you would have goosed our Hilda yourself – I know you would."

There was a general laugh.

"Well, gentlemen, "Devereaux said, "you are holding me up. Just remember I would like to talk to Kerr if you see him."

He pushed through the circle of men and hurried down the stairs.

So Kerr made passes at women, he was thinking. Maybe that was the motive. He had met the girl, made a pass at her, she had struck him, and in a drunken rage he had dragged her into the suite and strangled her.

But he knew it wasn't quite right: it didn't fit. There was an act of premeditation about this killing: there was the curtain cord, and the fact the killer had used the pass-key to get into the suite. No, this hadn't been a sudden act of rage or panic.

Guidet met the Inspector in his office.

"The hall porter identifies the beads," he said. "I haven't been able to find Thiry yet. I think he must be in the cinema. We have a good finger-print on one of the beads."

"You have? Well, that's something?" Devereaux sat down behind his desk. "Ricco of the *Nice Matin* says Kerr is staying at a hotel off the Rue d'Antibes."

"Every hotel in that district has been covered," Guidet said. "That was the first district to be checked."

"And no one knew him?"

"No."

"Then check again. It's possible someone is hiding him. Put twenty men on the job and tell them not to come back until they have found him. Have them cover the shops as well."

Guidet looked surprised.

"The shops?"

"Perhaps someone has noticed him going to and fro to the hotel. I want this man and I'm going to have him!"

At this moment the detective in charge of the finger-print department came in.

"I've found a print in the elevator that matches the print on the bead, Inspector," he said. "There's no record down here. I'm having it checked at Headquarters."

Devereaux grunted.

"If it's Kerr's print," he said softly, "then I think we have him."

He waved impatiently to Guidet to get off, nodded to the

other detective, then, pulling his massive notes towards him, he began to go through them again.

CHAPTER NINE

I

It was a little after five o'clock when Jay left the beach. He had driven over to Antibes because he was anxious not to run into Sophia until he had done what he had to do, and, in Cannes, it was impossible to avoid meeting anyone you didn't want to meet.

Now, driving slowly back to Cannes, caught up in a long stream of traffic, he decided he would go to La Boule d'Or for a drink, and he felt an anticipation of pleasure at the thought of seeing Ginette again.

Both his father and Sophia would be at the Nice Studios until late, and then they would be going to the cinema. So long as he got back to the Plaza before eight o'clock and away again, he wouldn't run into them.

Leaving his car by the Casino, he crossed the street and walked slowly into the busy shopping centre. He moved toward Rue Foch, spinning out the time by pausing to stare into the shop windows, and, as he wandered along, he became aware that there were several plain-clothes detectives in the long, busy street, and immediately his sense of caution was alerted.

These unmistakable men were going in pairs from shop to shop, spending only a few minutes in each shop, then coming out and entering another shop.

Coming towards Jay were two of these men, and, anticipating that they would be entering a bookshop close by, he went into the shop ahead of them.

The shop was empty and the assistant came over to him. Jay said he just wanted to look around and he stepped behind a counter piled high with books that screened him from anyone entering the shop.

He had to wait five minutes before the two detectives entered.

He heard one of them say: "Police. We're looking for a man who lives around here." The detective went on to give an accurate description of Joe Kerr. "Have you seen him?"

Obviously flustered, the assistant said he was sorry but he hadn't.

The detective grunted and the two of them left the shop.

Jay's mouth tightened. So they were still hunting for Joe, and they were getting warmer.

He told the assistant that he couldn't find anything to interest him and he went out into the evening sunshine.

Ahead of him, the detectives were going steadily down the street, entering one shop after the other.

Jay quickened his steps and reached La Boule d'Or. There was an elderly couple sitting at one of the tables, drinking wine. They looked hot and tired. Beyond, in the dim bar, Jay saw Ginette sitting behind the bar, her elbows on the polished counter, her fingers in her hair while she read a newspaper spread out before her. There was no sign of her father.

He walked softly into the bar and paused before her. She glanced up, and again he felt excited pleasure to see the blood mount to her face at the sight of him.

"Hello," he said. "I was passing so I thought I would come in. Isn't your father here?"

"No. He's out. He likes to sit by the harbour in the evening." It amused him to see the effort she was making to fight down the blush that stained her face. "You startled me. Look, you've made me go hot."

He laughed. His eyes behind their dark screens examined her face, and he thought this face was something he wouldn't grow tired of. It would be nice to look at even when it was old.

"It's quiet here." He climbed up on a stool. "I didn't mean to startle you."

"I was reading about this horrible murder. Have you seen about it?"

"Yes." He was sorry that she had read about it. This was a personal thing. He didn't want to discuss it with her. "Could I have a dry Vermouth with ice?"

"Of course."

She was wearing a white singlet and dark blue jeans, and as she reached up to get the bottle of Vermouth from the shelf he could see her full young breasts tighten under the thin stuff of the singlet and he felt a little stab of love for her dart into him.

"I saw her once in a movie," she said as she put the bottle on the counter before him. "She was pretty. I liked her."

Jay hunched his shoulders.

"The police are looking for a man," he said, watching her as she put a piece of ice into the glass. "They are going into all the shops along Rue d'Antibes."

"Then they know who did it?"

"I don't know, but they are looking for someone."

She poured the Vermouth into the glass.

"I hope they find him quickly. It isn't nice to think there is a madman loose in the town."

Jay stiffened. He hated to hear her talk like this.

"Mad? I don't think he is mad." He sipped his drink, frowning. "I think he is a man who had to test his courage."

She bent her head to stare down at the newspaper, and her hair fell forward, half screening her face.

"Of course he is mad," she said. "Look, it says so here."

"You didn't hear what I said." He was terribly anxious for her to understand. It was impossible to let her think that he was mad. "I said he must be a man who needed to test his courage."

She lifted her head and stared at him.

"What an odd thing to say!" she said and he could see the blank, puzzled expression in her eyes.

Jay felt a wave of irritation run through him.

"It's not odd at all," he said sharply. "After all, the man has put his own life in danger by killing the girl. You can see that, can't you? He may have had to do it – an inner compulsion – an urge that had been in him for a long time to find out what his personal and secret reactions to danger would be. To some people that is vitally important. Unless you put your courage, your wits and your intelligence to a test, how can you possibly know their quality?"

The note of urgency and tenseness in his voice made her stare at him.

"But surely not," she said. "I can't believe that. If you had to find out the quality of your courage, wits and intelligence, surely you don't have to make someone else suffer? That is a horrible idea. There are many other ways of testing your courage without murdering someone."

He shifted impatiently on the stool, and leaning forward, his fists clenched, he said fiercely. "You are wrong! To make an honest test, you must put yourself in a position where there is absolutely no escape. You might think mountain climbing tests your courage, but it doesn't. Of course it is dangerous and people risk their lives, but if their nerve fails, if they feel it is too dangerous to go on, they can turn back, but if you kill someone there is no turning back; there is no bringing the body to life

111

again." He began to pound gently on the top of the bar. "Imagine a situation like this one. Imagine having a dead girl on your hands in a crowded hotel, knowing you have killed her, and that one little slip will endanger your life. What a test that must be! It is the perfect test for one's courage! Can't you see that? If you commit murder, there is no possible escape except by your own nerve, cleverness and courage."

"But you don't really believe that anyone in his right mind would kill someone just as a test of courage?" Ginette asked. "I can't believe that! What about the victim? This girl who was killed – she was only just beginning her life. No one but a madman would have done such a thing."

Jay started to protest, then his caution warned him to be careful. This girl was intelligent. He must be careful not to talk too much. She must never become suspicious of him. It would spoil everything.

He smiled at her and shrugged.

"Well, it's nothing really to do with us, is it? If the killer is ever found, I'm willing to bet that he is as sane as I am."

It was while he was speaking that he became aware of two shadows falling across the bar. He looked around and saw the two detectives come in, and he felt a sudden tightening band around his chest as they came up to the bar and paused within three feet of him.

He looked at them out of the corners of his eyes. They were big, heavy men, their faces shiny with sweat, and he could smell the sweat on their shabby clothes.

They asked Ginette for beers, and, while she poured the beers into glasses, they glanced at Jay and then back to Ginette.

"Mademoiselle," the taller of the two said as Ginette put the glasses before them, "perhaps you can help us. We are police officers."

Ginette looked at Jay, but he kept his eyes fixed on his glass of Vermouth.

"We are looking for a man," the detective went on. "Perhaps you have seen him pass here from time to time." He gave a detailed description of Joe Kerr. When he had completed the description he asked, "Have you seen him?"

"Why, yes," Ginette said. "He always carried a camera hanging by a strap around his neck. Isn't that right?"

Jay felt a chill crawl up his spine. He sensed the excitement in Ginette's voice, and he was sure she had seen Kerr.

"That's the man!"

The two detectives leaned forward.

"The description fits the man who passes here every day," Ginette went on. "He came in here once for a drink. I remember he asked for whisky, and we hadn't any. He has a room down this street: either at the Beau Rivage or the Antibes hotel."

Casually, Jay finished his Vermouth, then slid off his stool and walked without fuss across the bar to the telephone that stood on a shelf away from the detectives. He picked up the directory, flicked through the pages until he found the Beau Rivage hotel number, then dialled.

He was quite calm, although his heart was beating a little faster.

The detectives were still questioning Ginette: both men seemed excited and tense.

There was a click on the line and a woman's voice, hoarse and deep, demanded: "Who is it?"

Cupping his hand around the telephone mouthpiece he whispered into it: "Is that Madame Brossette?"

"Yes." The hoarse voice sharpened. "Who is that?"

"Listen carefully. Two detectives are coming to your hotel within the next few minutes. They are looking for Joe Kerr. They have a warrant for his arrest."

Jay waited long enough to hear Madame Brossette catch her breath sharply, then he gently replaced the receiver.

As he did so, he saw the two detectives walk briskly out of the café and cross the street.

He watched them. If they found Kerr it wouldn't be very long before they would start looking for him. This was a moment of intense excitement, and when he saw them disappear into the Hotel Antibes, he drew in a quick breath of relief.

"Did you hear what they said?" Ginette said excitedly. "Why I've actually spoken to the man! Is he the one who did it? A horrible looking man! He could have done it."

Jay smiled at her, his lips stiff.

"They may only want information from him." He looked at his wrist watch. "I've just remembered I have to see someone. I'm late already. I'll see you to-night at the harbour."

Without giving her time to say anything, he left the café, crossed the hot sun-baked street and walked slowly past the Beau Rivage hotel.

As he passed the entrance he glanced into the dark doorway. The thin girl was sitting at the desk, running her fingers through her untidy hair and staring fixedly out into the hot evening sunshine. There was no sign of Madame Brossette.

This was not surprising, for Madame Brossette, as soon as she received Jay's telephone call, had called her daughter, Maria, told her to watch the lobby, and then she had plodded up the steep stairs to Joe's room.

She found Joe lying on his back on the bed in a heavy, drunken sleep. An empty bottle of Scotch lay by his side, his mouth hung open and he snored.

She shook him roughly, and Joe sat up, his eyes dazed as he stared at her.

"Wazzamatter?" he asked feebly, and would have toppled backwards if she hadn't caught hold of him.

"Wake up, Joe!"

The snap in her voice brought Joe's drink-fuddled mind awake, and he blinked, shaking his head as he heaved his feet to the floor.

"The police are searching the hotels. They are looking for you. Come on. I've got to get you out of sight."

"Me?" Joe's face lost colour. "Why? They came here this morning, didn't they?"

"Yes, and they're across the road at the Antibes right now. Come on, Joe."

He got unsteadily to his feet.

"What do you want me to do?"

"Just come with me." Her big hand closed over his and she dragged rather than led him to the door and out into the corridor.

"What's the idea?" Joe asked, trying to clear his fuddled mind. "Maybe I'd better talk to them. Maybe we'd better give up this idea. I don't like it. It's blackmail. I'll talk to them and give them the photographs. . . ."

She propelled him down the corridor, making soft soothing noises that one makes to a nervous cat. She opened a door into a cupboard full of brooms and pails.

"You leave this to me, Joe," she said, and, reaching for a hidden spring, she pressed it and the back of the cupboard slid aside. Beyond was a small room, equipped with a table, chair and a bed. It was lit by a tiny electric lamp let in the ceiling, and ventilated by a shaft that connected with the chimney in the room next door. "In you go, Joe, and stay quiet. I'll be back in a little while. Just stay quiet."

Protesting and mumbling, Joe felt himself propelled forward, and then there was a sharp clicking noise as the panel slid shut.

Moving with a speed remarkable for one of her bulk, Madame Brossette hurried back to Joe's room, bundled all his belongings into his shabby suitcase and put the suitcase in the cupboard, then she opened the window to let in some fresh air, snatched up the empty whisky bottle and went downstairs.

As she entered the lobby, the two detectives came in.

"You again?" she said, showing her white teeth in a grin of welcome. "What's troubling you now?"

Both the detectives knew Madame Brossette well. They had called on her from time to time trying to pick up evidence against the tobacco smugglers, and they both knew what went on in the hotel.

"Look, Jeanne," the taller detective said, "we have had a tip that Kerr is here. Do you want us to get a warrant or do you let us look the place over?"

Madame Brossette's grin widened.

"You're wasting your time, boys," she said, "but you can look. He's not here. Mind how you go." She closed one heavy eyelid. "Some of the rooms are occupied. Better knock before you walk in."

"Has he been here?"

Madame Brossette spread her hands.

"You didn't ask me that before, did you? This morning you asked me if he was here and I said that he wasn't. Now you ask me if he is here and I still say he isn't, but when you ask me if he has been here, then I say he has. Yes, monsieur, he has been here."

The detective hunched his shoulders in exasperation.

"Listen, you old fox, you know as well as I do when I asked this morning if he was here I meant was he staying here."

"I didn't. You can't expect me to read your mind. You asked me if he was here, and I said he wasn't."

"So he has been here?"

"Certainly. He stayed here for eight days. What is all the fuss about? This morning you gave me a description of the fellow, then asked if he was here. You can't blame me, monsieur. I told the truth."

"Then where is he?"

"He left this morning before nine o'clock. I think he was going to Marseille. He mentioned something about it but I was busy and didn't pay much attention. But he is coming back. He has left all his things here."

"Let's have a look," the detective said.

Madame Brossette turned to her daughter.

"You'd better run up and get the boys and girls out of here. These gentlemen will want to look at the other rooms. We don't want to embarrass anyone."

The detective looked over to where his companion was standing.

"Stay here and check them as they come out," he said, then as Maria hurried up the stairs, he turned to Madame Brossette, "This is a serious matter, Jeanne. Kerr is wanted for murder. He killed this Balu girl."

Madame Brossette's face remained impassive, but inwardly she was badly shocked.

"He wouldn't hurt a fly. What makes you think he did such a thing?"

"We have enough evidence to put his neck under the knife," the detective said. "Come on: show me his room."

Twenty minutes later, the detective came down the stairs, his face showing his disappointment. He had examined Joe's belongings and had gone through all the rooms in the hotel and had found nothing. He was satisfied that Joe wasn't in the hotel, and now he walked over to the telephone and called Inspector Devereaux.

Devereaux listened to his report, then he said: "Leave Evrard to watch the hotel and come back here. I'll send another man down right away. Is there a back exit?"

"No, Inspector."

"You're sure he isn't in the hotel?"

"Yes, Inspector."

"All right. Tell Evrard that, if Kerr enters the hotel, he is to bring him to me at once. You come back here," and Devereaux hung up.

Madame Brossette watched the two detectives leave the hotel. She saw the shorter of the two stroll over to La Boule d'Or café and sit down at one of the tables that gave him a clear view of her hotel, and her thick lips tightened.

She went into her private office and sat down. The situation was becoming complicated. She now regretted giving the Delaney woman so much time to hand over the necklace. She decided she had better hurry up the transaction. What possible evidence could the police have against Joe? She reached for the telephone and called the Plaza hotel.

"Connect me with Madame Delaney," she said.

There was a pause, then the girl on the switchboard said, "Madame Delaney is out. She is not expected back until after the film showing."

Madame Brossette grunted and hung up. She stroked the side of her fat face, frowning, then she got to her feet, went into the bar, took up a bottle of whisky and plodded up the stairs.

She found Joe sitting on the edge of the bed, his face glistening with sweat and she could almost hear the thudding of his heart.

"What's going on ?" he demanded anxiously. "Look, I don't like this! I'm going to the police right away. The whole thing was a mistake."

Madame Brossette sat down on the chair, which creaked under her weight. She poured two inches of whisky into the glass and gave the glass to Joe.

"Don't get excited," she said. "It's going to be all right."

Joe drank the whisky greedily, blew out his raddled cheeks and set the glass down. He needed the drink. It restored his shaken nerves.

"What do you mean – all right?" he demanded. "The police are looking for me, aren't they? If I'm not damn careful they may think I killed the girl. What do they want? What did they say?"

"They think you might have seen the boy," Madame Brossette lied smoothly. "They know you were in the hotel from the time the girl was killed until pretty late. They are looking for information. That's all. There's nothing to get excited about."

"I'm not excited," Joe said, sweat running down his face. "They don't think I killed her, do they?"

"Don't talk like a fool! Why should they?" Madame Brossette said. "All the same I think it would be better if we changed our plans." She tipped some more whisky into the glass. "I think we should ask for more money and settle for one payment. I think you'll have to tell them the truth, Joe, and show them the photographs, but before you do that, we'll get as much as we can out of the Delaney woman."

His hand shaking, Joe drank the whisky.

"I don't like it. I'm going to give the photographs to the police right away."

Madame Brossette moved impatiently. Although she was fond of Joe, she wasn't going to lose the chance of picking up an easy ten million francs.

"I told them you had gone to Marseille, Joe," she said, "but that you would be back to-morrow. Don't let's spoil this thing. By to-morrow I'll get the Delaney woman to part with her diamonds. As soon as we've got them, then you can go to the police. The diamonds are worth at least ten million."

The whisky was beginning to have an effect on Joe. He rubbed his hand over his face, trying to think clearly.

"What am I supposed to be doing in Marseille?" he demanded. "They're certain to check up."

"Relax, Joe," Madame Brossette said soothingly. "I know a fellow who'll swear you spent the day with him. You've nothing to worry about."

"But she won't part with the diamonds unless we give her the photographs and the negatives."

"She'll get them." Madame Brossette winked. "But the police will also get them. We won't give the police her photograph and I'll tell her I've kept one back. She'll keep her mouth shut if she knows we've still got her photograph."

Joe reached out and took the whisky bottle from her and sloshed a huge drink into the glass.

"You think she'll part with the diamonds?" he asked. "Phew! What one could do with ten million francs."

"Yes, Joe." Madame Brossette decided he was now over his scare and she could leave him. She didn't like leaving Maria on her own in the lobby. "Now relax. Take a nap. You can leave it all to me."

Joe lay back on the bed. He drank some of the whisky, then put the glass on the table beside him.

"Well, if you think you can handle it . . . I don't want any trouble. Still if we get ten million francs it'll put me on easy street for the rest of my life."

"And me too," Madame Brossette said gently. "We go shares on this, Joe."

"Sure," Joe said, but his face fell. Five million francs sounded much less attractive than ten.

Madame Brossette got to her feet.

"I'll be back again in a little while. You stay here for tonight. I'll call this fellow in Marseille and fix things for you."

His hand now much more steady, Joe finished his drink, then he closed his eyes.

As Madame Brossette left the room, he began to snore.

II

Jay sat at a table of a café near the Casino, reading the late edition of *Nice Matin*.

The time was ten minutes to ten. It was dark, not starlit, and there was a new moon.

Jay was wearing a dark blue light-weight suit and a dark blue open neck shirt. He made a drab figure in comparison to the other people at the tables around him in their bright holiday clothes.

He was reading the description of Joe Kerr that was printed on the front page of the paper with the statement that the police believed this man could help them in their inquiries.

Jay was a little worried.

Was Kerr still in the hotel or had he been smuggled away? He had satisfied himself that the two detectives hadn't found him, for he had walked past the hotel several times during the past two hours and he had seen the two detectives sitting outside La Boule d'Or, obviously watching the Beau Rivage hotel.

The watching detectives made Jay's plan much more difficult. They would see him enter the hotel and that could be fatal.

As the waiter passed with a loaded tray, Jay ordered another café espresso. He lit a cigarette, and, as he returned the lighter to his pocket, his fingers touched the coiled curtain cord he had brought with him.

He felt in his other pocket for the loose beads of the necklace he had bought, and then his fingers moved to the inside of his jacket and touched the leather case containing the razor.

He laid down his paper and stared across the small harbour, seeing the masts of the yachts sharply outlined against the sky, and his mind brooded on his problem.

The waiter put the espresso on the table in front of him and Jay paid him. When he had finished the coffee, he got up and walked slowly towards Rue d'Antibes.

He reached Rue Foch a few minutes after ten o'clock. The back street was deserted. The only lights came from La Boule d'Or and from the entrance of the Beau Rivage hotel.

Jay walked slowly down the street, his hands in his trousers pockets, his head slightly bent, his eyes screened by his dark glasses.

The two detectives were still sitting at the table. They had beers in front of them, and they were talking together in low tones. Neither of them paid any attention to him, and he slowed his stride to look into the bar.

Ginette's father sat behind the bar, staring emptily across the room. There was no sign of Ginette.

Jay moved on, and a few yards further on, he passed the entrance to the hotel.

Madame Brossette was sitting behind the reception desk, a cigarette between her full lips while she flicked over the pages of a magazine, the expression on her face revealing her disinterest.

He had hoped by now the detectives would have gone. This was going to make things difficult and dangerous. If he went into the hotel they might wonder who he was and what he was doing going into the place alone and without luggage. The woman, too, might be suspicious of him.

He paused at the street corner and taking out a packet of cigarettes he slit the seal with his thumb nail while he considered the problem.

It was solved for him when he heard a soft voice behind him say, "Hello, *chéri*, were you looking for me?"

He turned.

A girl stood on the edge of the kerb: a thin, shabbily dressed girl who was eyeing him speculatively as her red, full lips curved into a professional smile.

"Hello," he said. "Yes, I was looking for you as it happens."

She giggled and moved up to him.

"Well, here I am. There's a little hotel down the street." He could smell the cheap scent on her and her hard, young-old eyes made him feel a little sick. "Come with me, *chéri*. I'll arrange everything."

He walked with her down the dark street.

"Are you on holiday, *chéri*?" she asked, keeping close to him so her bare arm rubbed against his coat sleeve.

"That's right."

"You're American, aren't you? You speak very good French." She had the Midi accent and he had to listen carefully to understand her.

"Do you think so? Is this the hotel?"

He slowed his pace a little, his mouth suddenly turning dry.

To do what he had to do with the police within fifty paces of the hotel was tempting providence, but he had no other alternative. He had to get the photographs and the negatives if he were going to survive.

"Yes," the girl said, linking her arm through his as if she were suddenly frightened that he would lose his nerve and not go in. "It's all right, *chéri*. I come here often. It'll cost two thousand francs, and then there's my present."

120

"Two thousand francs? That's too much."

"It isn't, *cheri*. You can stay the night. Most gentlemen like to stay the night. . . ."

As they walked into the hotel, Jay didn't look towards the two detectives, sitting across the way, but he was sure they had seen them go in. The girl wasn't much shorter than he, and by slightly bending his knees and by keeping his head down he managed to screen himself by her so that the detectives couldn't get a good look at him.

Madame Brossette laid down her magazine and nodded to the girl.

"Well, Louisa?"

"My friend and I . . ."

"Of course."

Madame Brossette merely glanced at Jay as he put two one thousand franc notes down on the desk.

"The gentleman would like to stay the night," the girl said and giggled.

Madame Brossette picked up the notes.

How strong she looked! Jay thought. He looked at her red, rough hands. They were as big and as strong as the hands of a man.

"You know the room *chérie*? The usual one. . . ."

The girl took the key Madame Brossette pushed towards her and taking Jay's arm she led him up the steep dark stairs to a dimly-lit landing.

A man and a girl, coming down the passage, paused at the head of the stairs to let Jay and his companion pass.

Jay saw the two girls exchange winks.

Sheepishly the man pushed past Jay and started down the stairs.

His companion said: "Mind how you fall, *chéri*."

Louisa unlocked a door facing the head of the stairs. She turned on the light and walked in, followed by Jay.

The room was small and sordid. There was a bed, a chair, a washstand with a bowl and an enamel jug containing water on which floated a film of dust. A threadbare rug by the bed sent up a puff of dust as Jay trod on it.

The girl shut the door and turned the key. She moved up to Jay, smiling invitingly.

Jay slumped down on the bed. He took from his hip pocket two crumped five thousand franc notes.

"I'm sorry, mademoiselle," he said and smiled at her, "but

121

you must excuse me. I have changed my mind. I hope you will accept this. I regret wasting your time."

The girl stared at the two notes as if she couldn't believe her eyes. "Are those for me?"

"Of course. I hope you will excuse me."

She plucked the notes out of his hand as if she were afraid he would change his mind.

"What's the matter? Don't you like me?" she asked. Her voice was curious rather than hostile.

"Of course, but I have been walking all night and now I find I am very tired. Will it be all right for me to stay here a few hours and rest?"

The girl folded the notes and hastily put them in her purse. From her expression Jay could see she couldn't make up her mind whether to be insulted or indifferent.

"What kind of poor fish are you?" she said, moving to the door. "This is the first time any man has ever told me he was too tired."

"You must excuse me, mademoiselle. Will it be all right for me to stay a little while?"

"You paid for the room, didn't you?"

She went out, slamming the door.

Jay sat motionless, his clenched fists squeezed between his knees.

Somewhere in this dingy hotel was Joe Kerr, and where Kerr was the photographs and the negatives would be.

Now he had to find them.

He took the leather razor case from his pocket and took the razor from it, putting the empty case back in his pocket. The razor, closed, he slipped under the strap of his wrist-watch.

Then, moving silently, he crossed to the door, opened it a few inches and stood listening.

CHAPTER TEN

I

In the meantime. . . .

A little after six o'clock, Jean Thiry walked into the Plaza lobby. He had spent the morning and the afternoon in the cinema, watching two foreign movies, trying to make up his mind to the fact that, by Lucille Balu's death, he had now been reduced to the status of a third-rate agent, and if he wanted to survive, he would have to get back into the harness of solid, grinding work. He realized these two movies had possibilities. He hoped he could sell at least bits of them to a Polish agent who was looking for "shorts" at a cut-rate price.

So he had put Lucille Balu out of his mind and had watched the movies, noting the bits that might be commercial.

Now, as he walked into the lobby, he saw that people looked at him out of the corners of their eyes, and he knew they were thinking that, with Lucille Balu out of his stable, he was now of no account, and he knew the judgment was just.

A detective moved over to him and touched his arm.

"Pardon, monsieur, the Inspector would like to speak to you."

Devereaux sat behind his borrowed desk, his notes in a neat pile in front of him, and he waved Thiry to a chair, half rising, his face grave and his brow wrinkled.

"We have found a blue bead in one of the suites on the second floor," he said, taking the bead from a plastic envelope with a pair of stamp tongs. "We have reason to believe it is a bead from the necklace Mademoiselle Balu wore."

He placed the bead on the white blotter and pushed the blotter forward so Thiry could examine the bead.

"It is possible," Thiry said after looking at it. "She had so many necklaces. It could be one of hers. I don't know."

Devereaux moved impatiently.

"Surely, monsieur, you will remember this bead. You told me you were with her on the beach before she was killed. She was wearing the necklace at the time. Please try to think of the necklace which she was wearing on the beach."

Thiry frowned.

"She wasn't wearing a necklace," he said in a flat, definite tone.

Again Devereaux made an impatient movement.

"But I have evidence that assures me that she was, monsieur."

Thiry shrugged.

"She wasn't wearing a necklace. I can assure you of that."

Impressed by his manner, Devereaux scratched the tip of his nose while he stared at Thiry.

"Yet it was you who told me of her habit of wearing necklaces, monsieur."

"Yes, yes, but I didn't say she wore a necklace when she was on the beach. She didn't. As soon as she got out of her swim-suit she always put on a necklace, but she never wore one when in a swim-suit. I know what I'm talking about. I've known the girl for some years. She was not wearing a necklace when she was on the beach. That is final. If you don't believe me, we can get the photographs of her that were taken when she was posing on the beach, and you can see for yourself."

Devereaux suddenly felt vaguely excited.

"I would be glad to see the photographs, monsieur."

"That's easily done. If you will wait, I'll get them."

"Thank you, monsieur."

When Thiry left the office Devereaux again went through his notes and took, from the collection of the neatly written evidence, the interview he had had with Jay Delaney.

He read:

Q. You didn't see her when you went up to your suite?

A. No, I didn't. I would have told you if I had.

Q. And at no time after you had spoken to the girl on the beach did you see her in the hotel?

A. That is right.

He turned another page.

Q. I wonder if you could describe the bead necklace the girl was wearing?

A. Why yes. They were big sapphire blue beads. . . .

Devereaux laid down the notes and lit a cigarette. He sat staring up at the ceiling, his expression blank until Thiry returned with the photographs.

"Here they are, Inspector," he said and laid on the desk half a dozen pictures of Lucille Balu posing on the beach. "You see? She wasn't wearing a necklace."

Devereaux studied the photographs, then he swept them into a neat pile and laid them on top of his notes.

"Thank you, monsieur. You have been most helpful."

When Thiry had gone, Devereaux sat for some minutes thinking, then, getting to his feet, he went to the office door and beckoned to Guidet, who was waiting outside.

"I would like to speak to young Delaney. Is he in the hotel?"

Guidet inquired from the hall porter.

Returning to Devereaux, he said: "No, he's out somewhere. Do you want me to look for him?"

"Please tell the hall porter to let me know immediately he returns," Devereaux said. "We won't look for him. After all, he is the son of a very important man. We must be careful."

He smiled, lifting his shoulders in resignation. "It will be enough when he returns."

It was fortunate for Jay that, when he did return to the hotel, the hall porter was having trouble with an irate American film actress who wanted to know why there was no berth for her on the Blue Train to Paris.

So Jay was able to go up to the suite, and a little later leave the hotel without Devereaux being aware that he had done so.

It wasn't until after ten o'clock that Devereaux regretfully telephoned headquarters and gave instructions for Jay to be found and brought immediately to the Plaza.

II

In the meantime . . .

All the afternoon Sophia had been wrestling with her conscience. She kept wondering what Jay was doing.

Between now and nine o'clock I will have arranged something, he had said. *I don't think you will have to give her the necklace.*

What could he arrange? she kept wondering. The photographs were damning. Knowing the kind of woman she had to deal with, Sophia was sure Madame Brossette had either to be paid or she would carry out her threat and send the photographs to the police.

Several times during the afternoon and the evening, Sophia had been tempted to tell her husband, but she flinched from the inevitable explosion she knew would follow. She blamed herself for not giving Jay away at once. By not doing so, she had made herself an accessory to murder, and thinking about this as she sat at her husband's side, watching a French movie, she imagined herself in prison, and the thought sent cold chills up her spine.

Jay must do something! she told herself. He had got her into this mess, and he must get her out of it!

Then she came back to the thought that had nagged her ever since he had left her. How? How was he to do it?

It was while she was in the cinema, her nerves tense, her mind far away from the lighted screen, that Madame Brossette told her daughter to take over the reception desk, and then plodded up the steep stairs to see how Joe was getting on.

She was uneasy about Joe. The detective had said they had enough evidence to convict him for the girl's murder.

What possible evidence could they have except that he had been seen on the second floor of the hotel at the time of the

125

murder? And now *Nice Matin* had printed a description of him. If the two detectives continued to watch outside, how was she going to get Joe out of the hotel without his being seen?

She walked heavily down the passage to the broom cupboard. There she paused to listen and to look up and down the passage.

From a door close by she heard a girl protesting shrilly and a man cursing her. Shrugging, she opened the cupboard door and stepped inside.

Moving like a ghost, Jay stole out of his room and down the passage. He had taken off his shoes and he made no sound as he reached the cupboard door. It was shut now and he put his ear against the panel and listened. He heard a sharp clicking sound of a released spring, then a sliding noise. He waited, his heart beating fast, his ears straining.

"Anything I can get you, Joe?" he heard the woman ask. "Do you want something to eat?"

Jay's lips moved into his meaningless smile.

So Kerr was in there!

He moved away from the door and walked silently back to his room, pushing the door nearly shut. Then, leaning against the wall, he waited.

Joe Kerr moved uneasily as he frowned up at Madame Brossette.

"I'm all right," he mumbled. "What's the idea? You woke me up."

"I thought I'd see how you were getting on." She patted his arm. "Are you hungry?"

"No. I'm all right." He closed his eyes. She could see he was very drunk. "Just leave me alone, will you?"

"I'll be up again," she said, and she remained at his side until he began to snore, then leaving him, she walked down the passage, down the stairs and back into the lobby.

"All right," she said to her daughter. "You get off now. Don't be back too late."

Maria slid off the chair behind the reception desk.

"I won't be back until two," she said sulkily, "so don't expect me before then."

Madame Brossette grunted. She was long past worrying about her daughter. In another year the girl would be walking the back streets of Cannes and would be hiring a room at the hotel. Madame Brossette believed in sacrificing sentiment for profit. What had been good enough for her when she had been young should surely be good enough for her daughter.

She watched Maria leave the hotel, then, lighting a cigarette, she settled down on the chair her daughter had vacated and, with a bored grimace, picked up her magazine and began to leaf through its pages.

Jay moved silently to the head of the stairs and looked down at her; then, satisfied she would be occupied for a while, he moved on bare feet down the corridor to the broom cupboard.

He paused to listen outside the door, then he put his hand on the door handle and turned it gently. He eased open the door a few inches and was surprised to find himself looking into total darkness. He listened and, hearing nothing, he moved into the cupboard, closing the door behind him. For some moments he remained motionless, his breathing coming hard and fast while he tried to pick up any sound that would tell him he was in the room in which Kerr was sleeping. Finally, hearing nothing, he took out his cigarette lighter and flicked the flame alight. Then he saw where he was – in a broom cupboard, and seeing an electric switch, he put on the light.

Madame Brossette's conversation with Joe which he had overheard told him there must be a false wall in the cupboard, and it didn't take him more than a few minutes to discover the spring release that operated the false door.

He stood looking into a small room, not more than ten feet square. There was a bed, and, on the bed, lay Joe Kerr, his breathing heavy and punctuated with slow, strangled snores.

Jay moved back to the cupboard door and slid the bolt that was on the inside of the door, then he moved silently into the inner room until he reached the bed.

He stood looking down at Joe as he slept, the light from the outer room giving enough illumination for Jay to see the raddled, tired face in some detail.

He pulled the razor from his wrist watch strap, then he sat on the bed, and reaching out, gently shook Joe's shoulder.

Joe was dreaming of his wife, and for a change, the dream wasn't a nightmare. He was seeing her, in slacks and a flowered patterned shirt, weeding the flagged path that led up to the cottage Joe had rented for their honeymoon, and Joe smiled as he watched her in his dream.

Then he became aware of a hand on his shoulder gently shaking him, and the dream was spoilt, stopping abruptly the way the picture on a movie screen stops when the film snaps.

Jeanne again! he thought angrily. Why can't she leave a guy alone? He hunched his shoulders, mumbling a protest, then he tried to free himself from the persistently shaking hand.

Fingers gripped his coat more firmly, and into his dream-dazed mind came a sudden sense of danger, and a warning that these weren't Jeanne's thick, heavy fingers that had so often shaken him awake. Slowly he turned his head and opened his eyes.

He looked up at Jay, who sat motionless at his side, his left hand resting on Joe's shoulder.

Joe couldn't believe what he was seeing, then, with a gasp of fright, he started to sit up, but the fingers on his shoulder suddenly turned into steel claws and dug into his flesh, making him gasp with pain and fear and forcing him flat again.

He lay motionless, his heart thumping, sweat on his face, as he looked at the compact motionless figure who was sitting beside him, and for the first time in his life, Joe experienced real fear: fear that turned him cold, that dried his mouth, that paralysed him.

The pale, expressionless face with its dark glasses, the lips curved in a meaningless smile, struck a sick terror into him like a knife thrust.

"It's Mr. Kerr, isn't it?" Jay said, leaning forward slightly so Joe could see his own reflection in the two dark screens of the boy's glasses.

"How did you get in here?" Joe croaked. "You – you've no business in here."

The thin, pale lips moved into a smile that accelerated Joe's heart beat.

"Oh, but I have. I've come for the photographs and the negatives. Where are they?"

Joe tried to pull himself together. Again he attempted to sit up, but again the steel fingers bit into his flesh. He was horrified to realize this slight boy was so strong.

"Where are they, Mr. Kerr?" Jay repeated. "I want them."

"I don't know what you're talking about," Joe mumbled, shrinking back on his pillow. "You get out of here."

Jay withdrew his hand from Joe's shoulder. His very stillness made him seem more menacing to Joe.

"The photographs and the negatives, please," he said softly. "I haven't much time."

There was a threat in his voice that made Joe touch his dry lips with the tip of his tongue.

"I haven't got them. She's got them. You ask her for them."

Jay said gently: "I could persuade you, Mr. Kerr."

128

He lifted his right hand so Joe could see it. The razor lay in his open palm, and Joe suddenly felt very sick. He watched the boy open the blade that glittered in the electric light.

"The photographs, please," Jay said. He lifted the razor. "Unless you give them to me . . ." He paused and his pale lips moved into a smile that chilled Joe's blood. "I wouldn't wish to hurt you, Mr. Kerr."

The flashing strip of sharp steel filled Joe with horror. What was left of his drink-sodden courage disintegrated.

"Don't touch me!" he said, his voice quavering. "You can have them! I've got them here. . . . ."

He pulled out his wallet and spilled its contents out on to the bed. Among the few crumpled thousand franc notes, his press card and a faded snap-shot of his wife was a soiled envelope.

Jay picked up the envelope, got to his feet and moved away from the bed. He put the razor on the table, then he opened the envelope and took out three negatives and a number of prints. He checked them, then laid them in the ash tray on the table.

"Are there any more, Mr. Kerr?"

Joe shook his head.

Jay stared at him, and he felt certain the man was so frightened he was telling the truth.

"She hasn't any either?"

Again Joe shook his head.

Taking out his cigarette lighter, Jay applied the flame to one of the photographs. He stood over the little burning pile until there was nothing left but black ash which he scattered over the carpet.

"So now, Mr. Kerr, it is your word against mine," he said. "I wouldn't advise you to talk to the police. My father has a lot of influence. Besides, the police would want to know why you hadn't told them before. Attempted blackmail carries quite a stiff prison sentence. From what I hear a French prison isn't very comfortable."

Joe felt if he didn't have a drink, he would faint, and with a hand that shook violently, he grabbed up the bottle of whisky and poured whisky into the glass by his bedside. He half filled the glass with whisky before Jay moved up to him and took the bottle out of his hand.

The touch of Jay's cold fingers against his feverish skin made Joe start back. Then, as Jay moved away and set the bottle on the table, Joe picked up the glass and drank greedily.

The effect of the whisky on him was immediate. He felt as if he had been hit on the back of his head, and he realized the mistake he had made in drinking the whisky so quickly.

He felt the glass slide out of his hand and he heard it, as from a-long way off, thud on to the carpet. His brain now seemed to be wrapped in a hotbed of cotton wool. He lay back, feebly blowing out his raddled cheeks, feeling the violent acceleration of his heart beats.

He was aware that Jay was standing over him, and the dark glasses, reflecting the light, frightened Joe. Then suddenly he saw his wife standing behind Jay and smiling at him. She was wearing the white brocaded dress in which she had died, and he felt vaguely surprised that there was no blood on the dress.

She was beckoning to him, and he tried to lift his head to see her more clearly, but the effort was too much for him.

Then he became aware that the boy was doing something and his dazed eyes shifted from his wife to the boy's hands.

The boy was holding a scarlet cord between his fingers, and the cord formed into a loop.

Joe thought this was odd, and he made a desperate effort to try to understand what was happening, but the whisky fumes now had taken control of him.

He felt himself grinning stupidly as the boy moved slowly and silently up to him, the scarlet loop held in front of him.

Joe looked from the boy to his wife, and he saw a big patch of blood was now forming on the front of her dress. He started up, not feeling the loop of silk as it dropped around his neck, staring with drunken horror at the steadily increasing circle of red on the white dress.

It wasn't until the scarlet cord bit savagely into his raddled ageing throat that it flashed through his mind that he was being murdered.

III

It was a little after a quarter past eleven when Madame Brossette, bending over her magazine, suddenly lifted her head to listen.

Somewhere upstairs she could hear a tap running, and she frowned. The only person she allowed to use the bathroom was Joe. Surely he hadn't gone in there when she had told him to remain in the hideout? Maybe it was one of those wretched girls, although what they would want in the bathroom puzzled her.

Again she listened, and her frown turned into an angry

scowl as the sound of running water continued. If there was one thing Madame Brossette hated more than anything else it was waste.

Grunting with annoyance, she pushed back her chair and got up. She walked to the foot of the stairs and stared up them, listening.

Water was gushing out of the taps, she decided. Someone had been in the bathroom, and not only had left the taps open but had also left the bathroom door open.

"Turn that water off!" she bawled but without much hope that anyone up there would take any notice. The thought of climbing that long, steep flight of stairs in the night heat irritated her, but after waiting a few more seconds, she caught hold of the banister rail and started the long plod up.

Jay watched her come through the crack between the door and the door post. He had turned on the taps, and had left the bathroom door open in the hope the sound of the running water would bring the woman up the stairs.

He was very tense. He could feel a muscle twitching in his cheek, and he had difficulty in controlling his quick, hard breathing.

He watched the woman reach the head of the stairs, then move heavily down the passage to the bathroom.

Silently he opened the door, stepped out into the passage and, going down three of the stairs, he laid across the fourth stair the bolster he had taken from his bed. Then he stole up the stairs and back into his room as Madame Brossette, muttering angrily, turned off the tap.

She came out of the bathroom, turned off the light, then walked half way down the passage and paused outside the door of the broom cupboard.

Jay stiffened. This was the risk he knew he would be taking if he brought the woman up the stairs. Would she look in to see how Joe was?

But he relaxed as Madame Brossette shrugged her heavy shoulders and then continued on down the passage.

Jay watched her. He tensed himself, and as Madame Brossette reached the head of the stairs and turned to descend them, her back now to him, Jay silently opened the door and stole out behind her.

Madame Brossette had reached the third stair before she became aware that there was someone behind her. She suddenly felt hot, quick breath on the back of her neck and she had a vague idea that she could hear the thump-thump-thump of heart beats.

Her feet descended to the fourth stair as she turned her head. She saw a crouching figure of a man just behind her, his hands outstretched, and in the dim light the dark glasses he wore gave him an inhuman look.

She caught her breath sharply. Then she felt the stair give under her weight as she stepped on to something that had a horrible soft feeling.

She lost her balance. She made a desperate grab at the banister rail.

Jay put his hand on her shoulder and gave her a violent push.

She began to fall backwards, her mouth wide open, her eyes bulging with shock and a thin, wailing scream starting from her throat.

Jay reached down and snatched up the bolster as the woman's great body landed in the lobby with a crash that shook the house.

The thud of her body made an appalling sound, and it was immediately followed by a violent crashing of bottles on the shelf over the bar, jerked loose by the shock of the woman's fall.

Jay jumped up the three stairs and moved quickly into his bedroom, closing the door. He threw the bolster on the bed, then taking out his handkerchief he wiped his sweating face.

Was she dead?

He couldn't imagine anyone falling like that without being instantly killed, but there was a chance that she had survived the fall.

For a few seconds there was no movement nor sound in the hotel. It was as if everyone who had heard the sound of the fall were paralysed, staring at each other, listening and wondering.

Then doors began to open. There came the sound of running footfalls and girls screaming.

The two detectives, sitting at the table outside La Boule d'Or, heard the sound of the fall, and they started to their feet, staring at each other.

The senior officer, Lemont, said: "What the devil was that?"

He started across the street at a run, followed by the other detective.

As he entered the hotel, he pulled up short.

Lying in the dimly lighted lobby was the gross, broken body of Madame Brossette.

A girl, wearing only a brassière and a skirt, was standing over her, her hands in her hair, her mouth open as she screamed softly.

Looking up, Lemont saw several men and a number of girls leaning over the banister rail, staring down.

He shoved the screaming girl aside and knelt beside Madame Brossette. He put his finger on one of her staring eyes, and seeing no flicker, he grimaced, then touched the artery in her neck.

Farcau, his companion, moved closer.

"She's dead," Lemont said. "Better get statements. I'll call the ambulance."

The men at the head of the stairs, hearing this, started down the stairs, anxious to get away before their names could be taken, but found their way barred by Farcau.

From his room, Jay watched the activity. He had heard Lemont say Madame Brossette was dead, and his lips curved into a quick grin of relief. Now he had to get out of the hotel without being seen.

The stairs were blocked by men and girls trying to get down. Their backs were turned to him.

He opened the door, and moved out of the room, then he went softly and quickly down the passage to the broom cupboard, opened the door, stepped inside, groped his way to the back wall, found the spring realease and opened the false door.

Leaving it open, he left the broom cupboard, leaving that door also wide open.

Then he returned to his bedroom, took out a ten franc piece from his pocket, unscrewed the lightbulb, put the ten franc piece on the lamp socket and screwed it into the lamp holder.

The lights in the hotel were instantly fused and the place was plunged into darkness.

The men, caught on the stairs, realizing their chance to get away without getting involved with the police, plunged madly down through the darkness, swept Farcau aside, and rushed out into the street. At their heels ran Jay.

Once out in the open the men broke up, and Jay was on his own. He walked quickly to Rue d'Antibes, then crossing the car park, he made his way over to the harbour.

There were still a number of holiday makers taking advantage of the hot, perfect night, and they were wandering along the harbour, staring at the lighted boats, and Jay mingled with them.

He was in an exalted mood of triumph.

The experiment, he told himself, had succeeded. At one time it looked as if it were heading for complete disaster, but thanks to his ingenuity and his wits, he had pulled the thing off.

He was safe now! He had destroyed the negatives and the photographs. He had silenced two blackmailers. He had left evidence that would prove to the police beyond all doubt that Joe Kerr had killed the girl. One person in a million could have done what he had done! A million? That was ridiculous! Only he could have done it!

He reached the far end of the harbour where he could see Ginette's boat, and he sat on a bollard to wait for her. He had only twenty minutes to wait and he found he was impatient and anxious to see her again.

He was lighting a cigarette and preparing to settle down to wait when a tall, heavily built man strolled over to him and paused in front of him.

"Mr. Jay Delaney?" the man asked.

Jay stiffened. He felt a sudden cold knot of fear form inside him. The man was obviously a police officer, and for a moment Jay was too shocked to speak.

Then he said, "Yes, what is it?"

"I'm a police officer," the man said. "Inspector Devereaux would like a word with you, monsieur. If you will please come with me . . ."

Had he done something stupid after all? Jay wondered, his heart beginning to pound. Had he been seen leaving the Beau Rivage hotel?

"Please tell the Inspector that I will see him when I return to the hotel," he said, aware that his voice sounded stilted. "I have an appointment with someone now. I should be back just after two o'clock."

The detective made an apologetic gesture.

"I'm sorry, monsieur, but the matter is urgent. The Inspector won't keep you long. I have a car here," and he waved to where a black car was parked a few yards away.

There was another detective standing by the car, and he began to move slowly over towards Jay.

Jay stood up.

'Well, all right, but I must say this is most irritating."

The thought that he might miss seeing Ginette made him angry, and his anger forced down the fear that had flared up in him.

"I'm sorry, monsieur," the detective said in his flat, impersonal voice.

Jay walked with him to the car and got in the back seat. The detective sat beside him. The other detective got under the driving wheel and drove quickly off the harbour and along the Croisette towards the Plaza hotel.

Nothing was said during the drive. Jay stared out of the window, feeling very tense and angry, but he had got over his first scare.

If he had been seen leaving the Beau Rivage hotel, it wasn't likely they would be taking him to the Plaza, but he would have to watch out. This Inspector Devereaux was no fool. He wouldn't have sent two detectives to look for him unless it was something pretty serious – but what?

The car pulled up a few yards from the Plaza and the two detectives got out, holding the door open for Jay.

"Perhaps you would like to go on in, monsieur," one of them said. "No point in making the press curious. You will find the Inspector in the assistant manager's office."

"Thank you," Jay said.

He walked towards the Plaza, aware that the two detectives were strolling after him.

So it can't be all that serious, he thought. If they really thought I had killed her, they wouldn't let me out of their reach. But I must be careful. This may be a trick to get me off my guard.

He entered the Plaza lobby, which was fairly empty. Most of the people were still in the cinema, and, crossing the lobby, he went to the assistant manager's office, knocked on the door, turned the handle and entered the room.

CHAPTER ELEVEN

I

Inspector Devereaux was sitting behind his borrowed desk munching a sandwich. It was the first food he had eaten since he had begun the case, and he was hungry.

"You will excuse me, monsieur," he said as Jay came in. "I have had no time for supper." Regretfully he laid the half-eaten sandwich down on the plate at his side, took out his handkerchief and wiped his fingers. "You will excuse me too for disturbing you."

"I have an appointment at twelve," Jay said curtly and looked at the clock on the desk. The time was five minutes to twelve. "Perhaps I may use the telephone? I dislike keeping people waiting."

"Certainly," Devereaux said and pushed the instrument towards Jay. "I won't keep you more than five minutes."

Jay picked up the telephone book and quickly found the number of La Boule d'Or. He gave the girl on the switchboard the number. He didn't notice that Devereaux picked up his pencil and wrote down the number on the blotter as Jay gave it to the girl.

Ginette came on the line.

"This is Jay," Jay said. "I'm sorry, but I am delayed. I won't be able . . ."

"It's all right," she broke in. "I was going to call your hotel. I won't be able to come. We have just heard my father's brother is dangerously ill and my father has gone to St. Tropez to be with him. I can't leave the café."

"I see. I'm sorry. Well, then to-morrow. I'll come and see you to-morrow," Jay said, glancing at Devereaux, who was munching his sandwich and appearing to be paying no attention to the conversation.

"All right. I'm sorry too."

"I understand. Until to-morrow, then."

"Yes."

Until to-morrow, Jay thought as he hung up. To-morrow seemed suddenly a long way off.

"I'm afraid I have spoilt your evening, monsieur," Devereaux said.

"It's all right," Jay said irritably. "Well? What is it?"

Devereaux finished his sandwich. He again took out his handkerchief and wiped his fingers.

"There is a point I would like to raise with you, monsieur, to do with the statement you made this morning." He lifted a sheet of paper off the top of his pile of notes. "You said this morning that, after you had spoken to Mademoiselle Balu when you met her on the beach, you didn't see her again – that is to say, you didn't see her at any time after she had left the beach. That is correct?"

So that was it, Jay thought. The necklace. This man is no fool. He's spotted my slip. But I can get out of it. There's no need to panic.

"Yes, that is what I said and it is correct," he said and looked straight at Devereaux, again thankful for the blue screens of his sun glasses.

"A little later I asked you to describe the necklace she was wearing."

Jay nodded.

"I remember, and I described the necklace," he said quietly.

He saw Devereaux lift his eyebrows as if surprised.

"You described it accurately," Devereaux said. "Would you now look at this photograph?"

He handed Jay a photograph of Lucille Balu, posing on the beach.

Jay studied the photograph. Of course the girl isn't wearing the necklace, he thought. It was smart of him to have noticed that.

He laid down the photograph and looked inquiringly at the Inspector.

"Well?"

"You see nothing out of the way in the picture, monsieur?"

"No, I don't think so," Jay said and leaned forward and again studied the picture. "Is there something odd about it?"

"She is not wearing a necklace," Devereaux said, his voice sharpening.

Jay leaned back in his chair.

"That doesn't seem odd to me. I'd be surprised if she had been wearing one on the beach."

Devereaux drew in a deep breath.

"You said, monsieur, that you had seen the necklace. You said you didn't see her after she had left the beach. Then how could you have seen the necklace if she wasn't wearing it?"

This is the moment, Jay thought. I've got to convince him or this could be dangerous.

For several seconds he stared at the Inspector, a look of astonishment on his face.

"Do you mean to tell me you have made me break an appointment for such a trivial thing as that?" he said. "I never said she was wearing the necklace. I described it because it happened to fall out of her beach bag while we were talking and I picked it up and returned it to her. I remember I said I thought it was a pretty thing. Does that answer your question?"

Devereaux ran his fingers through his hair, frowning, then he gave an irritable shrug. The explanation was so simple and so obvious it made him feel foolish.

"Thank you, monsieur. You must excuse me. I'm afraid I have bothered you for nothing, but every statement I get has to be checked. I hope you understand."

137

Jay kept his face expressionless with an effort, but inside himself he felt a surge of triumph. He had done it! He had fooled this man! It had been so easy! Again it had been due to his ingenuity and nerve, and now – he was safe!

"That's all right," he said. "Of course, I understand. Well . . ." He got to his feet. "Is there anything else?"

Devereaux also got to his feet.

"No, monsieur. Only my regrets. . . ."

"It's nothing," Jay said. "I'm only too happy to help." He paused, then went on: "You have no suspect yet?"

Devereaux shrugged his shoulders.

"We are only just beginning the investigation, monsieur. I have been working on murder cases now for thirty years, and in my experience, very few murderers escape. There is always the unexpected factor that brings about their downfall. It is usually at the moment when they are quite sure they are safe that they get caught. I am a patient man. I ask questions. I write down answers. I check statements. That is all I do. It is the murderer who usually gives himself away. Solving a murder case is merely a matter of patience."

Well, this time, Jay thought, you will be disappointed, my friend. You can have all the patience in the world, but you won't catch me in a mistake.

At this moment the telephone bell rang and Devereaux reached for the receiver.

"Excuse me, monsieur," he said. "Don't let me detain you any longer."

"Thank you," Jay said and nodding, he went out of the room.

It was Guidet calling on the telephone and he sounded excited. He told Devereaux that they had found Joe Kerr at the Beau Rivage hotel.

"And about time too," Devereaux growled. "Well, bring him to headquarters. I'll be right over. Has he made a statement?"

"It would be better for you to come here, Inspector," Guidet said, unable to resist the drama of the situation. "He is dead."

Devereaux stiffened.

"Dead?"

"Yes. He's our man all right. I found one of the blue beads in his pocket. He hanged himself with a red curtain cord – the cord that is missing from the hotel."

Devereaux refused to give him the satisfaction of appearing startled.

"I'll be right over," he said and hung up.

II

As Jay crossed the lobby to the elevator, he saw Sophia come in with his father and four other men. The men paused to say good night to Sophia before going with his father towards the bar.

Sophia saw Jay and joined him as the elevator doors opened. They rode up to the second floor without exchanging a word, conscious of the attendant who kept looking at Sophia with furtive admiration.

It wasn't until they had left the elevator, and while Jay was unlocking the door to their suite that Sophia said in a tense, low voice, "Well? What have you been doing?"

"Arranging things," Jay said, opening the door and standing aside. "As I said I would."

Sophia entered the lounge, crossed over to the cocktail cabinet and poured a brandy to which she added a lump of ice and some soda water.

While she was making a drink, Jay closed the door and moved over to sit in one of the armchairs.

She turned and faced him.

"Well? For heaven's sake! Don't try to be mysterious! What have you done?"

How tense she looked! he thought. Smart as she is, she wouldn't have been able to have handled this thing the way I did. She would either have paid those two blackmailers for the rest of her days or she would have given up and weakly submitted to being arrested. It would never have crossed her mind to have silenced them.

"I have arranged things, Sophia," he said. "Everything is now all right."

His smug little smile made her want to slap his face, but she controlled herself.

"Don't talk like a fool!" she said angrily. "How can everything possibly be all right? Those two . . ."

He held up his hand.

"I said I would arrange things and I have arranged them. The photographs and the negatives are destroyed. I destroyed them myself."

She stared at him.

There was something about him she hadn't ever seen before. There was this smug little smile, but his cocky air of confidence disturbed her.

She sipped her brandy, then she sat down, frowning at him.

139

"You've destroyed them? But how?"

"I went to the hotel," he said airily. "I talked to the woman. She was difficult, of course, but I went prepared. Blackmailers are always cowards. I frightened her and I frightened Kerr. They gave me the photographs and the negatives and I burned them."

"You? *You* frightened that woman! I don't believe it!" Sophia's scorn made Jay flush angrily. "A callow boy like you couldn't frighten such a woman!"

"Don't you think so?" Jay's lips were in a tight smile. "I'm not saying it was easy, but I did it." He put his hand into his hip pocket and took out the razor. He opened it and let the light from the reading lamp glitter on its blade.

Sophia caught her breath sharply.

"You see? It even frightens you," Jay said softly. "It's odd – people have a horror of sharp steel. I threatened them with this. It had the required effect."

Sophia felt a little sick as she stared at him. Sitting there, his face pale, his eyes hidden by the dark glasses, a cruel smile on his lips and the razor in his hand, he looked horribly dangerous.

"Put that thing away!" she said; her voice was husky.

Jay closed the razor and began to tap his knee with it.

"So you have nothing to worry about, Sophia. You can forget the whole thing."

"You insane fool! Even if they gave you the photographs and the negatives that won't stop them going to the police and telling them!" Sophia burst out angrily.

He flinched.

"Of course, you are still thinking of yourself, Sophia," he said, "but I assure you it is going to be all right. They won't say anything. I can promise you that."

"But why are you so sure?"

"I just know." He paused and cocked his head a little on one side. "You can forget the whole thing. You do understand, don't you? It would be better if you forgot all about it."

She stiffened. The note in his voice was distinctly hostile.

"Is it my turn now to be threatened?" she asked.

His meaningless smile moved into place.

"After all, Sophia, you are now the only person who can do anything about this business. The other two won't, and you are the only other one who knows about it. If you hadn't returned when you did, everything would have worked out very well, so it does make it a little difficult between us, doesn't it?"

"I would like to get this quite clear, Jay," Sophia said. "Are you threatening me?"

He opened the razor and stared down at the glittering blade.

"I don't think it is necessary to threaten you, because you are clever," he said. "After all, if you did give me away, I would have to involve you as an accessory. You wouldn't want to go to prison, would you?"

She was suddenly so angry that she threw caution to the wind.

"Listen to me, you mad little fool!" she said furiously. "You don't imagine you are going to get away with this horrible thing, do you?"

"I think I have told you before," he said, his face set, "I am not mad. I am going to get away with it. Of course you have thought what you imagine is best to be done. No doubt you plan to tell father when we are out of France and persuade him to put me in a home, but I warn you, I'm not going to a home. Rather than that I will give myself up to the police and give you up too."

"You don't think you can be allowed to go free after what you have done?" Sophia said. "You are a mental case. You will have to have special treatment. Why, you could do this horrible thing again."

Then suddenly his inner voice began to whisper to him.

"It would be better if she died," the voice told him. "It would be safer. With her out of the way, no one would ever know. You can't trust her. Sooner or later, she will tell your father. You are alone with her. It would be quite easy to arrange. All you would have to do is to stun her, take off her clothes and put her in the bath. They would think she slipped in the bath, hit her head on the taps and drowned. An accident like that so often happens. Do it now. You have time. Your father won't be up for another half hour."

As Jay listened to the voice, he glanced at his wrist-watch. The time was twenty minutes to one. He had the time.

"I wouldn't ever do it again, Sophia," he said, his voice suddenly mild. "I have got it out of my system now. But if it would satisfy you, I would be willing to go to some doctor and let him talk to me. I can understand you wouldn't want me living with you and father any longer. I would be prepared to live alone if you would persuade father to let me have my own apartment."

He saw her hesitate, then she said: "If you are willing to submit to a thorough examination, and if you are willing to abide by the doctor's decision, then I won't say anything more about this." She made a little movement with her hand. "But you must have some kind of help and treatment to get you straightened out."

"You see?" whispered the voice. "She thinks you are mad. You can never have any safety until she is out of the way."

Behind the shield of his dark glasses, he looked around the room for a weapon with which to stun her.

He had now no compunction about killing her. She had brought it on herself. All she thought about was herself. She hadn't helped him because she was afraid of what would happen to him. She had helped him because she had been afraid of what would happen to her own social position and to his father's reputation.

He must first reassure her, and then, when she was off her guard . . .

"Well, all right, Sophia," he said as his eyes found the weapon he was looking for. It was a heavy paper weight in silver his father carried around with him that stood on the desk. It was an ideal weapon. He would have to be careful not to hit her too hard, he told himself, but he would have to hit her hard enough to make her unconscious. "I suppose I do want straightening out, as you put it. In fact, it would be a relief to have someone to talk confidentially to, and I would welcome living away from father. Do you think you could persuade him to let me have a place of my own?"

"I think so."

He wished she was a little more relaxed. It was disconcerting to see how closely she was watching him. She was, of course, extremely sensitive to atmosphere. Surely she didn't guess what was going on in his mind?

It mustn't be bungled, he thought. He could hear footsteps and voices as people passed the door of the suite, going to their rooms. She mustn't have a chance to scream.

"So if I agree to those conditions, Sophia," he said, "then you won't give me away?"

She got to her feet and put the scarcely touched brandy on the table.

"I'm tired now, Jay. We'll talk about this to-morrow. I'm going to bed."

He got up casually and strolled over to the desk.

"You haven't finished your drink," he said, his fingers closing over the paper weight.

"I don't want it. Good night, Jay."

He glanced at her.

She had reached her bedroom door.

She must be nervous, he thought. She hasn't once turned her back on me.

"I'm sorry about all this, Sophia," he said. He began to move slowly across the room towards her, the paper weight held down by his side, out of sight. "I wish I hadn't done it now. At the time it seemed important. I'll get straightened out. I'm relying on you to help me."

He felt his anger rising against her as she didn't react in any way to this.

She stood in the doorway of her bedroom, watching him, her expression alert.

"Good night, Jay," she said and before he could reach her, she stepped into the room and abruptly closed the door in his face. He heard the key turn in the lock.

For a second or two he remained motionless, then he moved silently to the door leading to the outside corridor and turned the key.

Would she forget to lock the door between her room and his father's room?

Moving softly, he crossed the lounge and opened the door into his father's room. Leaving the door open so he could see where he was going, he crossed the room to the door that led into Sophia's room. He listened, his head against the door panel. He could hear Sophia moving about in the inner room. He looked at his watch: the time was now ten minutes to one. His margin of safety was running out.

He put his hand on the door-handle and began to turn it very slowly. It seemed to take a long time before the handle fully turned.

Had she locked this door?

He pulled gently, and as he felt the door move towards him, he stopped pulling, and his lips curled into a triumphant grin.

Again he listened.

He heard Sophia clear her throat and then put something down on the dressing table.

He eased the door open a crack, his right hand gripping the paper weight so tightly his knuckles turned white.

He could see into the room now.

Sophia had taken off her evening dress and was peeling off her stockings.

143

Jay measured the distance between them. It was too great. She would have time to start to her feet and scream before he could reach her.

He watched her slip on a wrap, then undo her suspender belt and toss it on a chair, then she walked into the bathroom.

He heard the bath water running.

Better wait for her to get into the bath, he thought. He remembered she would be sitting with her back to the door once she was in the bath.

All he would have to do then was to move in silently and hit her before she even knew he was in there.

He waited, his breathing fast and hard, his heart thumping. He glanced at his watch. It was now three minutes to one. The margin of safety was narrowing.

He stiffened when he heard the bath water stop running, and then he heard the unmistakable sound of splashing.

She must be in the bath!

His lips moved into his meaningless smile as he opened the door and moved silently across the bedroom to the bathroom door.

He reached for the handle, turned it and pushed gently.

The door swung silently open.

III

Never before in the sordid history of the Beau Rivage hotel had the hotel been so quiet and dark as when Inspector Devereaux drove up in his car.

A small crowd stood outside the entrance, held back by three sweating gendarmes.

Guidet stood just inside the dark entrance and came across the pavement to meet Devereaux.

"Why in darkness?" Devereaux asked, staring up at the dark outline of the building.

"The lights have fused. As soon as we put in a new fuse, it blows." Guidet sounded exasperated. "I've got an electrician checking the wiring. In the meantime we have candles."

"So he is dead?" Devereaux said, walking into the lobby.

"Yes, he's dead," Guidet said. "He hanged himself."

On the reception desk were five flickering candles that threw a yellow circle of light on Madame Brossette's gross body lying where it had fallen at the foot of the stairs.

"Hello!" Devereaux exclaimed, coming to an abrupt stop. "What happened here?"

"My guess is she found Kerr, rushed downstairs to call the ambulance and fell," Guidet said indifferently. "The stairs are dangerously steep. Anyway, it's saved her getting into trouble with us. She deliberately lied when we asked her if Kerr was here."

At this moment the Medical Officer, Dr. Mathieu, came in. He went immediately to the body and made a quick examination.

"Her neck is broken," he said, looking at Devereaux. "A woman of such a weight . . . such a fall . . ." He shrugged his shoulders.

"And Kerr?" Devereaux asked.

"Upstairs."

Guidet turned on a powerful electric torch and guided Devereaux up the narrow stairs.

"So he was here all the time," Devereaux said as he walked into the room beyond the broom cupboard. "No wonder we didn't find him."

Lemont was in the room, lighting more candles.

Guidet threw the beam of his torch on Joe Kerr.

Joe hung from the scarlet cord that was fastened to a hook on the back of the door. His long, bony legs were curled up so that the weight of his body had tightened the running noose of the cord. His raddled face was a pale mauve colour; his lips were drawn off his teeth in a snarl of terror.

"He hanged himself with the missing curtain cord," Guidet said. "I've been through his pockets. In one of them I found a blue bead." He went over to the bedside table and pointed to the bead. "It's from the girl's necklace."

Devereaux glanced at the bead, then back to Joe.

"No confession or suicide note?"

"No." Guidet picked up the half empty bottle of whisky. "Looks as if he had been drinking heavily."

"Well, there doesn't seem much doubt that he killed the girl, and in a drunken fit of remorse, he hanged himself," Devereaux said.

While he was speaking the lights went on.

"Ah! That's better," Guidet said. "I'll have the body photographed and then taken down."

Devereaux nodded. He was feeling tired, but satisfied. The case had cleared up nicely.

"I wonder why he did it," he said. "You know, Guidet, this

145

seems almost too simple, but it often happens this way. Just when one thinks one has a difficult case on one's hands, the thing solves itself. Still, we'd better be on the safe side. Take his finger prints. Let's see if they check with the print we found on the other bead."

Guidet shrugged his shoulders.

"All right, but I don't think there's any doubt about it – he's our man."

Lemont, who had gone downstairs to fetch the police photographer, now returned, followed by the photographer.

Devereaux moved out into the passage to give the photographer room in which to work.

A man, carrying a metal tool box, came out of a room at the head of the stairs. He paused when he saw Devereaux.

"The blown fuse was caused by this, monsieur," he said and handed Devereaux a ten franc piece. "It was screwed into the light socket in that room."

Devereaux thanked the man. When the electrician had gone, Devereaux beckoned to Lemont.

"Did the lights go out before or after you heard the woman fall?"

"Some minutes after. They went out when I was examining the body. I imagine one of the men caught here fused the lights in order to get away. As soon as the lights failed, there was a rush for the exit. Farcau had no chance of stopping anyone."

Devereaux grinned.

"I can't say I blame them."

He dropped the ten franc piece into his pocket.

Dr. Mathieu came up the stairs.

"Another customer for you, doctor," Devereaux said. "Take a look at him. I don't think there's any doubt he's the one who killed the poor girl."

Dr. Mathieu nodded and went into the room beyond the broom cupboard. The photographer had completed his work and Guidet and Lemont got Joe's body on to the bed.

Ten minutes later Matheiu came out into the passage, a puzzled frown on his face.

"Well?" Devereaux asked. He was leaning against the wall, smoking a cigarette, thinking longingly of his bed.

"I'll arrange to have him taken to the mortuary, Inspector. I want to check him over much more thoroughly. There are a couple of points that puzzle me. He has a bruise in the middle of his back. It's a recent one, and I'm wondering how he got it.

146

I've seen a bruise like that before, and it is consistent with a knee being forced between the shoulder blades."

Devereaux stiffened.

"You mean he didn't commit suicide? That someone strangled him?"

Mathieu shrugged his shoulders.

"I don't know, but the bruise worries me."

"And the second point?"

"You remember I told you I found skin under the girl's finger nails indicating that she badly scratched her killer? This man has no scratches on his body."

Devereaux made a movement of exasperation.

"You are sure she scratched her killer?"

"There's no doubt about it."

"And there're no scratches of any kind on this man?"

"None."

Devereaux exchanged glances with Guidet.

"The finger prints?"

"They're being checked now."

As Dr. Mathieu moved down the stairs, Devereaux took the ten franc piece from his pocket and stared at it, then he called Lemont.

"You were watching outside the hotel. Did you see a man enter on his own?"

Lemont shook his head.

"No, Inspector. Every man who came here had a woman with him."

The finger-print expert came out into the passage.

"The print we found on the bead in suite 30 of the Plaza hotel doesn't match any of Kerr's prints."

Devereaux swore softly under his breath, then he thought for a moment.

"Go into that room," he said, pointing to the room at the head of the stairs, "and check the prints on the electric light bulb."

The finger-print expert went down the corridor and entered the room in which Jay had hidden.

There was a long pause while Devereaux continued to lean against the wall, smoking, his face set in a heavy scowl.

Recognizing the scowl as a danger sign that the Inspector was testy and tired, both Guidet and Lemont kept quiet.

A few minutes later, the finger-print expert came out of the room.

"A good guess, Inspector. There's a print on the lamp bulb that matches the one on the bead. No doubt about it."

Devereaux dropped his half-smoked cigarette on the floor, then stepped viciously on it.

"So we haven't solved the case," he said. "I had an idea it was too simple. Well, all right. We'll start again. At least we know whoever made that print is our man. It shouldn't be too difficult to find him." He beckoned to Guidet. "Come with me. We'll go to the Plaza hotel and we'll make a fresh start."

Lemont watched the two men walk down the stairs, then he took out a packet of cigarettes, lit a cigarette and gratefuly inhaled the smoke.

CHAPTER TWELVE

I

WITH her back against the wall, Sophia watched the bathroom door swing silently open.

She was tense, and her face was hard and pale and she was breathing rapidly, but she was much more curious than afraid.

She had sensed the sudden change in Jay while they had been talking and she had a feeling that he intended to silence her. She felt she had to find out just how dangerous he was, and, if he turned out to be as dangerous as she suspected, then she would no longer hesitate: she would tell Floyd and take her chance about getting into trouble with the police.

Her experience as a prostitute had equipped her to deal with all kinds of neurotic men, and there had been several occasions when her clients had turned out to be dangerous, but in each case she had been able to quell them.

She didn't think for a moment that she couldn't handle Jay, and she deliberately left the door between her room and Floyd's unlocked to see if Jay dare come into her room.

To make sure of her own safety, she had taken with her into the bathroom the ·25 automatic that Floyd had given her when they had been filming in the Mau-Mau country during the early part of the year.

Sophia had no experience of guns, but Floyd had made her fire the gun several times to get her used to handling it, but she didn't like the noise and had put the gun away, saying that, as she didn't intend leaving Floyd's side while they were in the jungle, he could do the shooting and she the screaming.

She carried the gun around with her on their travels because she liked its appearance. It had a mother-of-pearl handle and her initials let into the butt in gold.

She took the gun into the bathroom, not because she thought she would need it, but as a precaution. If Jay dared to come into her room, she was confident he would quickly come to heel when she turned the broadside of her tongue on him. Sophia hadn't forgotten how to tongue-lash a man, although it was now some years since she had had to use her startling vituperation.

Jay came to an abrupt standstill when he found himself face to face with Sophia. He stood motionless in the doorway, his right hand hidden behind his back, his head cocked a little on one side, his left hand holding on to the door handle.

For a second or so they confronted each other, then Sophia said in a cold, hard voice: "What do you think you are doing in here?"

The tip of Jay's tongue came out and moved over his lips. The movement made Sophia think of a snake.

"I'm sorry, Sophia," he said softly, and the tone of his voice was so menacing that it made her stiffen. "I promise you it won't hurt and it will be very quick. You shouldn't have been so interfering."

She then saw it had been a mistake to have put this to a test. The bleak expression on his face, the twitching muscle near his right eye, the thinness of his mouth made him a frightening stranger to her.

"Get out!" she cried. "If you don't get out at once, I'll tell your father!"

The thin lips moved into their meaningless smile.

"I don't think so, Sophia. I don't think you will tell anyone."

He moved silently into the bathroom and it was then she saw the heavy paper weight in his hand.

"Jay! I'm warning you! If you don't get out I'll shoot you!" Sophia exclaimed and lifted the gun and pointed it at him.

He paused, staring at the gun.

"Go on! Get out!"

Then he began to move forward again, his shoulders hunched, the paper weight balanced in his hand.

"Jay!"

He was almost within reach of her now. He seemed to be paying no attention at all to the gun she was pointing at him.

149

He was muttering under his breath. She caught the words. "I'm sorry . . . locked away in a home . . . a mistake . . ." Then she realized with a shrinking feeling of horror that she would have to shoot him. She lifted the gun to point at his shoulder and her hesitation was fatal.

He suddenly sprang forward as she pulled the trigger.

In that split second of terror, she realized she had forgotten to take off the safety catch on the gun. She saw Jay's hand flash up. She tried to get out of his way, but her movements were much too late.

A blinding light exploded inside her head as the paper weight caught her on the temple. Her knees buckled, the gun dropped out of her hand and she slid to the floor at Jay's feet.

Moving swiftly, Jay put the paper weight down on the toilet table. He reached over Sophia's still body and picked up the gun, which he thrust into his hip pocket.

He felt calm and elated and very sure of himself. Quickly, he rolled up his sleeves, then he bent over Sophia and stared at the broken, bruised skin by her temple. He rolled her over on her face, then stripped off her wrap.

He kept thinking to himself that this was so easy. Nothing could stop him now. Once she was dead, he would be completely safe.

He dragged Sophia's naked and unconscious body over to the bath, which was half full of tepid water. Bending over her, he lifted her and slid her down into the water, being careful to have her head towards the taps.

She stirred slightly and moaned.

He stepped quickly to the other end of the bath, reached into the water and took hold of her ankles. His lips were drawn into a tight, fixed smile as he lifted her ankles, pulling her forward so that her head and face went under the water.

Immediately he felt her legs stiffen and he had to grip tightly to keep her in this position.

It was while he was holding her like this that he heard a sudden movement in the suite. The sound was unmistakable. Someone had entered the suite and had pushed against a chair or some other heavy object.

His heart gave a great bound in his chest. It seemed to stop beating, and then began to race so violently, he felt suffocated.

How could anyone have got in? He had locked the door! Who was it – his father?

The reflex twitching of Sophia's legs had ceased. The little air bubbles that had escaped from her mouth no longer disturbed the water.

She must be dead now, he thought frantically. She had been under the water for at least three minutes!"

Then he heard his father's voice.

"Hey, Sophia! What's the idea – locking me out?"

Almost vomiting with panic, Jay released Sophia's feet, darted to the other end of the bath and caught her under the armpits, lifting her head clear of the water.

"Quick! Help!"

He didn't recognize his own voice. It was a high-pitched scream.

There was a sound of quick, thudding footfalls. Looking over his shoulder, he saw his father appear in the doorway.

Even though he was panic-stricken and his heart was hammering and he could scarcely breathe, he was still able to recognize his father's ruthless efficiency by his reaction to what he saw.

There was no panic on his father's face. He paused long enough to take one swift look at what was going on, then he jumped to Jay's side, gave him a shove that sent him reeling and caught hold of Sophia, supporting her. Then he had her out of the bath, slopping water all over the bathroom floor, and ran with her into the bedroom.

Jay felt bile rush into his mouth. He had just time to get to the toilet before he began to vomit. Crouching over the toilet, cold, shivering and deadly sick, he felt his humiliation, knowing that stark fear was making him do this.

"Come here!"

The snap in his father's voice brought him to his senses.

He grabbed a towel and wiped his mouth and sweating face, then he staggered unsteadily into the bedroom.

Sophia was lying face down on the floor. His father was kneeling over her. His face was hard and tight and his eyes were glittering as he went through the routine motions of artificial respiration.

A little trickle of water came from Sophia's open mouth every time Delaney pressed down on her back.

"Pull yourself together, you damned stupe!' his father shouted at him. "Get the hotel doctor up here! Get him up here fast!"

Jay went unsteadily into the lounge. With a shaking hand he picked up the telephone and, when the girl answered, he said huskily: "The doctor! Quick! There's been an accident!"

He dropped the receiver back on to its cradle, then walked over to the liquor cabinet and poured two inches of whisky into a glass and drank it.

For some moments he waited for the spirit to knit his quailing nerves together, then he went unsteadily to Sophia's bedroom door.

His father was still giving Sophia artificial respiration and he looked over his shoulder at Jay.

"What happened?"

Jay had never heard his father speak like this before. The words seemed to cut the air like a whip lash.

"She must have fainted," Jay said, his voice a croak. "I heard her scream and a splashing noise. I went in there and found her."

"Where's that goddamn doctor?"

"He's coming."

"Go and drag him up here. Don't stand there like a dummy! Get him up here!"

As Jay went back into the lounge, he heard a knock on the door and the door jerked open. It was then he saw the key of the door lying on the floor. His father must have got the floor waiter to let him in. The waiter had pushed out the key in the lock with the pass-key.

The hotel doctor, bag in hand, came in.

"In there," Jay said, pointing to the open door, then, as the doctor walked into Sophia's room, Jay moved silently to the door, keeping just out of sight.

She must be dead! he told himself. She had to be dead!

He heard his father say: "She fainted in the bath, hit her head and was under the water. I think I've got most of the water out of her. Here! Take over!"

Then followed three minutes of agonizing silence.

Was she dead?

Jay leaned against the wall, his heart thumping, listening and waiting.

Finally, he heard the doctor say: "She'll be all right. She has a pretty bad concussion, and she'll be unconscious for several hours, but she's going to be all right. It was a close thing. If you hadn't thought of artificial respiration . . ."

"Oh, skip it!" Delaney barked. "Let's get her on the bed. Get nurses! Get everything you need. The sky's the limit! I love this woman, and I'm not going to lose her! Come on . . . get things organized!"

Jay drew in a long, slow breath. So he had lost out. It had

been a gamble. He had been lucky with Kerr and the fat woman. If only he had had another minute before his father had come in!

Now he must think of himself.

Sophia would be unconscious for at least a couple of hours. He was sure she would give him away as soon as she could speak, and his father would then hand him over to the police, so, if he was to get away, he had to act at once.

He was suddenly aware that perhaps after all this was the experience he had been looking for. The police would come after him. They would hunt him. He would have to rely on his wits and ingenuity to elude them.

There could be nothing more exciting than a man-hunt nor any greater test for his courage and ingenuity.

What did he need?

Money, of course, then clothes, toilet things and a weapon.

He touched the ·25 automatic in his hip pocket. He was lucky to have that, he thought. Now money . . .

His father came out of the bedroom. There was sweat on his face and he looked fine-drawn, but otherwise he was his ice-cold ruthless self.

"That was a close call, Jay," he said and went across to the liquor cabinet and mixed himself a whisky and soda. "She's out of danger now, poor kid. It's damn funny. I've never known her to faint before." He looked at Jay and grinned. "You were certainly in an uproar. Well, I don't blame you. I was in a bit of an uproar myself. Thanks for going to her help."

Jay muttered under his breath and began to edge towards his bedroom.

The doctor came into the lounge at this moment and allowed Jay to escape into his room.

He shut the door, then went to the wardrobe, took from it a canvas sack he used when he went fishing and began hastily to put the various things in it he wanted to take with him.

He had just completed packing and had dropped the sack out of sight behind the bed when his father looked in.

"Better get some sleep, son. Don't worry about her now. There're a couple of nurses with her. I'm going to hit the sack myself. As soon as she regains consciousness, I'll be called. You turn in."

"Yes," Jay said.

Delaney nodded and withdrew,

Jay waited until he heard the shower going in his father's bathroom, then he went into his father's bedroom.

On the chest of drawers was his father's wallet, stuffed with ten thousand franc notes. Without bothering to count the money, Jay emptied the wallet, pushed the notes into his pocket, then went quickly back to his room.

This then was the beginning of a new adventure, he thought, as he picked up the canvas sack. By to-morrow morning the police would be looking for him. The man-hunt would be on!

He had money, a gun, his wits and his ingenuity. What more could he want?

He walked softly to his bedroom door, opened it, glanced into the empty lounge, then, moving quickly, he crossed to the door out on to the corridor, looked to right and left, then walked down the corridor to the stairs.

The lobby was still crowded. People standing about discussing the film they had just seen. The clock over the reception desk showed that the time was now twenty minutes to two.

As Jay made his way through the crowd towards the exit, he felt a hand on his arm and he looked quickly around, fear gripping him.

Harry Stone, his father's business manager, massive and perspiring in his tuxedo, grinned at him.

"Hey there, son," he said. "Where do you think you're going?"

"That's my business," Jay said curtly, and pulling free, he continued on his way towards the revolving doors, leaving Stone staring blankly after him.

II

Inspector Devereaux pushed aside his pile of notes and reached for a cigarette.

Guidet, hot and tired, reclined in an easy chair and watched his chief. He wished he could go to bed, but he knew the Inspector wouldn't give up now until he had decided on a new course of action.

"As it isn't Kerr," Devereaux said, leaning back in his chair and blowing a thin trail of smoke up to the ceiling, "we have to decide who is our next likely suspect. I have only one other man on my list who could have done it, and that's Jay Delaney."

Guidet lifted his shoulders.

"Is it likely? Why should a boy like that want to kill the girl? Anyway, what makes you think he's even a suspect?"

Devereaux frowned.

"There's something very odd about him." He leaned forward to flick the ash off his cigarette. "He was the last to talk to the girl as far as we know. He was in the suite when she was up on the second floor. He had the opportunity."

"You'll have to watch your step," Guidet said. "His father's rich and has a lot of influence. Besides, Madame Delaney was in the suite at the time the girl was killed."

Devereaux began poking holes in the blotter with a paper knife.

"I know, and that bothers me." He scowled at the blotter. "Then who could have done it? Some unknown who was up there who met the girl and killed her for no reason at all? I can't accept that. I'm now almost positive the girl wasn't killed in suite 30. I think it was faked to make us believe that's where she was killed, as Kerr's death was faked to make us believe he killed her. I'm sure of it. It's a feeling I have."

Guidet struggled with a yawn.

"It's not feelings, Inspector, we have to work on: it's evidence."

Devereaux nodded.

"Yes. Well, let's see if we can get some evidence. Who was on duty watching the second floor during the day?"

Guidet thought for a moment.

"Sergeant Humbert."

"Is he still on duty?"

"I doubt it, but I'll see."

"If he isn't get him here, and get Lemont down here too."

While Devereaux waited, he again went through his notes. He saw as he read his neat handwriting that he had been immediately suspicious of Jay Delaney once he had discovered him in the apparent lie about the necklace. Then his suspicions had subsided when he had had Jay's obvious and very simple explanation.

I never said she was wearing the necklace. I described it because it happened to fall out of her beach bag while we were talking and I picked it up and returned it to her.

An obvious explanation, but at the same time it could have been a very obvious lie: a lie calculated to cut the ground from under the Inspector's feet, which it had done.

Suppose it had been a lie?

Then Delaney was obviously suspect No. 1.

It wasn't until after one that Guidet was able to bring both Sergeant Humbert and Detective Lemont into Devereaux's office, and it was at that moment, as they sat down in easy chairs, facing the Inspector that, upstairs, Jay was making his attempt on Sophia's life.

Devereaux looked at Humbert, a fat, solid man with a sun-tanned face and clear, lively blue eyes.

"Do you know Floyd Delaney's son by sight?" Devereaux asked.

Humbert nodded.

"Yes, Inspector. Before this happened, I was on duty organiz-ing the crowd outside the hotel. I got to know the various film people and I know him by sight very well."

"During the day, did you see him leave and later return to his suite?"

"Yes, Inspector."

"Did he visit any of the other suites while you were on duty?"

Humbert, after thinking for a moment, nodded.

"Yes. A little after ten o'clock he visited suite 30. The occupier seemed to be a friend of his. They talked for some minutes, then Delaney left. He went to his suite, then came out shortly with swimming trunks and took the elevator to the ground floor."

Devereaux and Guidet exchanged glances. Both of them were now a little tense.

"You are quite sure he went into suite 30?"

"Absolutely sure, Inspector. I logged it in my notebook."

"This took place before we searched the suites?"

"That is correct."

Devereaux nodded, then said: "All right. You can go off duty now."

When Humbert had gone, Devereaux turned to Lemont.

"Do you know Jay Delaney?"

"No, Inspector, I can't say I do."

"He is about twenty-one or -two, good-looking, dark, slightly below average height and wears dark glasses," Devereaux said. "While you were watching the Beau Rivage hotel did you see a man to match this description go into the hotel either alone or with a woman?"

Lemont wrinkled his sweating forehead, then shook his head.

"No, Inspector, I can't say I did. Two or three of the men who entered the hotel were screened by the women they were with. I was watching for Kerr, and I was paying more attention to those who came out of the hotel rather than those who went in."

Devereaux nodded.

"Yes. Well, all right. You get off."

When Lemont had gone, Devereaux said to Guidet: "At least we know Jay Delaney had the opportunity of planting the bead and taking the curtain cord from suite 30. I'm not saying he did it, but he could have done."

Guidet moved uneasily.

"Aren't we wasting time, Inspector? Madame Delaney was with him at the time of the girl's murder. You're not suggesting she had anything to do with it, are you? Besides, what possible motive could a young fellow . . . ?"

Devereaux waved him to silence. He was staring fixedly at the telephone that stood on the desk.

"Now, wait a moment," he said, his voice sharp with excitement. "I believe we can settle this. When young Delaney came in here, he asked me if he could use the telephone. Maybe he's left his prints on it. We know the print we are looking for. Get Leroy here and get him fast!"

The snap in Devereaux's voice brought Guidet hurriedly to his feet, and he went out of the office.

Devereaux lit another cigarette and sank lower into his chair. His legs ached and his body longed for sleep, but his mind was alert enough.

There was some delay in bringing Leroy, the finger-print expert, from the Beau Rivage hotel where he was still working, and it was during this delay that Jay slipped out of the hotel, unseen by the hotel staff, who were at this time fully occupied in handing out keys and taking orders for breakfast. The only man who noticed him leave was Harry Stone, and he, seeing the fishing bag, assumed Jay was off on a night's fishing expedition.

It was a little after two o'clock in the morning that Guidet and Leroy came into the office where Devereaux waited patiently.

As soon as Devereaux saw Leroy, he pointed to the telephone.

"Check that. I'm hoping to find a print on it that matches the one you found on the bead and also on the electric lamp bulb at the Beau Rivage."

Leroy looked a little startled, but he didn't say anything. He opened his kit and set to work. In five minutes he gave a sudden little grunt, a sound he always made when he had done a satisfactory job.

"A beauty," he said. "Yes, you're right, Inspector. Here it is: on the side of the instrument. Whoever handled the electric light bulb in the Beau Rivage, also handled this telephone and he also handled the bead found in suite 30."

Devereaux rubbed the back of his neck while he stared at Leroy.

"Are you absolutely certain?"

"I'm always certain," Leroy said cheerfully. "Finger prints don't lie. There's no question of a mistake."

There was a long silence while Devereaux stared down at his desk. He said finally: "We'd better go up and talk to him if he's there. Guidet, ask the hall porter if he is in the suite."

Guidet went out and returned a few minutes later.

"He's up there, and so are his parents."

"It'll be interesting to see if he has any scratches on his arms," Devereaux said, pushing his chair back. "You'd better come, Leroy. I'll want you to take his prints."

The three men left the office.

Pausing in the lobby, Devereaux said to Guidet: "Go up there and wait outside the door. I'd better get the clerk to announce us, and I don't want the boy to have a chance of bolting. I'll give you five minutes before calling the suite."

Guidet nodded and hurried up the stairs.

While they waited, Leroy said: "This case, Inspector, will make you famous. Your name will be in every paper in every country in the world."

Devereaux shrugged his shoulders.

"We'll have to handle the boy tactfully. He may have an explanation. This is dangerous ground. His father has a lot of influence. I hope to goodness you haven't made a mistake."

Leroy grinned happily.

"We'll soon see when I take his prints. I'm willing to bet all the money I own that he is our man."

"I think you are right."

Devereaux went over to the reception desk.

"Will you call Mr. Jay Delaney and tell him I want to speak to him and I propose going up to his suite?" he said to the night clerk.

The clerk looked pointedly at his wrist-watch.

"It's a little late now to disturb Mr. Delaney," he said. "Won't to-morrow do?"

"Please call the suite and tell him. I will apologize when I see him."

The clerk, shrugging, put through the call. There was a delay,

158

then he said: "Will you hold on, please?" and, looking at Devereaux, he said: "Mr. Jay Delaney isn't in the suite."

Devereaux frowned.

"I understood he went up an hour ago."

"Mr. Delaney senior says he is not in the suite," the clerk repeated.

Devereaux took the telephone receiver out of the clerk's hand.

"Monsieur Delaney? This is Inspector Devereaux speaking. Cannes police. I would be glad if you would see me for a few minutes. May I come up?"

"Well, for heaven's sake!" Delaney sounded irritable. "I was in bed. Well, all right, come up, Inspector, but you mustn't keep me long," and he hung up.

Devereaux went over to the hall porter.

"Did you see Mr. Jay Delaney leave the hotel?"

The hall porter shook his head.

"No, Inspector. I don't think he has left."

Harry Stone, waiting for his key, said: "Yeah, young Delaney went out about half an hour ago. He's gone fishing."

Devereaux thanked him and, jerking his head at Leroy, he crossed the lobby and took the elevator to the second floor.

Guidet was prowling about the corridor.

"He hasn't appeared," he said as Devereaux and Leroy joined him.

"He isn't in the suite. They say downstairs he has gone fishing."

"Shall I have him picked up?" Guidet asked.

"Not yet. I'd better talk to his father first. You two wait here. When I want you, I'll call you," and, leaving the two detectives by the elevator, Devereaux crossed the corridor and rapped on the door to suite 27.

The door opened immediately and Floyd Delaney, in pyjamas and dressing gown, stood aside.

"Inspector Devereaux?"

"Yes. I'm sorry to disturb you . . ."

"Come in. What's it all about?"

Devereaux entered the lounge.

"I understand your son isn't here?"

"That's right. I guess he's gone out for a breath of air. He wasn't well. We've had a nasty shock. My wife had an accident. She slipped in the bath and pretty nearly died. It upset the kid."

159

"I'm sorry to hear that," Devereaux said, glancing around the room. "Is Madame better?"

"Yeah, she's coming along. Why are you interested in my son?"

"I'm investigating the murder of Lucille Balu," Devereaux said. "I wanted to ask him some questions."

Delaney stared at him.

"What the hell for?" Then with a sudden apologetic wave of his hand, he said, "Sit down, Inspector. I didn't mean to sound touchy, but I've had quite a night."

Devereaux sat down in an armchair.

"I appreciate that, monsieur, and I regret having to trouble you. Your son was the last person to speak to the girl."

"He was? I didn't know he even knew her. Well? What's that to do with it?"

"He made a statement to me this morning, and the statement wasn't entirely satisfactory," Devereaux said, choosing his words.

Delaney crossed over to the table, picked up a box of cigarettes and offered it to the Inspector.

Devereaux took a cigarette and lit it with his lighter. As he returned the lighter to his pocket, it slipped out of his sweating hand and dropped into the chair, sliding down between the cushion and the arm.

Delaney said sharply: "In what way – not satisfactory?"

Devereaux paused to retrieve his lighter, and his finger closed over another object that had slipped down between the cushion and the chair arm. He pulled it into sight.

He found himself looking at a narrow lizard-skin handbag, with the initials L.B. in gold in one of the corners.

He stared at the bag, remembering what Jean Thiry had said: *Yes, she had a handbag. It was one I gave her. It was quite small. She carried a powder compact, handkerchief and lipstick in it. It was a narrow lizard-skin bag with her initials on it.*

Delaney moved forward, frowning.

"What have you got there?"

"Mademoiselle Balu's handbag," Devereaux said quietly. "There's no doubt about that. Look, it has her initials on it. The girl was murdered in this room."

Delaney stiffened.

"What the hell do you mean? In this room? What is this?"

Devereaux got to his feet.

"I'm afraid, monsieur, it is very serious. I must ask you to allow my men to examine your son's room."

"My son?" Delaney suddenly remembered that Sophia had told him Jay had had a girl up in their suite. Could the girl have been Lucille Balu? "What's my son got to do with this?"

"I have reason to believe he is responsible for the girl's death," Devereaux said.

"That's a lie!" Delaney said, his voice even and quiet. "Are you suggesting that my son murdered the girl?"

"I have reason to believe that he did."

Delaney drew in a long, deep breath.

"You have? Then you'd better state your reasons pretty damn quick or you could find yourself out of a job!"

"Have you any objections to my men examining your son's room, monsieur?" Devereaux asked. He felt sorry for this big, powerful American whose eyes plainly showed his increasing anxiety.

"Go ahead! I am quite sure my son has nothing to hide!"

Devereaux stepped to the door, opened it and beckoned to Guidet and Leroy.

The two detectives entered the suite.

"Look for prints," Devereaux said to Leroy in an undertone, "and hurry."

The two detectives went into Jay's room, and there was a long, awkward pause.

Delaney sat down and stared at the carpet, his face was pale.

He remembered what Sophia had said about Jay being queer. He also thought of Harriette, and how she had crept towards him, knife in hand, with that animal-like, insane expression on her face. Surely the boy hadn't done this thing! But if he had! Delaney's mind shied away from the consequences of such a thing. And the premiere of the picture he had sunk so much money in was on to-night!

Leroy came out of Jay's bedroom.

Devereaux looked anxiously at him and Leroy gave him a cheerful nod and a grin.

"No doubt about it, Inspector," he said briskly. "The room is full of the print we've found."

Delaney got to his feet.

"What print?"

"If you will give me a few seconds, monsieur, I'll explain everything to you," Devereaux said gently, then, turning to Guidet, he went on in an undertone: "Get him as quickly as

161

you can. He may have bolted. Put as many men on the job as you want, but get him!"

Guidet nodded and he and Leroy left the suite.

Devereaux sat down in the lounging chair.

"I'm afraid this is going to be a great shock to you, monsieur," he said quietly. "Your son is now wanted for two murders."

"Two murders?"

Delaney's face went white and he sat down abruptly.

"Yes," and, speaking rapidly, Devereaux gave him the facts of the case.

CHAPTER THIRTEEN

I

The unexpected telephone call that had sent Ginette's father off hurriedly to St. Tropez had left Ginette on her own to handle the café trade.

As the café offered a vantage point to watch the Beau Rivage hotel, a number of people, curious to see why there was so much police activity going on in the hotel, had crowded into the café, and Ginette was kept busy attending to their needs while they sat at the tables gaping at the lighted entrance across the way.

It wasn't until half-past one that the spectators decided there was nothing further to see and began to drift away to their homes, and Ginette was able to shut the café.

This was the first time she had been left entirely alone in the café, but it didn't worry her. After locking the café door and pulling down the blind, she turned off the lights in the bar room, and then going into the kitchen, she set about the business of washing up the fifty or so glasses and the dozen or so coffee cups before going to bed.

While she worked she thought of Jay. She was disappointed that she hadn't been able to see him this night, but she was pleased he had suggested coming to see her in the morning.

She liked him, she told herself. She knew he liked her. It was an instinctive feeling and she was sure she wasn't mistaken.

Perhaps the word "like" was too mild a word to express her feelings, she thought, as she slid coffee cups into the sink. Could she be falling in love with him?

It was while she was drying the cups and putting them in neat rows on the shelf, her mind still occupied with her thoughts of Jay, that she became aware that someone was gently tapping on the street door.

She paused to listen, surprised and a little uneasy. The knocking continued.

She hesitated, then she turned off the light and moved silently into the dark bar room.

The faint light from the moon reflecting into the room gave her enough light to find her way to the street door.

Against the blind that covered the glass door, she could see the shadowy outline of a man, and she stopped, wondering who it could be, her uneasiness growing.

Knuckles continued to knock against the glass, then a voice said very softly: "Ginette? Are you there? It's Jay."

She went immediately to the door and pulled aside the blind.

They looked at each other through the glass panel. The moonlight fell fully on her, while he was in the shadow, and she smiled at him as she turned the key in the lock and opened the door.

"Why, hello," she said. "What are you doing here at this time?"

He stood motionless, looking at her. She couldn't see him clearly, but she did see he had taken off his dark glasses and over his shoulder he carried what looked like a canvas sack.

"I've come to stay," he said. "You said there was a room for me."

She hesitated, then, as he moved forward, she gave ground, and he stepped into the room, closing the door behind him. She heard him fumble with the key and turn it.

" I – I don't think you can stay here to-night," she said a little breathlessly. "You see I'm alone here. Father had to go to St. Tropez."

"Yes, you told me. I'm sorry," he said, dropping the sack on the floor. "But you can't turn me away. I have nowhere else to go."

She found it exciting and disturbing to be in the semi-darkness so close to him. She could feel the heat of his body as he stood by her.

"Wait a moment," she said. "I'll put on a light."

"No, don't do that." His voice sharpened and surprised her. "Wasn't there a light just now at the back?"

163

"Yes, I was clearing up. When I heard your knock I was startled. I put the light out."

"Clearing up? Let me help you." He walked past her into the kitchen and turned on the light. "You have all this to do?" he asked as she came to the door, and he waved his hand at the trays of glasses on the table. "Don't you have any help?"

She laughed.

"I'm used to it. It won't take very long."

She moved into the kitchen and over to the sink.

"Have you really nowhere to sleep?"

"No. I've left my hotel. You said you had a room for me, so naturally I came here."

She began to slide the glasses into the sink.

"Well, I suppose you could have a room, but I don't think my father will approve." She smiled at him. "Will you want it for long?"

"Two days. When is he coming back?"

"I don't know. His brother is very ill. He may be away for a week."

"Then it doesn't matter if he approves or not, for he won't know, will he?"

He picked up a cloth and began to dry the glasses as she rinsed them.

"I don't like doing anything that I know he would disapprove of," she said, wanting him to stay, but making excuses to her conscience.

He watched her, his heart beating rapidly, thinking how beautiful she was and loving her.

"Then I'll go. As soon as I have finished helping you, I'll go and I'll sleep on the harbour somewhere."

She laughed.

"I'm sure you don't intend to do any such thing. You are trying to worm your way into my heart."

"Would that be very difficult?"

She paused, her hands in the water and looked over her shoulder at him.

"I don't think it would."

He put down the glass he was drying and let the cloth drop out of his hand, then he moved towards her. She smiled as she faced him.

"You're like no other girl I have ever known. Up to now, girls have never meant anything to me but you . . ."

She put her hands on his chest, pushing him back.

"I don't think we should be doing this, Jay."

"You are only saying that because it is the conventional thing to say. You don't really mean it, do you?"

She hesitated, then shook her head.

"No, you're quite right. I don't mean it at all."

She dropped her hands and let him draw her against him, and she leaned against him, her heart beating violently.

Jay thought, this is something I have never experienced before. Why have I been so utterly stupid? Why have I put my future in jeopardy? I could have found everything I have been searching for in this girl.

His kiss was clumsy, but Ginette reacted to it in a way that set his blood on fire. They clung to each other, their bodies hard against each others, her fingers moving gently up the back of his neck and through his hair.

Then suddenly she broke free and turned away, her breathing quick and hard.

"We mustn't do this, Jay. Please . . ."

For some seconds, he remained motionless, his mind in a daze, then he said unsteadily: "Why not? I love you."

The words sounded horribly trite to him. Every character in every one of his father's movies said *I love you* sooner or later: the cheap, stylized jargon of the commercial cinema.

She looked over her shoulder, her eyes searching and questioning.

"I know so little about you," she said. "You are a stranger to me. I can't understand why I should feel as I do feel about you. We've only met for an hour or so and we talk of love."

"I know." He lifted his hands helplessly. "For me it is different. I've been lonely and unwanted all my life. Then I meet you and I'm no longer lonely."

She turned, smiling at him.

"We won't do any more of this," she said, waving her hands at the glasses still to be washed. "I'll show you your room."

He looked at her, and he saw how bright her eyes were and how quickly she was breathing, and because the excitement inside him was almost too strong for him to bear, he went out of the kitchen into the semi-darkness of the bar room and picked up the sack he had left on the floor.

She turned out the light in the kitchen and moved to a door leading to a steep flight of stairs. She paused in the doorway, turning on the light so he could see the stairs and he looked at

165

her; seeing the expression in her eyes he knew for certain what was going to happen, and he hesitated.

Sexual experience was an unknown factor in his suppressed, enclosed life. He had never considered it because he had never expected any girl would want to yield to him. Now he saw Ginette was ready to offer herself to him, his nerve quailed. He thought of the girl he had killed and he regretted the act. The excitement, the test of his ingenuity, wits and courage seemed suddenly petty and ridiculous. What Ginette would offer him was the ultimate thing in a man's life, he told himself. He was suddenly sure of it. The other – the act of killing, the false excitement, the pitting of wits – was a sham and he was sickened at the thought that now he could never again lead a normal life. He would never know when the police would catch up with him.

"It's on the first floor," Ginette said.

He watched her climb the stairs, and he was now acutely aware of her body in the tight-fitting singlet and cotton trousers she was wearing.

He picked up the sack and followed her up the steep stairs to a door at the head of the stairs.

As she turned on the light in the room, she smiled at him.

"It's not much of a room, but the bed is comfortable," she said.

He moved up to her, looking beyond her into the small, clean room with its bed, its strip of carpet, its chest of drawers and the bright oil painting of Cannes harbour on the wall.

"It's wonderful," he said. "I couldn't wish for anything better."

He tossed the sack down by the bed, then deliberately went over to the window and faced her.

They looked at each other, then Ginette came into the room and closed the door.

"Jay . . . I know I shouldn't be doing this, but I can't help myself. I love you so," she said. "Please be kind to me."

"Kind?" His breathing was quick and his heart hammering. "Why, of course." He put his arms round her and drew her close to him. "You need never be frightened of me, Ginette." He pressed his face against hers. "You are the special thing in my life."

II

The hot sunlight coming through the shutters and lying across the bed woke Jay.

He moved drowsily, and then lifted his head, staring around the unfamiliar little room.

For a moment, he didn't know where he was, then looking around, and seeing Ginette asleep at his side, he relaxed back on the pillow.

He lay still, staring up at the ceiling, listening to the sounds in the street below.

Then, languidly, he reached for his watch, lying on the bed-side table, and saw it was twenty-five minutes past six.

He raised himself up on his elbow to look more closely at Ginette, who moved in her sleep, her hand sliding across his naked chest.

His mind came alert.

By this time the police would know he had killed the Balu girl, and they would be searching for him. His description would probably be in the morning papers.

He lay back, sliding his arm under Ginette's shoulders, draw-ing her close to him and he thought of what he must do.

It would be better, he told himself, for him to remain out of sight in this room until the first intensive search for him had died down.

He would be safe here. When he was sure the search had slackened, then he would slip away one night and make for Paris.

There would be difficulties. His description would be in all the newspapers. Ginette might see the description and recognize him. How would she react? Without her co-operation, he might easily fail to get away.

He turned his head to look at her and, as he did so, she opened her eyes, smiling sleepily at him.

"What is the time, Jay?" she asked.

"Half-past six."

She gave a little sigh of content and pressed herself against him.

"We don't have to get up until nine. Go to sleep," she said, her lips now against his neck. "I've never been so happy . . ."

He lay motionless, his arm tightening around her, and in a moment or so, her quick, light breathing told him she was sleeping.

I've never been so happy . . .

Remorse bit into him as he thought of that ghastly moment when he had tightened the scarlet cord around the girl's throat.

Why had he done this thing? he asked himself. It wasn't

167

because he had been bored. That was a lie he had told Sophia to try to justify his act. Neither was it because he wanted to test his courage and his wits. He realized that now. That had also been a lie to try to justify what he had done to himself.

He felt a cold chill creep over him as he was forced to recognize the fact that he had killed the girl because of an inner compulsion. Something inside him had urged him to kill her: a force he had been powerless to control.

Was this then the thing people called insanity? Was he really out of his mind? Yet, lying here, with this girl at his side, feeling her breath against his neck, he felt as sane as he imagined any sane person would feel.

He drew Ginette closer. His thoughts were of the activity that must be going on at the Cannes police headquarters. The police were already hunting for him. If he made one slip, he would be caught.

Guilty but insane.

If the jury brought in that verdict, what would they do with him?

He would be put away in a cell, away from Ginette, shut up like a dangerous animal, not just for a few months, but for the rest of his days.

Sweat broke out on his face at the thought.

What a fool he had been! To have deliberately put himself in such a situation!

Unable to remain any longer in bed, he drew his arm gently from under Ginette's shoulders, moved the sheet aside and silently left the bed. Moving over to the window he lifted the blind a few inches.

Already the early sun felt hot against his face as he looked down the narrow street.

A few people were walking to work. The shutters of the shop windows were still drawn. A man pushing a handcart on which were piled vast bunches of white, red and purple carnations passed just below the bedroom window.

Jay looked over at the Beau Rivage hotel. A gendarme stood in the shade, just inside the entrance, his face tight with boredom. A little further up the road stood a police van, its long radio aerial pointing like an accusing finger towards the blue sky.

The sight of the gendarme and the police van made Jay feel sick. He remained motionless, watching the gendarme, unable to drag his eyes away from this symbol of his possible destruction.

"Jay . . . what have you done to your arm?"

He started and looked quickly around.

Ginette had thrown aside the sheet and lay outstretched on the bed. She made a picture of beauty that quickened his heart beat.

"My arm? Why, nothing."

He moved away from the window.

"But you have . . . look."

Then he saw the three long ragged scratches, the marks from Lucille Balu's finger nails. They looked inflamed against the brownness of his skin.

"Oh, that . . ." He shrugged. "It is nothing. I scratched myself on a nail."

"But doesn't it hurt?" She was solicitous and he was pleased. No one had ever bothered before when he had hurt himself.

"It's nothing."

He came and sat beside her, and bending over her, he put his mouth gently on hers. She gave a little sigh, and her arms slid around his neck, pulling him to her.

"Dear, dear Jay . . ."

And no one had ever spoken to him like that before, and he felt hot tears sting his eyes as he gripped her fiercely and lovingly.

The hands of the clock moved on from six-thirty to eight o'clock.

When Jay woke again he found Ginette no longer at his side, and immediately he started up, his mind crawling with alarm.

Where was she?

Had the police come for him?

In sudden panic, he scrambled off the bed and darted across the room to where he had left his clothes. He was groping frantically for the gun he had left in his trousers pocket when the door swung open.

He felt a kick of fear against his heart as he looked over his shoulder.

Ginette came in carrying a breakfast tray. She was wearing the blue jeans and a yellow cotton shirt. She was smiling, but her smile faded as she paused in the doorway and stared at him.

The stiff motionless way in which he was crouching, the expression on his face, gave her the idea that he was frightened.

"What is it, Jay?"

He made an effort and pulled himself together.

"Nothing. I woke suddenly, and I wondered where you had got to," he said, his voice a little unsteady. He pulled on his pale blue cotton trousers. "Breakfast? Good. I'm hungry."

She gave him a puzzled look, then set the tray down on the table. There was crisp bread, a large pat of butter, jam and coffee.

They sat side by side on the bed while they breakfasted.

Ginette said suddenly, "Jay . . . I don't even know what work you do, except you do something in the film world."

"I'm in publicity," Jay said. "It's not much of a job."

"Will you be working this morning?"

"Oh, no. My work's finished here now. I'm taking a vacation. Then I'll have to go to Venice."

"Won't you be coming back, Jay?" she asked as she refilled his coffee cup.

"I don't know. Would you like to come to Venice with me?"

She stared at him, her eyes opening wide.

"Venice?" She shook her head. "I'd love it, but it's not possible. I couldn't leave my father."

He said what he knew was now impossible because he would never again be able to use his real name in safety.

"We could get married."

She smiled at him, and put her hand on his.

"My father is helpless. He has no other means of earning a living. We French are loyal to our parents. It is a tradition. It's something in our blood. I can't marry so long as he is alive."

"You're wasting your life," Jay said impatiently. "When he dies what will happen to you?"

She shrugged her shoulders.

"Don't let's talk about it. What are you going to do this morning? I won't be free until half past two; then we can go for a swim. The café reopens at six."

"I'll stay here," Jay said. "Do you mind? I'm tired."

"Of course you can stay here, but wouldn't it be better for you to go out in the sun?"

He finished his coffee and then lay back on the bed.

"I've had enough of the sun. I like it here." He smiled at her. "We have a few days together, Ginette. We are going to be very happy."

She touched his face gently.

"I must go now. I have a lot to do."

"Is the café open yet?"

"We don't open until ten."

She bent over him and kissed him, her fingers smoothing back his hair, then, smiling at him, she picked up the tray and went out of the room.

He put his hand to the place where she had kissed him and he had to struggle against the desire to weep. For some time he lay in an emotional vacuum, then he forced himself to think how he could get out of this trap he had dug for himself. If he could get to Paris, he felt he might be safe.

As he lay thinking, he heard a murmur of voices downstairs. Immediately, he stiffened and sat up.

The police?

He went over to the window and looked out. The gendarme still guarded the entrance to the Beau Rivage hotel, but the police van had gone.

Leaving the window, he crossed the room and eased open the door, his hand closing over the butt of the gun in his hip pocket.

He heard a man's voice say something and Ginette reply, although he couldn't hear what was said. He moved silently into the passage and peered over the banister rail.

He could see Ginette's slim legs and small feet as she stood by the bar. The man she was talking to was out of sight.

"It was murder," Jay heard the man say. "There's no doubt about it. I was talking to the gendarme just now. He says it was a clumsy attempt to make it look like suicide."

Jay's fingers gripped the banister rail as he leaned forward to catch what the man was saying.

"He told me the killer is insane. They know who he is. You'd better be careful who comes in here to-day."

Ginette laughed.

"I'm not worrying. He isn't likely to return to this district," she said.

"That's where you are wrong. Killers often come back. They can't keep away from the scene of their crime. Still, you don't have anything to worry about. The gendarme is across the way. He'll keep an eye on you."

"Well, I must get on. I have work to do."

"You'll be busy to-day. People will come to look at the hotel. I'll see you to-morrow."

Ginette moved out of Jay's sight. He heard the café door open, then close and the key turn in the lock.

How had the police found out that Kerr hadn't killed himself? Jay wondered. If they were as clever as this, how was he to get away?

171

Moving like a ghost, he started down the stairs until he could see into the bar.

Ginette was bending over a table on which was spread a newspaper, her back turned to him. He watched her, and, after a few moments, she became aware of him and she turned.

"The police have found the man they were asking about yesterday – Joe Kerr," she said, a little breathlessly. "They fo ·nd him dead in the Beau Rivage hotel across the way. They s .y he was murdered and they think the man who killed Lucille Ba.u did it. They say he is insane."

"He isn't insane," Jay said, suddenly angry. "I explained that to you before. Of course he isn't insane."

"But he must be," Ginette said, turning to the newspaper. "Inspector Devereaux is in charge of the case. He is very clever. He comes here quite often to talk to father. The paper says the Inspector knows who did it and he says that this man killed Kerr to make the police think it was Kerr who killed the girl."

"How do they know Kerr didn't kill himself?" Jay asked, his lips stiff.

"They don't say." Ginette paused while she studied the account in the newspaper, then she began to read the account aloud: "A quantity of human skin was found under the dead girl's finger nails. It is believed she put up a desperate struggle while the killer was strangling her, and she inflicted deep scratches on his arms and hands. The police ask anyone who has noticed a man with recent scratches on his arms to notify them at once." She straightened and turned. "It's strange, isn't it, how it is the little things that give murderers away? The scratches on his arm . . ." She stopped short, staring at Jay, who had begun to back away, his face white, his eyes glittering, his left hand trying to cover the inflamed scratches that ran from his wrist to his elbow.

They stood staring at each other, then Ginette's eyes opened very wide and she put her hand to her mouth as if to stop a scream.

CHAPTER FOURTEEN

I

Soon after eight o'clock, as Floyd Delaney was finishing his morning coffee, the night nurse came into the lounge.

"Madame Delaney is asking for you, monsieur," she said. "You'll be careful not to excite her?"

"Sure, sure," Delaney said, getting hastily to his feet. "How is she?"

"She has a bad headache, but otherwise she is doing very well."

Delaney went into Sophia's bedroom.

Sophia, her head in bandages, lay flat on her back. She looked very small and fragile and beautiful, and Delaney felt a tug at his heart as he sat by her side and took her hand.

"Hello, honey doll," he said. "Gee! You certainly gave me a fright. I thought I was going to lose my lovely."

Her fingers tightened on his.

"Where's Jay, Floyd?"

This was unexpected, and Delaney's face stiffened. Ever since Devereaux had explained why he suspected Jay of killing Lucille Balu and Joe Kerr, Delaney had been in a fever of apprehension. He had told the Inspector that he didn't believe his son was guilty, but, after the Inspector had gone, and he had had time to recover from the shock and to think over what the Inspector had told him, he was forced to accept the fact that the insane fool of a boy had done this thing.

He didn't intend to tell Sophia while she was in this condition, so he said casually: "I guess he's out taking a swim or something. Look, baby . . ."

"He tried to kill me," Sophia said huskily. "I'm so frightened."

Delaney stared at her.

"Jay? He tried to kill you? Why, the boy rescued you. If it hadn't been for him . . ."

"He hit me with the paper weight. He intended to silence me. Oh, Floyd darling, I've been so stupid. I knew he had killed the girl. I didn't tell anyone, as I wanted to protect us from the awful publicity."

Delaney drew in a sharp breath.

"Now take it easy, Sophia. The nurse says you're not to get worked up."

"Oh, damn the nurse!" Sophia exclaimed. "Where's Jay? I must know! I'm frightened he'll come back here and finish me. He's mad, Floyd! He's not safe to be free."

"It's all right, kid," Delaney said soothingly. "The police are hunting for him now, and you have nothing to worry about. Do you think you feel like telling me about it? How did you know he killed the girl?"

Speaking rapidly, Sophia poured out the whole story right from the moment she had walked into the suite and had suspected the girl was in Jay's bedroom to the moment when she had realized the safety-catch was still on the gun and she had seen the paper weight flashing down on her head.

Delaney sat motionless, his face hard and lined, his hand covering hers as he listened. When she had finished, he bent and kissed her, then he got up and began to prowl around the room.

"Darling, what about the film to-night?" Sophia asked, her eyes bright with tears.

"Never mind about the film," Delaney said. "It's good enough to ride this. I'm not worrying about that. It's the boy! I never realized he was that crazy. I blame myself for not realizing the condition he was in." He frowned suddenly. "I'll be right back." He went into Sophia's bathroom and looked around. On the toilet table stood the heavy paper weight, but he wasn't interested in that, he was looking for Sophia's gun. When he was satisfied it wasn't in the bathroom, he went back to Sophia. "Look, honey, I must talk to the Inspector. I must tell him how dangerous the boy is. I'll keep you out of this. Maybe it'll have to come out that you knew what was happening, but we'll take that when it comes. For the moment, I'll say nothing about it, but I must tell him the boy attacked you." He patted her hand, then said casually: "By the way, honey, was your gun loaded?"

"Yes."

He saw her eyes open very wide. She tightened her grip on his arm.

"Has he taken the gun?"

"Yeah. I'm afraid he has. At least, it's not in the bathroom. I'll look in his room just to make sure, but I think he's taken it."

"Oh, God!"

Sophia closed her eyes, and began to weep.

Delaney went to the door and beckoned to the nurse.

"Don't leave her for a second. I'll be back in a little while."

He went briskly into Jay's room and glanced around. It was so obvious that the two detectives had searched the room thoroughly that he didn't waste time looking for the gun. If Jay had left it in the room, the detectives would have found it.

He left the suite, carefully locking the door after him, then went downstairs to Devereaux's office. The time was now five minutes past nine.

Devereaux sat behind the desk, drinking coffee. His face was drawn with fatigue and his eyes were deep-set, but he got to his feet briskly enough when Delaney came in.

"Have you found him?" Delaney asked as he shut the door.

"No, monsieur; not yet."

"Have you released the news to the press?"

"It will be soon enough when we've caught him."

"You may have to get the press to help you," Delaney said, grimly. "He has a gun."

Devereaux stiffened.

"You are sure of that, monsieur?"

"Pretty sure. He's not only got a gun, but he has a cut-throat razor as well. You'd better warn your men to be careful how they corner him."

Devereaux crossed to the door and opened it. He beckoned to Guidet, who was trying to keep awake as he lolled in a lounging chair waiting for orders. Devereaux spoke to him, then he returned to the office.

"I'm afraid the boy's completely out of his mind," Delaney said. "His mother was the same. She killed herself after trying to kill me. Now this boy tried to kill my wife." He went on to give Devereaux the details of Sophia's escape.

"Why do you think he tried to kill your wife, monsieur?" Devereaux asked, poking holes in the blotter with the paper knife he had picked up.

"I don't know. It looks as if he gets the urge to kill, and he just kills."

"Have you a photograph of him, monsieur?"

"Not here. I have a number in my New York home, of course. I don't know if my publicity man has any."

"I'll have to give this to the press now. There is no sign of him, and we'll have to ask the public to help. He may have left Cannes. He may be anywhere by now. He's had a seven-hour start. A photograph would be helpful."

"I'll see if I can get one for you," Delaney said. "He has money. He took nearly three million francs from my wallet."

Devereaux looked at him.

"I realize what this means to you, monsieur, but I am afraid the consequences are inevitable. At least, it won't be necessary to tell the press about the attack on your wife."

Delaney nodded.

"Thanks, Inspector. Well, I guess I asked for it. I should have taken more interest in the boy. I'll see if I can dig up a photograph for you."

When he had gone, Guidet came in.

"The warning has gone out that he is armed," he said, closing the door. "There's still no sign of him."

"Monsieur Delaney tells me the boy took nearly three million francs when he bolted, so he's not short of money," Devereaux said wearily. He laid the paper knife down on the blotter, and then suddenly paused to stare at a pencil scribble just by the point of the knife. It was a telephone number that Jay had given the operator when he had been in the office for questioning. Devereaux remembered the brief conversation. The boy had arranged to meet someone this day.

Devereaux became alert.

"Here, find out whose telephone number this is," he said, scribbling the number on a slip of paper and giving it to Guidet, "and hurry."

A little bewildered Guidet took up the telephone receiver and asked the switchboard girl to connect him with *Information*. A few seconds later, he hung up.

"It's the telephone number of La Boule d'Or," he said.

"That's Jean Bereut's place," Devereaux said, frowning. "What would the boy want with him?" He rubbed the back of his neck as he thought. "Of course! It's the girl . . . Bereut's daughter. He must have made an appointment to see her this morning. Call the café and ask Bereut if he has seen the boy."

Guidet gave the number, and after a long wait, he shook his head and hung up.

"There's no answer."

Devereaux stared at him.

"But someone must be there at this hour. . . ." Then he jumped to his feet. "We'll go down there! Get twenty men and see they are armed. Hurry!"

As Guidet went quickly from the room, Floyd Delaney came in.

"I have a photograph for you . . ." he began.

"I don't think it will be necessary," Devereaux said. "I think I know where he is. I would be glad if you would come with me. You may be able to help us."

"Sure," Delaney said, his face paling. "Anything I can do, I'll do."

"In a few minutes, then," Devereaux said.

They waited.

Delaney prowled around the room while Devereaux sat on the edge of the desk. Then Guidet came in.

"All right, Inspector."

Devereaux stood up. He looked at Delaney.

"Let us go, monsieur," he said.

II

Moving unsteadily, her eyes fixed on Jay's white, frightened face, Ginette backed away until she reached the bar, then, unable to back further, she remained motionless.

It couldn't be possible, she was trying to assure herself, that he was the killer the police were looking for. This boy she had been moved to love so passionately and in whose arms she had passed the night! It couldn't be! Nothing could be more horrible! But if he wasn't this man, then why was he looking at her like this, his eyes glittering, a muscle twitching in his face, his lips twisted in a frightened, meaningless smile and his hand trying to hide the three livid scratches on his arm?

Neither of them spoke. They just stood in the shadowy bar room, facing each other, with the sounds of the traffic in their ears.

Then suddenly, unexpectedly, the telephone bell began to ring: a strident, nagging noise that made Jay start violently.

Ginette made an effort and fought down the faintness that gripped her.

"I'll answer it," she said, her voice trembling.

The telephone was across the room and Jay stood between her and the instrument. With a cold feeling of dread, she saw that he remained motionless, watching her with this frightening expression on his face.

She began to move slowly forward, circling him so she wouldn't pass close to him, and he pivoted on his heels, his eyes never leaving her.

177

Then as she was nearly within reach of the telephone, he said softly: "Don't touch it, Ginette."

"But why not?" She stopped abruptly, aware of the hidden threat in his voice. "It – it may be my father."

"Let it ring," he said. "You mustn't answer it."

Then she felt weak because she was now certain he was the man the police were looking for.

"Don't look so frightened, Ginette," Jay said. "You don't have to be frightened of me. I told you last night I'll always be kind to you, and I mean it."

She sat down abruptly in one of the chairs by a table.

The telephone bell continued to ring.

They waited. Then, after what seemed an endless age, the bell abruptly ceased to ring.

The silence in the room was almost unbearable to Ginette after the strident clamour of the bell.

"I want to tell you about it," Jay said, speaking urgently and abruptly. "All that stuff in the paper about me being mad is a filthy lie. I'm not mad. You know that. I'm as sane as you are. I didn't mean to kill her. It was an accident. She tried to make love to me. I told her to get out. We were in my father's suite. She began to scream. I had to stop that. I took her by the throat . . . but it was an accident. You must believe me."

Ginette put her hands to her face and shuddered.

"Kerr was trying to blackmail me," Jay went on, his words coming faster, his eyes more desperate. "You're listening, aren't you? He was trying to blackmail me. I said I would tell the police. He was frightened then. All blackmailers are cowards. He hanged himself. It's ridiculous for anyone to say I killed him. He took his own worthless life. I admit he did it because I said I was going to the police, but no one can say I murdered him."

Ginette put her hands over her ears. The tense, guilty voice carried no sincerity, and she knew he was lying.

"Please don't say any more," she begged, not looking at him. "Will you go now? Will you please, please go?"

He stared at her, his hands turning into fists.

"Go? Where can I go? I'm relying on you to help me get away. You love me, Ginette. You said so last night. When two people love each other, they help each other. I must have help. I'm relying on you. To-night we'll leave here together. We'll go to Paris."

She was recovering from the shock now, and she realized the danger she was in. If he were insane, he might turn on her if she didn't pretend to co-operate. But was it possible the newspaper had exaggerated? Perhaps he wasn't insane. He hadn't acted that way last night. She had loved him, and yet she was sure he was lying when he had said the girl's death was an accident. There was a horrible glibness in his tone and a callousness that shocked her.

She looked at him. That dreadful, meaningless smile gave her the key. No one sane would smile like that.

"But I can't go to Paris with you," she said, trying to steady her voice. "My father . . ."

"Oh, yes, you can. I have plenty of money. I'll see your father doesn't suffer." He moved towards her. "You want to help me, don't you?"

Before she could control herself, she cried out in a wild, terrified voice: "Don't come near me!"

He stopped abruptly.

A sudden vicious spurt of anger shot through him. Was there no one who would try to understand him? She had said she loved him. She had given herself to him, and now she was crouching away from him, staring at him as if he were dangerous. So she did believe he was mad, as Sophia believed he was mad.

"I told you you don't have to be frightened of me," he said, his voice hardening, "but if you are going to be stupid and if you prefer to believe the lies in the paper, then I'll have to take precautions."

Ginette shrank further back.

"Please don't touch me," she begged. "I'll help you if I can, but please don't come near me."

Then into his mind came the stealthy voice whispering to him that it would be safer to kill her. It was the same urgent, compelling voice that he had heard when he had been watching Lucille Balu on the beach and when he had been talking to Sophia.

The voice said in his mind: "You can't trust her now. She thinks you are mad. You can never get away if you leave her here alive. Why should you hesitate? A girl who could give herself to you and then won't believe you isn't fit to live. Kill her quickly and then go. You can get down to the harbour and take her boat. They won't think of looking for you in the boat. Do it now! Do it quickly!"

179

As he hesitated, trying not to listen to the voice, he thought of last night and what he had said to her.

You need never be frightened of me, Ginette. You are the special thing in my life.

He thought: it would be better for me to be caught than to hurt her. She gave me the loveliest and happiest experience of my life. I mustn't repay her by death.

But the voice was growing louder and more insistent in his mind.

"See the way she is looking at you," the voice said. "Do you call that love? She thinks you are mad. Kill her, you sentimental fool! You'll never get away unless she's dead. The moment you leave here, she'll raise the alarm. You'll never even reach the harbour."

Jay found himself beginning to surrender to the urgency of the voice and his hand moved behind him, his fingers closing over the butt of the ·25 automatic.

"Don't use that!" the voice shouted at him. "Don't shoot her! The noise of the gun will bring the police! Hit her over the head. There's a bottle on the table. Use that! Hit her now!"

Jay moved over to the table, slightly away from the one at which Ginette was sitting.

I mustn't do it, he thought, as his fingers closed around the neck of the bottle. She is the special thing in my life. I mustn't hurt her.

"Do it now!" the voice inside his mind raved at him. "Quick! Don't hesitate! She'll start to scream in a moment, and then you'll never get away!"

He picked up the bottle.

Ginette sat paralysed, watching him. She was so frightened the scream forming in her throat made no sound.

"Now! Now! Now!" the voice urged. "Quickly!"

But with an effort that brought sweat to his face, Jay put the bottle back on the table.

"Get out of here! Go quickly!" His voice was strangled. "Quick! Get out of here!"

Instinctively she realized that for her sake he was holding on desperately to his tottering sanity and fighting to control a mad urge to kill her. She could see the struggle going on from the expression on his face.

She scrambled to her feet and darted across the room. She began to tear blindly at the bolts on the door.

Jay felt his control leave him. The voice inside him was

screaming abuse at him. He felt himself turn and his hand reach for the bottle.

As he picked it up, Ginette wrenched open the door and stumbled into the street.

She fell on her knees on the pavement, hiding her face in her hands, and she began to scream wildly.

Police cars were pulling up at this moment.

Devereaux and Delaney were the first out of the cars.

Devereaux ran to the screaming girl and pulled her to her feet. "It's all right! It's all right!" he cried. "Stop screaming! Where is he?"

Ginette pointed to the café, then her eyes rolled back and she went limp in the Inspector's arms.

"Here – take her!" Devereaux said, thrusting the unconscious girl into the hands of the nearest gendarme. He moved towards the café entrance as the police, spilling out of the cars, began to control the crowd that had immediately collected.

Floyd Delaney caught the Inspector by his arm.

"Wait!" he said. "I'll go in there. If he sees you, he'll probably use the gun."

"Better not," Devereaux said, uneasily. "He's dangerous. Better leave him to us."

"Do you think I'm frightened of my own son?" Delaney said. "I can handle him. Keep out of the way!"

He walked into the café and paused just inside, looking into the gloom.

"Jay? Where are you?"

He heard no sound except the murmur of the crowd behind him. Without hesitation, he walked further into the bar room.

"Jay? Come on, son. I've come to take you home," he said quietly. "There's nothing to be frightened of. You and I can work this thing out together."

And as he said this, he realized the futility of his words. He had left it far too late now to help the boy.

Then the sudden sharp bang of the ·25 automatic made him start. The sound came from the half-open door that led into the kitchen.

The bang of the gun was immediately followed by the sound of a heavy fall, then a gasping, sobbing sigh.

Delaney flinched and turned away.

Through the half-open door, a thin wisp of cordite smoke drifted on the still air. It hung for a second or so, then dispersed like a departing spirit.

181

Devereaux came quickly into the bar room.

He looked at Delaney, who was pressing his hands to his face, then he walked across the kitchen and pushed the door wide open.

>>> If you've enjoyed this book and would like to discover more great vintage crime and thriller titles, as well as the most exciting crime and thriller authors writing today, visit: >>>

The Murder Room
Where Criminal Minds Meet

themurderroom.com